THE DOUBLE LIFE OF BENSON YU

THE DOUBLE LIFE OF BENSON YU

A Novel

KEVIN CHONG

ATRIA BOOKS

NEW YORK   LONDON   TORONTO   SYDNEY   NEW DELHI

ATRIA
BOOKS

An Imprint of Simon & Schuster, Inc.
1230 Avenue of the Americas
New York, NY 10020

First Atria Books hardcover edition April 2023

ATRIA B O O K S and colophon are trademarks of
Simon & Schuster, Inc.

For information about special discounts for bulk purchases,
please contact Simon & Schuster Special Sales at 1-866-506-1949 or
business@simonandschuster.com.

The Simon & Schuster Speakers Bureau can bring authors to your live event.
For more information or to book an event, contact the Simon & Schuster Speakers
Bureau at 1-866-248-3049 or visit our website at www.simonspeakers.com.

Interior design by Lexy East

Manufactured in China

1   3   5   7   9   10   8   6   4   2

Library of Congress Cataloging-in-Publication Data is available.

ISBN 978-1-6680-0549-1
ISBN 978-1-6680-0553-8 (ebook)

This book is dedicated to the memory of Kam Sau Cheng

A NOTE FROM THE AUTHOR

This work contains indirect references to child sexual abuse and scenes that depict suicidal ideation.

My transliteration from Cantonese and Japanese was done in an ad hoc fashion from various online sources and translators. All errors are mine.

Hey there,

Found this address in one of your old comic books in the library, and I figured I'd say hello. Still mad about everything? It occurred to me that the reason you haven't stayed in touch is because you've remained upset about what happened with your dad. Or maybe there's some other sore point. Heh-heh. It's been over thirty years and so I am taking a chance that things have cooled down. You might not know much about what I've been up to. Still teaching karate. The factory closed down so I am in semiretirement. To be honest, I'm just scraping by.

You might be pleased to know that I've followed your career. I even saw the first Iggy Samurai movie. I guess it's for kids. But I did get a chuckle out of your Coyote Sensei character. I made an impression on you! I swear, some of the things that character said came right out of my mouth. Maybe you'd like to kick some of your residuals my way before I talk to that intellectual property lawyer. I sure could use the cash. Heh-heh.

A librarian helped me with the internet. She clicked on a link to a recent interview in which you say you've moved. My sister lives two towns over from where your wife teaches. I owe her a visit. We can meet up.

Maybe you're not mad at me. Maybe you've forgotten about me. If that's the case, and that seems highly unlikely, here's a reminder of my existence. Write me back when you get a chance.

C.

PART ONE

Chinatown, 1980s

CHAPTER ONE

A few days after I receive that noxious letter from C., the boy appears for the first time. The picture fills my eyes, and the most expedient way to clear them is by writing it down. I see the boy, on the street, cowering behind his grandmother. That's his default pose. He's holding a fold-up cart. His ailing poh-poh nudges him forward. Up until a month ago the old woman pulled the two-wheeled cart herself. Then, one morning, after she'd been coughing through the night, she made the boy do it. On that initial outing, as they embarked on their errand running, she made a point of moving at her typically brisk pace. "It's just my hand," she said in Cantonese, with a village accent she used only around family, like a pair of ugly slippers. "It hurts, that's all. It'll be fine tomorrow." But then she asked him to pull the cart again the next day.

Every week, on Sundays, this depleted family unit makes their rounds to the markets for dried scallops, for pea shoots and watercress, for oxtail and tripe. Everyone knows Poh-Poh. She used to teach Chinese school to half of them in the church basement. Everyone stands up straighter, eyes jittering, the second she appears.

Whenever he's out with Poh-Poh, the boy worries about seeing kids from his class. Their side-eyes and smirks could strip paint. Those jerks will wait until they're in the schoolyard to tell the boy they recognize his clothes from gift-shop clearance racks and church donation bins. They'll ask him where his parents are, as though he *hasn't* told them already.

Now that he pulls the cart, the shopkeepers direct their attention to him first, as the person who handles the business. They all know better than to see him as in charge, but this way they don't have to meet the gaze of the woman who would pick their Chinese names from a roll to recite classical poetry.

Today, it's Mr. Mah, who runs the convenience store across the street.

"Dai lo!" he says from the back of the store. He's finished stacking cans of soup. "How may we serve you?" he says in Cantonese.

Poh-Poh tuts, her voice like the rasp she uses on her feet before bedtime, and allows the boy—I guess we're gonna call him Benny—to choose a shrink-wrapped package of snack cakes for acing his math test. One indulgence he's earned from pulling the cart is getting to stop here first. He no longer has to wait until their errands are done for his weekly treat. "You're acting as though he's the one paying for everything," she reminds Mr. Mah.

"One day he will. Big head, big brain, woh!" says Mr. Mah, rubbing his hands on his flannel shirtsleeves as he follows them to the front of the store. The sides of his face are crinkled from all the smiling he does.

His daughter sits behind the cash register. Benny's cheeks warm at the sight of the girl. I cringe to picture him this way, fluorescent with hormonal yearning around Mr. Mah's daughter, Shirley. I've changed her name, although the real one is pretty similar. Only a few years ago, Benny and Shirley did everything together—watching TV, playing Transformers, drawing, even eating, on most days, from the same bowl of macaroni, peas, and ham in broth—back when his mother had grown too weak to work and babysat her for extra cash. Now he can't speak to her.

"Why can't I have at least one smart child, laa?" the shopkeeper says to her. Shirley's older brother, Wai, works at the store, when forced, but otherwise runs with the wrong kids, the ones who wear clothes their parents can't afford. "Look at him," Mr. Mah tells his daughter. "Always on the honor roll. Nose in books, teem."

"He takes after his grandmother," Shirley says in English, staring at her lap as she struggles to wipe her mouth clean of a smirk. She has an oblong face with wide cheekbones and tendrils of hair that escape from her ponytail. Her bright eyes and a readily pursed expression complement a thorny demeanor that the boy will always be drawn to. "Look who I have to take after."

Mr. Mah wags an open palm at her, his eyes glinting with amusement. "Begging to be hated."

Poh-Poh slides the cupcakes across the counter and produces a folded five-dollar bill from the lanyard money pouch where she keeps her senior's bus pass. Shirley opens the register and calculates the change in her head.

"Your girl is even better with numbers than my grandson, gwaa," Poh-Poh says. "Every child has a different strength."

The shopkeeper seems stumped by this praise from a woman who offers so little of it. Praise from her always feels unprecedented. As they're leaving, Mr. Mah gathers his wits and holds out a candy bar.

Benny stares at the treat. *Flake*. He's never heard the name before. It's probably chocolate. It's probably good. It's free. But why can't it just be a normal candy bar? A Snickers or a Mars bar, and not something that came over on a boat?

"A gift for dai lo," Mr. Mah says to Poh-Poh. "Free of charge."

"Nonsense," Poh-Poh says, and hands Benny two quarters to pay for it.

Shirley reaches out. He wishes his fingertips weren't so grimy as they glance along her palm. She turns away when she takes the money.

Benny eats the snack cakes once they step outside, eats them so fast it's as though he's trying to hide them from himself. Poh-Poh would chide him for eating so quickly except that she's in a hurry. He'll save the candy bar for later.

"That shopkeeper doesn't pay taxes, woh. That's why his girl is so good at numbers. Don't tell her you know all of that, laa," Poh-Poh says to him once they reach the next block. "Why were you standing around, acting so dopey around Mr. Mah?"

"I wasn't," Benny insists, moving a step ahead of her down the hill to their first stop. At night, he will picture Shirley, the way she flutters her eyelashes and tucks in the left corner of her mouth when she's embarrassed. He sits behind her in their history and English blocks so he can watch her ponytail sway for up to two hours a day.

They pick up vegetables at a greengrocer, chicken feet at the butcher shop. The people at those stores don't fawn over him as much. At the butcher's, Poh-Poh slips on the wet linoleum but reaches for the counter to prevent a fall.

Throughout their walk, the big hill back to their cream-colored concrete housing development looms for Benny. The first few days pulling the cart were muscle-scorching slogs, ones that underscored his softness, and he wondered how Poh-Poh managed that task all these years. But the sum of that effort has made him more resolute, if not stronger. Today, he feels as though he can sail up that hill.

When he turns around to see Poh-Poh midway down the block, her body seems to be twisting, hands aloft like a surfer's along a concrete wave. She clamps a handkerchief to a face that's purple with distress. As Benny starts to hurry back, the cart turns over. Stooping over to pick up the scattered groceries on the sidewalk, he sees Poh-Poh reaching for a lamppost but missing it. Then crashing.

He abandons the cart and races down the hill. When he gets to her, she swats him away. No, she can't grab hold of his hand. Finally upright, she reveals an abacus of scrapes along her cheekbone.

"Mom!"

Benny sees Steph, still in her waitressing uniform, hurry down from the top of the hill. "It's nothing," Poh-Poh says to her. "It looks worse than it feels, gwaa."

Benny marvels at his aunt's brisk competency. First she recovers the cart and walks them back to their apartment before jetting off to the pharmacy for disinfectant and bandages. Then, while Poh-Poh rests, she cooks dinner, humming along to Perry Como on the oldies station while Benny watches her. Steph reminds Benny of Mommy. She has Mommy's long nose, the kind he wishes he had instead of a flat nose with the hump of a chocolate hedgehog. She has her double-folded eyelids, a pair more than Benny, who always looks sleepy. She has her ability to tease Poh-Poh, darting her eyes at him with complicity when Poh-Poh grows huffy. In his aunt's presence, Benny, who'd never dare tease his grandmother, always feels the courage to crack up.

Whenever Steph visits, Chinatown shrinks and the world beyond it emerges. Poh-Poh always complains that Steph isn't Chinese enough. Because Steph was born here nearly a decade after Mommy—Poh-Poh blames their age gap on the hardships of immigration—she is more westernized. Unlike Mommy, who worked a job preparing taxes, his aunt insisted on attending art school. Gong-Gong was dying when she enrolled, Poh-Poh says, so she didn't have the energy to force her to abandon her dreams. Now Steph lives on the other end of town, where she serves breakfasts with funny names. The "Jacked

Stack." "Benny from Heaven" (one of her nicknames for him). "Huevos Ran-
cheros." And she's in a punk rock band. The last time Steph visited, she gave
him her old Walkman and a cassette of her band's album. The cover shows the
band members leaning against a brick wall in their jeans and leather jackets.
They stand with their arms to their sides, blindfolded, with cigarettes at the
corners of their mouths. "Do you really smoke?" he asked his aunt, to which
she only answered, "In spite of yourself, you are so cute."

After they finish eating, his grandmother tells him he can either watch TV
or play video games. He gets an hour of TV, but only half an hour of gaming—
to Benny, a cruelly unfair ratio. She doesn't wait for him to choose, turning on
their thirteen-inch set and, for the first time in his life, cranking up the volume.
In his peripheral vision, he sees Poh-Poh lead her daughter into the bathroom.
Noticing this, Benny is too distracted for *Growing Pains*. It's a rerun anyhow. He
stands by the door. Their voices are so low he can barely hear.

"Ah-neui," he can hear Poh-Poh say.

"I know, Mom," Steph says in English. "I've got it."

"Do you promise?"

"I *promise*."

Benny doesn't have time to ask Steph what she assented to. When she
emerges from the bathroom, a quarter hour after Poh-Poh, she stretches out
in a yawn. "Bedtime," she announces. "Nice and early, as usual." She winks at
him. She's changed out of her work uniform and into clothes from her bag. In
makeup, hair done, in a leather skirt. Better places await her. Steph only comes
by every couple of weeks, and he feels cheated that she cuts out so early.

I too had an aunt who helped take care of me, but not someone like Steph,
who's modeled after the older sister of a friend—another hopeless crush.

Benny doesn't know it, but he'll see his aunt tomorrow when she shows
up after the worst day ever at school. That Monday afternoon, the final bell
rings and he can't wait to get home. He pushes through the outer doors but
stops when he sees Steph. His chest soars. She's here for him, and he's too grateful to wonder why. He hopes she takes him out for hot chocolate and cracks
a few jokes. Just the thought of her kindness, given everything that happened
that day, steams him open like a mussel.

"What's the matter, little man?" she asks him. Her hands, which she had on the straps of her backpack, reach for his shoulders.

He wants to chew her out for calling him "little man," a nickname he's told her not to use, but he bawls harder instead. "Mrs. Renzullo asked me a question about Christopher Columbus," he begins. The rest of the story is too painful for him to tell.

As it happened, Mrs. Renzullo, his English and history teacher, always called on him. Nobody else could respond to her questions. Half the class could barely speak English. When he gave the answer, "King Ferdinand and Queen Isabella," something collapsed in his mouth, a wounded bird's death honk, on the third syllable of Isa*bell*a. "Faht yuhk," Poh-Poh had said with an indulgent smile when his voice cracked the other night.

His classmates, even Shirley, who sat in front of him with her loose but perfect ponytail, would find his voice breaking no less funny than if he had answered Mrs. Renzullo's question with a tuba-timbred, split-toned fart.

At lunch hour, it started. "Isa*bell*a" was croaked behind his back. He was shoved by someone as he stooped over the water fountain. He turned to see his tormentors, Bronson Su and Roderick Chow, cackling. Both of them were broad-shouldered (in a preteen way), with gel-swept hair and tapered trousers. If only he knew, I think now, how easy it would be to punch them, to fight back. He might take his own blows, but they would leave him alone.

Now, secure in his aunt's arms, he thinks all of this, and yet he can't utter one off-key word of explanation. Steph hugs him tighter anyway. If Poh-Poh were here, she would say, "No crying," and turn her back on him until his eyes had dried. He can see some of his classmates hurry past him, but he doesn't care if they know he's crying. He's dirt to them anyway. Soon his face is back in Steph's argyle sweater. Because he can't remember how Mommy smelled anymore, he likes to think she smelled like Steph. Like secondhand-store clothes, patchouli, and cigarettes.

"Tough day? Hormones?" she asks. "Whatever it is, I'm sorry."

As he expected, they get hot chocolates at the Chinese bakery Poh-Poh avoids on account of all the white people stepping out from tour buses to crowd the place and justify its stiff prices. Steph also buys cocktail buns, egg tarts, and pork turnovers that the woman behind the counter places in a box and ties with a pink plastic ribbon.

"That is for you to take home," Steph says once they settle into a booth with their drinks.

Benny figures that the promise she made to Poh-Poh has something to do with why Steph is visiting only him today. His aunt is on edge this afternoon, her fingers tapping the glass that covers the menus on the tabletop.

"Why are you here?" he asks finally.

"Um, I've brought something for you," she announces. "A little listening."

Steph unzips her backpack. From the bag comes a bundle of cassette tapes with handwritten track listings. "I'm sure you wore out my album by now. You liked my album, right?"

He nods, and reads the names scrawled on the spines of the tapes. The Clash, the Velvet Underground, Kate Bush. He gets preoccupied for a moment.

"We're going on tour tomorrow," she finally tells him. "Los Angeles to Chapel Hill to New York to Montreal. And a bunch of other cities."

He stares down at the chocolate sediment still gathered at the bottom of his mug. "How long will you be gone?"

"Two months," she says. "That's why I wanted to see you, and not you and Mom. Your poh-poh doesn't want me to go. You know how dramatic she can get, right? She thinks our van will crash. She worries so much."

He remembers what Poh-Poh says about her two daughters. "Your mother was so responsible—the only mistake she ever made was marrying your father, gwaa," she would tell him. "Your aunt just wants to have fun." Normally, Benny loves the lightness Steph brings. He remembers tinkling on the electronic keyboard Steph would lug over when Mommy and Poh-Poh went to the hospital for tests. Later, she would play Go Fish with him in the hospital cafeteria when Mommy was too sick to see more than one visitor at a time. Now her shine feels like gloss as she sets aside family responsibility for personal fulfillment.

They know Poh-Poh is weakening with age. She can care for herself, even for her dead daughter's boy, but she can't manage without help. Even Steph knows this, as her eyes won't meet his. She smiles at her hands. "We've been setting up the tour for months. We've all been working double shifts and over-time to pay for the van. Your poh-poh is a worrywart, isn't she?"

Benny thinks about Poh-Poh. As long as he's lived with her, she's been getting up in the morning to make him jook for breakfast. It's impossible to stay asleep when she has risen in their one-room apartment and the soup pot is clattering on the stove. And yet he will lie on the pullout, eyes closed, until she tells him to eat.

But for the past two mornings, Poh-Poh has stayed in bed. Through the night, she coughs and coughs. Sometimes, she will get up to rinse her mouth with salt water. For dinner, she bakes yams and serves them with rice cooked in the pot with lap cheong and doused in soy sauce. It's the kind of dinner she prepared when Mommy was dying, less a meal than a gesture that acknowl-edges the biological necessity of eating.

As I hash out this scene, I'm glad I'm not drawing it. The only withheld emotions in *Iggy Samurai* come at swordpoint, the noble feelings of martial arts heroes keeping mum about their sacrifices. In this case, knowing her mind is set, Benny makes sure not to broadcast his concern to his aunt. He tries being happy about her decision. He hopes Steph can see through it. But her face is glowing in relief. The warmth of the hot chocolate receding, he waits with Steph until her bus comes. She tells him to call her if he needs anything. One thing, though. She has disconnected her line. She writes down a phone number on a slip of paper. "When I moved out of my place, I left all my stuff at our drummer's house," she says. The drummer's roommate has a list of the clubs she's playing while the band is on the road that he can share if necessary. "You can call me in an emergency."

The bus comes. They hug. She asks him how many postcards he wants. He blurts out, "Four or five." She says, "How about two?" "Three?" He waits for her to board. Once she's inside, she holds up three fingers and nods. He watches her turn away and slip on her own set of headphones. Her face relaxes. The smiles and jokiness vanish from her face. Her eyes grow distant. She looks freed.

CHAPTER TWO

As for the Samurai, I was at my drafting desk, on my laptop, when I first saw him. In welcoming the boy a few days earlier, I had ducked away, hyperventilating, from the memory of C. Blue-eyed and golden-hued, built like a bus. From this void emerged a funhouse version of C., outwardly similar to him but with all his venom drained.

The Samurai, he's winding around a grimy aluminum-sided shed until he finds an open door. Once inside he meets the guy who owns the company, sharpening a set of shears on a belt sander. The landscaper squints as the Samurai bows—the Samurai needs to stop doing this—and puts down his shears to look at his résumé. The landscaper barely glances at it and asks him whether he's ever mowed a lawn. The Samurai nods.

"Then why do you look so nervous?" the landscaper asks.

"It's been a while since I applied for work."

His answer prompts the landscaper to finally look at the résumé and notice that the last job the Samurai held was as a dishwasher at a restaurant that shuttered five years back. Where has he been since? Once the Samurai tells him, the landscaper stitches together a tight smile. He talks about second chances and roads taking unexpected turns. Handing back the résumé, he promises to call him when something opens up—after speaking to other applicants.

The Samurai's baby sister, Iulia, is waiting outside in her Hyundai Pony. The real-life Samurai, C., has a sister with an eastern European name, like Nadia or Alina. But I've never met her. I know nothing about C.'s family. In the car, Iulia tries to be encouraging. "No one gets the first job they applied for," she tells the Samurai. The steering wheel digs into her pregnant belly. She asks him to repeat the questions the landscaper asked. He does, and she suggests that he say, in future interviews, that he spent the time since his last job caring for a sick family member. "It's a lie, I know, but not really a lie." She adds, "You're your own family."

Although it's dishonorable to spread falsehood, the Samurai accepts this suggestion without protest. When he behaves properly and takes his medication, the Samurai knows he must answer Iulia's questions with enthusiasm. He must introduce himself to his brother-in-law's buddies as Iulia's brother. And answer to the name of Constantine. What choice does he have? He's been a masterless ronin ever since he lost contact with his daimyo.

Perhaps if he weren't so "normal" they would have let him stay. It was never quiet at the hospital, but he missed the feeling that every object had its place. A small white bed, orange desk, pink chair. His homemade bokuto. He could hear the assuring voice of his daimyo, who wanted him prepared for his ultimate mission. He missed the orderlies who would kindly bow when they saw him. He was allowed to practice his sword work.

But then, Iulia explained, there was a budget deficit, a big one that made folks angry. And other people complained that taxes were too high. The guy with the white teeth and cornsilk hair went up for election. The guy with the arctic-wolf-blue eyes, who looked bitter not to have a great head of hair, took his place. "He wanted to say that he had streamlined the government," she told the Samurai. "He wanted to announce budget surpluses." One day the Samurai was informed by a caseworker he'd never met before that his sister had arrived to take him "home."

Not only is my Samurai a gentle soul, he's also afflicted by some unspecified mental illness. His actions don't originate from malice, but rather from faulty brain chemistry and a savage upbringing. He's like an actor being fed the wrong lines.

It's nearing the end of February, when the Samurai promised Herb he'd leave. Back in the house Iulia has shared with Herb since they married, he goes through the paper and sees an ad for work at an ice factory. The next morning, he calls and is asked to come in.

He lets Iulia sleep late—she's not hairdressing today—and takes the bus to the address he was given. He spends his first day loading bags of ice onto pallets in the warehouse. When he gets home, he watches the relief pass over his sister's face when he tells her about working a full shift. On the second day, he's asked to make deliveries with a driver, an Oriental guy who looks a little younger than the Samurai, in his midtwenties. He's small and skinny, with a rattail that peeks out of his shirt collar. He speaks with a faint accent. His name is Mickey. "Like Mick Jagger or Mickey Mouse," he says when they shake hands, "but not like Mickey Rooney."

"Are you Japanese?" the Samurai asks. They load the truck in the morning light. "I know the language. A bit of it. I would like to practice."

"Am I speaking Jap to you, man?" Mickey says. He shakes his head. "No, I'm Chinese, but I won't speak any Chinese to you either." He spins the radio dial and starts singing along to Bon Jovi until he grows bored. *"That's Bon Jovi, 'Livin' on a Prayer' and hitting all the high notes as we take our show to the top of the hour,"* he says in a radio announcer's voice. *"This is DJ Mick Cheung and his sidekick, Silent C., hoping you're getting through hump day.* How do I sound?"

"Really good," the Samurai tells him. "Like a pro."

"Yeah, man, that's because I am," he says, heaving his thumb toward his chest. Mickey spent a year studying radio broadcasting before he was shot and robbed by his childhood best friend. He shows the Samurai the scar from the bullet. It looks like a penny had been pressed to his arm. "I used to get in trouble. Now, only a little—to keep things saucy. What's your story? There's something about your eyes." He snaps his fingers. "Like you're looking at everything for the first time."

The Samurai shrugs. He has been living in the hospital since he was twenty-four. After losing a kitchen job, between homes, a voice he later recognized to be his daimyo's instructed him to stab someone in the shelter he was living in. "I'm a private person," he says, repeating what Mama once told him to say. "But a friendly person."

"You were in prison?" Mickey says. He grins. *"Shit.* You look too soft to be an inmate."

"Not exactly," the Samurai says. He's relieved that Mickey has come close to the truth without recoiling. "But I guess you're not completely wrong."

"Oh, okay, be that way, Mr. Mystery."

In fact, the ice factory job was real, real to C. But I'm inventing Mickey, the kind of blustery dude I grew up with in Chinatown, as a sidekick. I don't know if the real-life Samurai, my sensei, had any friends. How could I? I was just a kid when everything happened.

Mickey follows his route without a hitch. Convenience stores, green-grocers, and fish markets in the morning. Restaurants and bars in the after-noon until the shift ends. At each stop, the Samurai climbs into the back of the truck. He throws a piece of cardboard on the ground and then drops the bagged blocks of ice onto it so they break and loosen. Then he and Mickey load the handcarts and deliver bags of ice. Mickey leads them through back doors, around kitchens and storage areas. He deals with the transactions. He talks sports with the white guys. He flirts with women.

"You look familiar," he says to the manager of a fifties-themed diner. "You're not on TV, are you? A weather girl? Just in case you're famous, may I have your autograph?" The manager rolls her once-unamused eyes and accepts the in-voice on Mickey's clipboard. Moments later, she gives him a milkshake to go.

With the Chinese convenience store owners, he talks to them in Chinese until they notice the Samurai and their eyes fall. Mickey runs back into the truck and reappears with a carton of cigarettes under each arm. Afterward, they vanish into a back room for several minutes. The Samurai waits in the truck until Mickey returns.

"Remember how I said I like things saucy? I get the cigarettes from some friends," he says as he flips through a wad of twenty-dollar bills. It's easy to let Mickey talk. How fortunate the Samurai feels to be spared from commenting on the weather or sports. "Driving this truck is what I do during the day. I like to keep busy. The driving pays my bills, but if you want to have fun, man, you need a side hustle. Anytime someone needs something, they come to me," Mickey boasts in the truck. He juts out his chin. "What do you need?"

The Samurai hesitates before he blurts it out. "A place to live."

Mickey hunches over his steering wheel at a red light. When he's certain the intersection is clear, he guns the car through. "Easy," he says afterward. "I know the place. When do you need it?"

"As soon as possible."

"I'll make a call, okay?"

He pulls over at a pay phone, gets out, and the Samurai overhears him negotiating in Chinese. When Mickey returns to the car, he names a price for rent, in cash, which the Samurai agrees to. "Can you get me that money tonight?" The Samurai nods. And even though he hardly has anything, he accepts Mickey's offer to help him move.

On his way home, he goes to the bank. The clerk who's normally there when he visits with Iulia isn't around, but the Samurai overcomes his panic and makes a withdrawal with a new teller for a sum totaling the deposit and first month's rent. He leaves with so much cash that his wallet won't close.

When he gets home, his brother-in-law, Herb, waits for dinner with his nose in a paperback and one hand holding a pipe. He grunts when he sees the Samurai. Iulia is at the stove making an old family favorite. Cabbage rolls and sausages, served with a green salad and an opened jar of store-bought pickles. In her final month of pregnancy, she totters over to the table carrying a casserole dish. Finally seated, knees fanned out, she releases a yawn. She seems to remind herself to perk up and launches into a detached monologue to blanket over the gaping silence. "Well, how was my day, you might ask?" she says. "Pretty good. I was tipped very nicely by a woman who said a lot of mean things about Jewish people. I found a stroller I like. And the cabbage rolls aren't too salty, so that's good too."

He doesn't know how to interrupt this odd banter to tell her he's leaving.

Even while the dishes are familiar, she tries to replicate the dinner conversation they never had. Growing up, they didn't know exactly what they lacked, only that the details of their domestic lives were off-kilter and not to be shared. On those nights as children, they would eat in silence. The Samurai would count the number of times forks would clink against the plate—sometimes sixty-five or eighty, sometimes two or four—before Tata would scream at Mama for letting vegetables overcook, or until Mama would complain of a headache and retreat to her bedroom. He preferred it when Mama would forget dinner altogether and he would instead get to eat one of her buns, freshly made in the morning, alone at the table while Tata stewed in his workshop. Before Tata got drunk and looked for someone to hit.

"I'm moving out tonight. I found a place in Chinatown," the Samurai announces when Iulia takes a sip of water. "Sorry to interrupt."

Iulia looks to Herb, whose silverware stops its scraping. "Oh," she says. "Why didn't you tell us earlier? We could have celebrated. Great news."

The Samurai looks down at his lap. "It just popped into my head."

Herb pushes his chair back and finally cracks the can of Diet Coke he drinks every night. He's a little guy, slightly shorter than Iulia, and probably half her size even when she's not pregnant. He wears flowery polyester button-ups and makes fun of Iulia for not appreciating wine. Tata would hate him for many things but mostly for being a member of the Socialist Party. At the news of the Samurai's departure, Herb can barely contain his exuberance. "Do you need help?"

The Samurai shakes his head. "My Oriental—my Chinese friend is helping me."

Iulia erupts with questions. Then Herb makes a joke about the Samurai's good fortune to leave before the screaming baby comes, confirming the Samurai's suspicion that he's done them a favor by finding his own place.

He takes his dish to the sink and then heads to his basement room. He rolls up the futon he's been keeping on the floor next to Herb's desk. This is Herb's house, which he inherited from his parents. Even though Iulia's lived here for two years, most of her furniture and photos are still in boxes in the garage.

It doesn't take him long to pack. Just a duffel bag with his donated clothes and a box of his practice weapons. He's finished reading an issue of *Inside Karate* magazine that he borrowed from the library. He skims an article entitled "Modern Samurai: Countering World Terrorism." Maybe Iulia can return his copy to the library with her romance novels. He sits on his heels and tries to meditate, but there's a knock at the door.

"Hey, man," Herb says, scratching the back of his neck. "Just wanted to say we liked having you here. I may not have acted that way all the time. Sorry. You're still welcome here for dinner whenever Iulia's cooking. Don't be a stranger."

They shake hands. The Samurai appreciates this fool's efforts, although they exhaust him. He's been in his space long enough, sponging off his generosity. He's eaten Herb's meals and slept in his study. He bows deeply to him.

In return for the hospitality, the Samurai had tried to help out. When Herb took Iulia to birth class, they asked him to babysit Herb's kids from his previous marriage. The Samurai initially said no. "I'm not good with kids," he said. Herb stomped off, and Iulia insisted that he try. The Samurai should have known better. Despite his true intentions, his good deeds inevitably misfire. Wherever he goes, he leaves hurt people, and, knowing this, he realizes that a lonely life is the best one.

The first time minding Herb's kids passed uneventfully. The boys just sat in front of the TV for two hours while the Samurai read *Inside Karate* at the kitchen table. The second time, the other week, was when it went sideways. The two boys wanted to hang out in his room. They wanted to use his nunchucks and shurikens, the ones he had bought the day after his release. He knew that was a bad idea. But they insisted. And so they compromised. He showed them the homemade bokuto that he had made from a hockey stick, how to bow. And then he demonstrated the first few katas that he had learned in karate class. C., the real-life Samurai, my sensei, had mentioned his own unremittingly cruel instructor. "Thank me later," he would always say as I felt the bruises rise on my body.

Herb's boys got warm in their bulky sweatshirts and insisted on taking them off. Then they wanted to remove their shirts. They loved Bruce Lee movies and he was always shirtless. The boys, who got into periodic scrapes with each other, wanted to spar until they were sweaty and wild-eyed.

"I'll do it if you put on your shirts," the Samurai told them. They agreed.

He went upstairs to get a broom handle to use as a second sword. He found it, unscrewed it from the broom head. The boys were too much, and he needed to calm himself before he returned downstairs. He was on the steps when the younger boy, who was maybe eleven, started screaming in pain. The Samurai could hear the gravel crunching as the Hyundai pulled into the backyard driveway. Running downstairs, he saw the Samurai's weapons removed from his closet and on his bed. The younger boy had a ninja star embedded in his bloodied hand. His older brother, thirteen and girthy, was trying to laugh away his tears. To make matters worse, the boys were still shirtless. He couldn't stand to look at them.

Herb didn't speak to the Samurai for a week after that. Tonight, however, the Samurai shakes Herb's hand again, jogging it with conviction. They share a couple of glasses of white zinfandel and then the Samurai accepts Herb's offer to carry his bag to Mickey's little red sports car. Everything is better now that he's leaving.

"You ready?" Mickey asks.

CHAPTER THREE

All words. No pictures. Child abuse, I warned my publisher, in an email about this project. Gory ending. It's gonna be a bummer. I expected that they'd be turned off by the change in direction. And I didn't even know they published books without pictures. But they saw this as a comeback opportunity and threw a deadline in my face. I wasn't so optimistic. Even as I drew from my own life, I found myself repelled by the material. Take, for instance, Poh-Poh. In these Asian immigrant tales, Grandma is always a selfless, sentimental placeholder for a child's failure to honor their family and uphold cultural traditions. The grandmother, recruited to raise a child she did not bring into the world, executes her task with diligence until her body can no longer comply. In my story, I hew unerringly close to the stereotype.

For the boy, it means caring for his caretaker, and realizing that even an obedient, clever child cannot stem an old woman's precipitous decline. For three days, Poh-Poh does not rise from her bed. Between coughing jags, she asks the boy, Benny, for cups of hot water from her water boiler. But she hasn't eaten. Not that there's anything to eat. All that's left in the house are instant noodles, some blotchy gai lan, a loaf of Wonder Bread, and a jar of peanut butter. Even the rice bin is only a fingertip deep.

On the third day, he calls out her name when he comes home from school and sets his backpack by the door. He hears her groan and then the squeak of the mattress as Poh-Poh sits up for the first time.

"Get a pencil, laa," she spits out. "And some paper."

He pulls out a pencil and a piece of loose-leaf from his school bag. Poh-Poh recites a list of ingredients for a soup. To Poh-Poh, soup is magic, a potion to reset the imbalanced body. Benny himself disputes its curative effects and place of honor at every dinner in their apartment, and resents the way the musky scent of shiitake mushrooms and ginseng seeps into his clothes, but for once, he hopes his grandmother is right. *See what I said about oppressive superstition? Soup will fix everything.* She hands over money from her lanyard money pouch. "Get a small bag of rice. And buy things for yourself too," she says.

He grabs the folding cart. There's a bite in the air outside, so he slips on Poh-Poh's gloves and an ugly scarf she knitted for him in a brown argyle pattern—as though it were modeled after a piece of stewed tripe. He makes the stops in the same order as he would have with his grandmother. The Chinese medicine shop is the exception, and he doesn't know where to find the dried roots that Poh-Poh wrote down for him. He points to the ingredient on the list, and the pharmacist, a man with a whiskery mole, totters, holding out one hand as if leaning on an invisible cane, to the bin Benny needs to scoop the roots from.

Benny buys a whole silkie chicken from the butcher. He has four dollars left, but he still needs a package of peanuts.

Outside the corner store, he sees Shirley's brother, Wai, watching men unload bags of ice from a truck. Wai nods at him. He's about seventeen, not much taller than Benny, but his chest is three times as wide as Benny's in a leather bomber jacket. He wears gold chains over a black turtleneck, Reebok sneakers Benny would die for, and dark jeans. Cologne insufficiently masks the smell of the cigarettes the older boy smokes. To Benny, he's off-the-charts cool. The available male role models for him are, well . . . slim pickings. "Are you here to see Shirley or to look at the magazines?" Wai asks him, smirking.

Benny hides his reddening face as he steps inside. Last year, Benny and his best friend, August Pham, were caught by Mrs. Mah flipping through an issue of *Juggs*. If Wai knows all about it, then Shirley does too.

Benny finds peanuts on a shelf next to the bags of potato chips. With the money left over, he picks up a shrink-wrapped package of three lychee juice boxes. And a package of frozen potstickers.

"How did you do on the English quiz?" Shirley asks him. She starts ringing up the items. "Did you ace it?"

Laying out his four dollars in change on the counter, his heart starts thumping. "Maybe," he says tentatively. "How did *you* do?"

Her eyes sink to the floor. "My parents can't help me. They just tell me to try harder."

He hesitates. "I can help."

"Really?" She notices the money on the counter. "It's $4.40."

"Oh." He's forgotten about tax.

She catches him from the corners of her eyes. "Do you think I got the amount wrong?"

He takes the juice boxes from the counter. "I don't need these."

She pushes four quarters back to him. When he gets home, Poh-Poh is upright and dressed for the day. Her bed has been made. She still looks weak, but Benny's optimism flares seeing her lift a soup pot filled with water onto the stove.

The soup takes a few hours to cook. They eat dinner late. Poh-Poh makes a pot of rice and fries up the remaining gai lan in ginger. Normally, Benny would drink only the minimum portion of Poh-Poh's medicinal soups. But this is the first real dinner that he's had all week. His hunger has been a car alarm bleating in the background. He fills his rice bowl three times. When he's finally done eating, his body applauds.

The soup has restored Poh-Poh, and instead of going straight to bed she plays Chinese chess with Benny. She beats him handily, but when he begins to reset the pieces on the board, she tells him she needs sleep.

He basks in his allotted hour of TV. By the end of it, Poh-Poh's eyes are shut and her breathing audible. Benny drags her legs to the end of the couch and gets her bedding, wedging a pillow under her head and draping a duvet over her. Poh-Poh's coughing resumes in the middle of the night. And she is still on the couch when he wakes up from her bed. Benny prepares another peanut butter sandwich to take to school and leaves with her sleeping.

It feels as if the day will throttle his capacity for joy out of him. In his history and English blocks, his classmates have forgotten about his voice cracking, but he doesn't speak up, not once. He staples his hands to the desk until the end of time. He eats his subpar sandwich alone and studies in the library during lunch hour. Back in class, he finds a piece of folded paper on top of his desk.

Do you still want to study with me after school? Meet me outside today.

He stares at Shirley's ponytail for the rest of class, but there's no difference
in her behavior. She never turns back to acknowledge him, much less her invitation.

When the final bell sounds, he gathers his things. Wandering outside, he
finds Shirley by the sidewalk in the exact place Steph found him the other
week.

"Is my house okay?" she asks when he approaches.

They walk three blocks in silence before they reach her house with its
gray stucco siding and shingled roof. Inside they ascend the creaky steps until
Benny recognizes the altar with incense and a statue of Kwan Kung in the
landing outside the door, which Shirley opens with a key she wears around
her neck, just like Benny. Poh-Poh may look down on Shirley's family for not
being well educated—Poh-Poh's father was a xiucai, a scholar who passed
the Imperial examinations—but they live in a house, or at least the top half
of one. In the front room, Shirley's mom, who works as a seamstress when
she's not at the store, keeps a VCR with stacks of cassettes hand-labeled with
the titles of Hong Kong soap operas and a tub of dried plums. Shirley's dad's
place is marked off by a black leather armchair that reclines with a lever, its
seat messy with empty peanut shells. Shirley and Wai each have their own
room. Benny stands outside hers while she retrieves a pencil sharpener. Instead of a door, there's a curtain that she pulls open, as the room is more like
a glorified storage closet. And yet, to Benny, this nod toward privacy makes
his heart churn in envy. She even has her own desk with drawers and a lamp.

They take their schoolwork to the kitchen table. As he sits opposite Shirley
at the round table, Benny eyes the phone behind her on the wall, thinking he
should call Poh-Poh. Normally she'd be worried that he wasn't already home.
He'd get a scolding. But not now, not when she's still sleeping. It's better not to
wake her up and force her out of bed.

Shirley serves them both a plate of lemon crackers with lychee juice boxes.
The ones he wanted to buy the day before. She remembered! She turns the

lazy Susan to advance the plate toward the boy, who sits so far apart from his inamorata that it looks as though they're negotiating a nuclear missile treaty and not studying together.

"Why don't you pull over your chair?" she asks at last.

He drags his seat toward her, his cheeks flushing, as she cracks open her binder. He hadn't known his palms could get so damp. For their English homework, Mrs. Renzullo has assigned three reading response questions to the third chapter of *Never Cry Wolf*.

"What's the right answer?" Shirley asks him after reciting the first question.

"Well, there's no right answer," he says. "At least, not one."

Her eyes cross in exasperation. "But what's *your* answer?"

When he doesn't respond, she stares through him as though he doesn't exist. Benny is reminded of how the two of them used to play when they were kids. If she wanted something from him, she would point her eyes at him until he relented. If he didn't, she would punch him and wake Mommy in her room to tell her he'd uttered the F-word. Mommy would laugh about it after Shirley's mother picked her up. "She gets what she wants, one way or another," she would say to Benny.

Shirley starts writing down what Benny tells her, but then, in a pique of frustration, throws her pen onto the lazy Susan. "Can't you talk more slowly?" she says.

He reaches for her pen. "Let me write for you."

She clucks at him. "Teacher will know." Swiveling on her seat from side to side, she holds up his worksheet at eye level, the way Mrs. Renzullo does, standing in front of the class when she shows Benny's immaculate cursive.

"It's not my fault she does that."

"Isn't it?"

He helps her through the rest of the answers, trying to answer them in her voice. How she ends every statement like a question, how she cabooses her thoughts with qualifications. *"And so mankind, and not the wolf, is the ruthless killer? And the vicious killer? But not the Inuit."* After a while, he does it for effect.

"Stop it," she says, her voice hitching when she laughs. "Stop copying me."

They finish right around when Shirley's mother comes home. Entering the kitchen, Mrs. Mah asks Shirley if she's seen her brother. "He's probably out selling drugs," Shirley says, hunching over fearfully as her mother starts slamming cupboard doors in response. Mrs. Mah doesn't acknowledge Benny. Ever since she caught him and August poking through that copy of *Juggs* at the store, she hasn't met his gaze. Or maybe he's the one who can't meet hers.

Benny gathers his things. Shirley waves from the door when he leaves the foyer. He knows he's just her homework mule. But he's happy. And a little worried. He should have called Poh-Poh. No doubt she's awake by now. She's probably worried about him. She'll scold him. She'll pull his ear and slap him with the ruler she used to teach Chinese school, the one she keeps only for smacking him. "Your mother should have given birth to a piece of barbecue pork instead," she will say. "At least we could have eaten that." And now he hurries his pace. He runs down the street to their building. He sprints into the elevator.

"Wait!" he hears someone say. Benny jabs the button to close the elevator doors.

A hand slips between them before they shut. In come a small Chinese man and a towering white dude. The big white guy's really noticeable. He's as big as an outhouse and smells like one, with the cloying stink of someone sweaty and hairy. He's in baggy sweatpants, holding a box. A laundry bag at his feet. His Chinese friend is chattering about the apartment he's moving into. "Fourth floor, best view," the friend says. "Four is not a good number for Chinese folks, but for a Caucasian like you—it's very lucky." The big white guy grunts. For a man who takes up so much space, he's oddly disengaged from it—as though you could walk through him. Benny shudders at the thought of how Poh-Poh will react when she sees this big white guy living down the hallway from them. He pictures her cowering and smiling reflexively the way she always does around white folks.

When the doors open to his floor, he dashes down the once-red runner carpet, now brown, until he gets to the door and braces himself for his grandmother's fury. That's another thing that the Asian grandma represents. Rebuke and corporal punishment.

At the door, Benny realizes something is off. He doesn't smell anything from the other side. He doesn't hear her cough.

He stands there a moment, knowing who's not behind the door but not wanting to believe. It's not impossible for her to be there, only unbearable.

Poh-Poh isn't there. And she doesn't come back that night.

For dinner, he eats the leftover rice in the fridge. He tries to finish the homework he started at Shirley's. He changes into his pajamas and tries to sleep. The night feels like a week. It feels like a net that he can't untangle himself from. Lying in bed, eyes open, he waits for Poh-Poh to come through the door, plotting his reaction. Will he scream at her for leaving him, as a way to stave off his tears, or will he be too happy to care and cry anyhow? At the sound of footsteps, he bolts upright. Eventually, he dozes off. When he wakes up, it's morning and he's tired. And still alone.

He gets dressed and makes another peanut butter sandwich for lunch. Should he even go to school?

He watches the clock. At a little past eight, the phone rings. He lunges for it.

"A-Benny," his grandmother says. The voice is faint.

"Poh-Poh." His voice trembles as he utters her name.

Slowly, she relates her story. She decided she was strong enough to go outside. She was across the street at the park when she felt dizzy. "The next thing I know, I woke up here," she explains. "Someone found me passed out and called an ambulance, gwaa."

He hears a jostling sound as the phone is taken away from her. A woman's voice speaks to him in English, in a British accent. She tells Benny that she's a nurse, and that his grandmother was admitted last night. "We're running some tests on her heart this afternoon," she says.

This pretty much happened to my own grandmother, except I was a college student—technically, an adult—when my poh-poh called from the hospital. I was as shocked as Benny when I learned the news, but of course I was a grown-up. When it happens to a twelve-year-old, as I've depicted here, compressing and intensifying events, it not only escalates the situation but gets closer to the emotional truth of the moment. The helplessness, I mean. It's less embarrassing for a twelve-year-old to feel that way too.

"When will she be home?" Benny asks.

"That's hard to say. Would it be possible to speak to your mother?"

"She's at work. But I can get her to call you back."

He doesn't know why he lied, only that Poh-Poh would want him to. Otherwise, he'd get sent to his father, a man he barely remembers, and the person Poh-Poh blames for Mommy's death.

"Get her to phone right away," the nurse says. She gives him phone and room numbers to take down.

He hears Poh-Poh in the background. She's asking to speak.

"Call A-Yi to look after you," she tells him.

After he assents, he hangs up to find Steph's number with his other personal items, in the dresser he shares with his grandmother. His clothes take up the top two drawers, but in the back of the second one, he keeps his treasures in a shoebox. Before he gave it to August Pham, that's where he kept Optimus Prime—the last gift from his mother. There's forty-two dollars left over from the Lunar New Year and his honor roll certificates. There's the only family photo with his father, taken when Benny was just born. Mommy, in a purple turtleneck, seems tired but smiles her froggy, closed-mouth smile. His father was a handsome man, like my own father—tall and broad-shouldered, with high cheekbones and a playful scowl—who resented the job he had selling insurance. Even Poh-Poh would admit that he looked like a movie star. "The trouble wasn't his looks, or his manners," she would say. "It was his dishonesty." His father cheated on Mommy, spent her hard-earned money on clothes and a sports car, and then later a scheme to import electronics from Hong Kong. Like my own father, as well, he left the family for good right after Mommy got sick.

When not lying outright, Benny's father made promises he failed to keep, or kept poorly. Benny's strongest memory of him is of a trip to the amusement park that his father was two hours late to take him on, and the single ride—a cup that spun—they shared before the park closed and his father tried unsuccessfully to bribe an attendant, with a five-dollar bill, to run the ride one more time. For Benny, that counted as a good memory. Even though his dad has a mustache in the photo, Benny thinks he can see the expression on himself in his school portraits. Maybe that mustache is gone, and maybe that clean-shaven version of his father, who's found work in another city managing his uncle's nightclub, is a more honest one of a man who misses his only child.

Putting the photo away, Benny finds Steph's old Walkman. Folded between two of the cassettes she gave him is the phone number of the drummer. He dials the number. He lets it ring for minutes, but there's no answer. He waits five minutes and calls again.

"What . . . is it?" The voice is whimpering and groggy.

Benny pauses. "Hi, do you know where my aunt is?"

"Who?"

"Stephanie Choi."

"Wrong number. Bye—"

"Wait, is your roommate in a band?"

Benny hears a sigh. "Yep."

"My aunt is the lead singer. They're on tour."

"Right, *Steph.*" Benny hears a throat clearing. "Sorry to be a dick about it. I had a late night."

So did I. "Um, Steph said you had a list of clubs that her band was playing. Could I get that?"

"Oh yeah, it's somewhere in the house, but I'm going to level with you, I'm a little too wasted to find it."

The voice on the other end tells him to call again in the afternoon and then the line clicks dead.

CHAPTER FOUR

As I imagine the Samurai's life, I dress him up from scraps of memory. I put him in C.'s one-room apartment, with its kitchenette and balcony. His window is so different from mine, which looks out into the yard and the Orientalist garden. Where I live now, semidomesticated deer roam free. It shocked me, a city kid, to see them when we first relocated here for my wife, Trina's, teaching job. Now my daughter, Adele, and I sometimes leave lettuce and cobs of corn in the winter when they get scrawny. We stand at my office window and watch them come over the pond on the footbridge to graze, and the two of us sketch them in crayon. After all these years here, the emptiness, the quiet of this place I call home, still make me want to scream.

From his own window, the Samurai sees clothes hung from other balconies. In the hallway, he hears Chinese and the scrape of spatulas on woks from other apartments. His neighbors keep wall hangings with Chinese characters and small altars at their doors. Just like at C.'s old place.

The Samurai stands out, of course, but only for being white, and for being so big. But not for looking crazy. The old folks on his floor, who live on their own, shudder at the sight of him. Passing them, he smells reused cooking oil, mothballs, and musty smells that he doesn't know are stewed mushrooms and bitter melons.

On his first day there, he goes to work, takes home seventy-five-cent slices of pizza from a place near the ice factory, and reads his karate magazines until he falls asleep. When he arrives home from work on his third night, Iulia and Herb are waiting by the building entrance with a bag of groceries, a shower curtain, and a box of secondhand cookware. The baby is due in two weeks and Iulia's face is pale and drawn. The first thing she mentions, once she's inside his empty apartment, is that he doesn't have a phone. "We couldn't reach you.

How will you know when the baby is born? Or when to visit? What if you're bored and you want to talk?"

Herb, who often describes himself as a cinephile, has brought a movie poster. "You don't want to stare at bare walls, bro. That's depressing."

On the poster, a grimacing, bearded samurai holds his katana upside down, so the blade is parallel to his forearm. It's a nonstandard kata. Above the samurai's topknot, in bamboo script, reads the movie title. SANJURO.

"You've seen this, right?" Herb asks.

The Samurai nods. "It's super good." He really hasn't seen it, but he doesn't have the patience to hear his brother-in-law wax on about a movie—a "film."

Herb unrolls the poster and tapes it to the wall opposite the kitchen. "This should really be framed."

I still remember that poster from C.'s nearly identical apartment. C. said he had a tiny apartment by choice. In reality, my abuser's place was meticulously cluttered with his trophies, the adult magazines opened up on a coffee table, the shag rug and hide-a-bed. The bottle of Jim Beam he kept above the refrigerator, the memory of which burns in the back of my throat. The crusted smell of a bachelor corralled with cologne and deodorant. I take all of that away from the Samurai's apartment. In my imagination, I give that apartment a deep clean.

The Samurai is a minimalist by intent and necessity. A few days in, though, this oddball unrolls a second tatami mat and begins practicing his kata with his homemade bokuto. He does that for an hour and is winded. He follows the set of illustrated nunchuck exercises in a magazine he's taken out of the library. He does that for another hour and then showers with the sliver of soap that he took from Iulia's house. Samurai are prepared. Samurai are clean. Samurai keep ruinous secrets. Even the masterless samurai.

At some point, I need to give the Samurai an actual sword. Every samurai has one, even this big white-guy samurai. One night, the Samurai wanders out farther so he's not in Chinatown, where the Chinese shopkeepers follow him with folded arms. In this part of town, people are hunched over, drinking from brown paper bags, men walking by muttering "Skunk" and "Hash" at him. As night falls, he orders bacon and eggs at a diner next door to a pawnshop where the sword catches his eye.

The next day, when the pawnshop is open, he shuffles inside to look at the swords. The first one he's shown is a flimsy replica. *Made in Hong Kong* is written in English on the bottom of the tsuka, or handle. It's meant to be a wall decoration. If he were to swing it, the blade would fly off the tsuka.

"It's fifty bucks," the pawnbroker says. "But I can give it to you for thirty-five."

The Samurai points to another sword, in a glass counter next to a set of war medals. "What about that one?"

The pawnbroker steps back. His wolfish smile recedes. "Well, that's pricier."

"Let me see it."

The pawnbroker digs out a set of keys from his pocket. He steps back and holds the sword in his hands for the Samurai to inspect from a distance. He removes it from the black lacquer saya, or scabbard. The polish and point of the blade are exquisite. The steel gleams, even in the store's fluorescent light. On the blade itself runs a milky streak with glittering grains. They look like sparks of fire.

"It's the real thing," the Samurai says.

"Don't have any authenticity papers," the pawnbroker says with a shrug. "It belonged to a family that came over from Japan before the war. They were sent to an internment camp and their belongings auctioned off. An 'enthusiast of the Orient' bought it for a few bucks. And then his son inherited it. He has a gambling problem."

The Samurai asks for a price. When the shopkeeper shows him the tag on the tsuka, $2,000, the Samurai shrinks back.

"Thought so," the pawnbroker says, sheathing the blade again and replacing it in its case. "I've got more of a midrange model in the back, if you like, for a couple hundred."

"I've got money. It's in the bank."

The pawnbroker smirks. "If you have the money, why don't you go get it?"

"The bank is on the other side of town."

He folds his arms across his chest. "Can't promise anything."

The Samurai finds himself unable to shake the idea of a real katana in his hands. A katana is not just a weapon but a talisman. It scares off demons.

He counts the money in his slacks. Thirty-eight dollars and change. He's going to be paid soon, and he doesn't spend much, but he's not going to have two grand until the end of the year. Who knows where the sword will be?

When he goes to the bank, he's told his sister has power of attorney, and that he was only able to withdraw money for his rent last week because the bank teller working that day was a trainee.

It's for the best. The Samurai owes it to Iulia to be good with his inheritance, the proceeds from Tata's life insurance policy, and take his medication. He remembers how his parents used to fight over Mama's spending. Tata made Mama use a chalkboard in the kitchen to account for every penny she spent. When Mama behaved, she would be scrupulous with these rules. Because Tata worked hard installing telephone lines. But then Mama would have her days (and weeks and months) when the rules no longer mattered. Not even if Tata threatened her with his belt. She would donate, to the church, money that had been set aside for Constantine's and Iulia's new shoes. The Samurai spent one year walking around with his big toes poking through his shoes. She would order from catalogs, buying booties and formula to send to the children of relatives in Bucharest, kids who were already teenagers. Mama had some trouble recognizing people's ages. She even insisted on bathing him when he was a teenager, scrubbing his changing body with a sponge. "Feels good, no?" she would say.

The Samurai gets the shaft in both nature and nurture. Born to a sociopath and a crazy lady with boundary issues. Never make things easy for your hero, who broods over that sword the next day at work and flies through his tasks more silently than normal. Mickey's joking around and smiling exceed his baseline exuberance. The Samurai's new friend doesn't keep secrets, not for long, so he admits that he's got a date. "I was reading in a magazine that the supermarket is better than a nightclub on a Friday night," he says. "I think, sure, let's give it a try. And so I spot this nice-looking girl while I'm in the produce aisle squeezing melons. I tell her I like her . . . eyes." He starts to snicker.

Spring has come ahead of schedule. Business has picked up in the early swelter, and they make more than their usual round of deliveries. Mickey doesn't seem to be in a hurry. "Like I said, I'm my own boss!" After the first stop, he pulls over by a pay phone to make a call. Seeing him, the Samurai thinks he should check in on Iulia. He misses her but knows she's relieved to be free of him.

Mickey doesn't talk much on the way to their next delivery. He keeps the radio off. He looks like someone trying to solve a riddle as his expression becomes blank. The Samurai figures he should ask what's wrong. He holds off.

"Hey, Mickey," he says instead. "How do I find a side hustle?"

Mickey laughs. "Well, let's see. What are you good at?"

The Samurai thinks. "Delivering ice."

Mickey shakes his head. "Can't help you if you can't help yourself." He laughs. "Oh man, there are so many jobs for a white dude like you. Legit stuff. You could sell encyclopedias or shampoo carpet treatments door-to-door. You could manage a newspaper delivery center. So many options."

None of them appeal to the Samurai. And none are as lucrative as Mickey's extra work. In between unloading bags of ice, his friend drops off more cartons of cigarettes and comes back with envelopes of cash. At other stops, the Samurai waits as Mickey disappears into alleyways. He sees Mickey trading his envelopes for plastic shopping bags that he tucks under his arm as he saunters back to the truck. As Mickey takes the driver's seat, his pager buzzes. "I need to make one more call," he tells the Samurai. He takes the truck around the block to a pay phone.

When Mickey returns to the truck, he needs a favor. "She wants to bring a friend," he says. "You can come with me. Dinner, drinks, all that foreplay. Do you have nice clothes? No offense, but you dress like a homeless veteran."

The Samurai shakes his head. "No."

"Okay, I can find a jacket that will fit you."

"I can't go out."

Mickey flashes the smile he's used the few times the Samurai has seen someone call him a "chink." He turns on the music. "Come on, man. You're not bad-looking. You don't need to be alone every night. When was the last time you went out?"

The Samurai's next "No" is forceful enough to silence Mickey. They make another stop at a supermarket, and his coworker is slower to exit the truck to help him unload.

When they leave, Mickey won't look at him. The Samurai knows that the silences he enjoys are painful and awkward to others. But now, with Mickey silent, he too can feel the tension of the moment.

"I'd only ruin things," the Samurai says at last. "Your friend will want to go home early."

Mickey slams his fist on the steering wheel. "When are you going to pull your weight? I help you with your job, with your apartment. I can even get you a nice jacket that you can wear to a wedding. Anything you want, I do it for you. For nothing, for no reason. So why aren't you helping me?"

He pulls over and looks toward his window, sucking his teeth aggressively. When the Samurai realizes that they won't finish their shift on time, he agrees to help. He'll go out. Mickey starts the engine again. He turns the radio on to something upbeat and cranks the volume. He lets out a laugh to express his embarrassment that their dispute became so heated. He starts joking again.

They veer off from the next stop listed on the clipboard and park in another alley in Chinatown. Mickey disappears through a door next to the dumpster and comes out with a black velvet sports jacket on a wooden hanger. He asks the Samurai to step out and try it on. It's snug around the shoulders but wearable.

"How does it feel?" Mickey asks. "My buddy rents out suits and tuxes inside." He's got another jacket for himself.

"It's okay." The Samurai tries, and fails, to raise his arms over his shoulders.

Mickey brushes lint from the Samurai's shoulder. "You won't need a jacket when it's time for *gymnastics*."

The Samurai grows red at his suggestion. *When people talk that way*, Mama said as she ran a sponge along his teenage torso, *tell them you're a gentleman*. But whenever he did say that, people looked at him as though he had admitted to being a pedophile. So he smiles instead. They finish the shift the way they always do, with Mickey dragging out each interaction with a manager and taking smoke breaks to chew up the afternoon. Sometimes, he drops off one of his shopping bags. The money he comes back with is now in a bigger, manila envelope. The Samurai again wishes he had a side hustle.

When the day comes to a close, what he really wants to do before he socializes is bathe. But Mickey takes a whiff of his armpit and pronounces him "fresh as a daisy." At the end of their shift, they collect their pay. In the staff lot, they climb into Mickey's cherry-red Pontiac Fiero and go to a check-cashing place. "You might need some cash," Mickey says. Afterward, he suggests they get a shave, and they find a barber who slaps hot towels on their faces, lathers them with soap, and scrapes their necks with a straight razor.

Mickey pays with money from his manila envelope. "You can get the drinks," he says before he reaches across into the glove compartment for a square blue bottle and douses them both in cologne.

After they get burgers, their next stop is the brick-lined tavern where Mickey has chosen to meet their dates. The Samurai hasn't had alcohol in years. He remembers that the first time he heard his daimyo's voice was after he'd finished an entire bottle of Southern Comfort given to him by a coworker he'd helped move furniture. When the bartender takes his order, he points to the drink in front of a barfly sitting alone.

"Vodka soda," the bartender says before he pours a tall glass.

The Samurai's first sip calms him down. At Mickey's suggestion, they've arrived early to get buzzed. "Normally, I would suggest we share a bottle in the parking lot," he says, "but I like to shoot pool."

They play a game, and once the pool balls break, the Samurai knows that Mickey's an ace. He sinks every shot, as matter-of-factly as someone stepping into slippers. "Oh yeah," he says, when the Samurai gasps at a bank shot. "I used to shoot a lot."

They give up the pool table when Mickey's date and her friend arrive. Their names are Donna and Lorna. Donna is Black and Lorna is white, but they look alike in high-waisted jeans and hair that is center-parted and fluffy. They have matching silver-sequined handbags. The four of them sink into a leather couch by the dartboard. As the bar fills up, the music swells in volume. Mickey suggests they shoot pool, but first he and Donna have to win a game against another couple to gain control of the table.

As Lorna and the Samurai watch Mickey and Donna, he wonders how long it'll take before he scares her off. The countdown starts with his first awkward question. "What are your interests?" She smiles like someone ignoring a bad smell. He wishes he were back in his hospital room with the small white bed, orange desk, pink chair.

Corny as he sounds, Lorna fulfills his request. She works at a bakery and is studying for a certificate in baking and pastry arts at a community college. When the Samurai's eyes brighten as she talks about baking, she seems embarrassed. "You don't need to pretend that's interesting," she says. He responds with more questions about her work. She's several years younger than him, in her early twenties. Reassured of his interest, she tells him about her plans to open a shop that specializes in the strudels and other German treats her grandmother made.

When another couple settles on the couch, Lorna and the Samurai squeeze together knee against knee. His drink has a pleasant effect, throwing a veil onto his awkwardness. He can't see it as acutely. Time passes and he doesn't remember how it does. He worries that he's talking too loudly, but when he asks her, she shakes her head and laughs and tips back her glass as though he's said something charming. Lorna asks if he wants another drink, but the Samurai offers to get up and replace her emptied light beer.

At first, as I imagine this, I tell myself that if only C. had gone out like this with Lorna, if only he were a social drinker who asked nervous questions to fluffy-headed bakers, nothing would have happened. But then I remember how C. would give me advice on meeting girls, about how to "loosen them up" and "wear them down," and I feel a little sick. I need to break up this scene for his alter ego.

When the Samurai returns from the bar, a burly Chinese kid at the pool table is pushing Mickey. The kid, short like Mickey but double his width, looks familiar. Another burly friend of the kid's stands in the background, hands already set in fists. Mickey tries to laugh off a disagreement the way he does with a meter maid who finds the ice-factory truck beside a fire hydrant. But the burly kid pushes Mickey's shoulder. Now the Samurai recognizes him. They delivered ice to his family's convenience store a few days earlier. He remembers

Mickey and the kid chatting in the alleyway, Mickey muttering in displeasure when he got back to the truck—the kid cursing him from the mouth of the alleyway. Mickey swings the pool cue at him, but his attacker's friend, who has stepped toward him, grabs the shaft.

The Samurai hears his heartbeat over the music. And then he sees himself levitating toward the pool table. What happens next escapes the Samurai's understanding. In retrospect, he remembers the kata and how his adversaries seemed to line up to his positions as though they were performing in a gymnasium. Rising punch, side kick, upper rising block. It's probably the adrenaline, but their bodies give way like padded fighting dummies.

The bartender rushes toward the pool table wearing a look of betrayal on his face that is borderline farcical. He asks Mickey and the Samurai to leave. Their opponents still lie curled on their backs. Once they exit, Mickey and the Samurai see Lorna and Donna huddled in their little jackets together on the street, their matching silver handbags glinting in the streetlights. They're startled. "We thought you two would get killed," Donna admits. They decline Mickey's offer of a nightcap and climb into a cab idling outside. Lorna seems to hesitate at the curb, then runs up to the Samurai and hands him a scrap of paper. "We gotta run," Donna says, pulling her into the taxi.

"So much for that," Mickey says in the car. He explains that the burly teen had shortchanged him in a deal last week and wanted to intimidate him into calling off the debt. "The kid thought I was there by myself. He didn't think I had backup." Mickey makes like he's dusting his hands, wiping himself clean of that trouble. "You're pretty quick for a big guy. Where'd you learn to do that tough-guy shit?"

"I used to practice karate," says the Samurai.

"It was like in a movie. It was choreographed."

The Samurai is more ashamed of his actions than pleased. In the past, in other altercations, he hurt people more than he thought he would, leaving him unsure that he actually could restrain himself once he started. When he waves off Mickey's praise, he notices a range of motion in his gesture that he hasn't had all evening. He looks over his shoulders and realizes he's torn his borrowed jacket at the shoulders. He turns around to show Mickey, apologizing. Mickey's eyes bulge and then he laughs.

"You're the Incredible Hulk, man," he says. "But the real deal!"

Later, in his building's elevator, the Samurai unfolds the scrap of paper with Lorna's name and phone number. He knows he should throw it away and save them both pain, but he tucks it into his wallet. Right now, he's feeling too much adrenaline. He's certain about himself only when he's alone. Around others he becomes the place their heartache begins.

CHAPTER FIVE

Shortly after Adele was born, I suffered from panic attacks that left me sweaty and twitchy, hiding in a closet for hours at a time with only a bottle of Diet Coke and some Ritz crackers. Trina, my wife, who had first thought I was trying to outdo her postpartum depression, asked me to see a therapist. The professional I found online received high ratings, and I liked how she swore a lot and offered me chewing gum (because she went through a few sticks herself during a session). Mostly we talked about my day-to-day concerns, but once I mentioned C., she stopped smacking her gum. She sat up on the edge of the chair. "Tell me more," she said. And when I became the laconic, taciturn Asian man Trina grappled with daily, the therapist doubled back to my work as a writer and illustrator. "Why don't you fucking write about it?"

What an original idea from a therapist who seemed to be working from some kind of *Dummies* guide to counseling. Still, I liked her more than the marriage counselor Trina made me go to last year. As it happened, I was always writing about what happened with C. I used my relationship with him as a foundation for the anthropomorphic animals that I pitted against each other in sword battles. In those illustrated stories, the hero always emerged triumphant through a combination of his own wits and the abilities of his teachers and bodyguards. Now I'm moving closer to domestic realism, if not, strictly speaking, nonfiction.

Even with Poh-Poh in the hospital, his aunt still unaccounted for, Benny knows he should go to school. Poh-Poh would insist on it. When Mommy was dying, the only time he missed a class was the day of the funeral. Even then, Poh-Poh insisted he go back to school after the jie hui, or consolation feast. Does he have any other options? He slides into his shoes and slips on his backpack. He feels almost normal.

When he doubles his pace to school and rushes into the classroom, panting as the morning bell sounds, he almost forgets about his dire situation. His day back at school proves to be a balm, and he's content until he returns to his empty apartment. He waits for Poh-Poh's call but it doesn't come, and the drummer's roommate doesn't pick up when Benny tries him. The next day is harder. He can't focus on geometry with Mr. Mason, or science with Mr. Fung. In English, he can't focus on *Never Cry Wolf*. On his third day, he's noticeably distracted. In history, as Mrs. Renzullo lists off the ancient peoples that students can present on, he stares out the window in the direction of the hospital his grandmother is lying in, the one where his mother died, until Mrs. Renzullo snaps her fingers in front of his face.

The classroom divides into groups to discuss their projects for the next half hour. He's been put in a group with Shirley—a situation that normally would leave him skittish—along with Bronson and Roderick, who hold back on delivering Benny's daily dose of scorn to await his directions. Those boys need Benny's grade-boosting. Benny stares at his hands as other groups busy themselves with the task, even after Shirley asks him if he's okay.

On this third day, when the final school bell chimes, the tension has ratcheted to the point of disobeying his grandmother's instructions. He fishes out change and heads to the bus stop. Once he's there, he studies the map under the awning and figures out his route. He gets hungry for the first time all day and eats the peanut butter sandwich he ignored during lunch hour. When the bus arrives, he takes a seat up front, where he normally sits with Poh-Poh, but realizes it's reserved for seniors when an old white lady glares at him. There are no other seats and the bus fills as it moves toward a stop. At first, he's worried that someone will notice him traveling on his own, but why would anyone care? He's a kid, not a baby.

He doesn't recognize the area he's in. Everyone here dresses the way his aunt does, artfully ragged. Unwholesome. As the bus continues, the Chinese riders step off until he's the only one. He's afraid to ask if he's on the right bus. Even though seats have opened up again, he imitates the twentysomethings standing with their hands thrust into their leather jackets, listening to their Walkmans. One day, on his way to campus, this will be him. He wishes he brought Steph's old Walkman. Finally, he sees the hospital in the distance and disembarks.

Poh-Poh will probably be mad at him for disobeying her orders and visiting. The hospital staff might figure something out. But he doesn't care. She hasn't called, he's worried, and he's prepared for her anger. The hospital feels enormous to him, and when he steps inside a maze of corridors and elevators, he feels lost. He asks for directions from someone in coveralls with a mop but gets so many he can't follow them completely. He leans against the door of a supply closet, trying to remember to breathe, until a nurse takes notice and leads him to Poh-Poh's room.

But when he arrives, it's not the right one, even if the room number is the one he wrote down over the phone. Poh-Poh isn't there.

"Hello?"

He turns around to see a nurse. "Do you know where my grandmother is?"

He catches her wince before she opens her mouth to speak.

She has a British accent, like the nurse on the phone. "Is your mother here, love?" she asks, looking past him. "I would very much like to talk to her. We've had trouble reaching her. The contact information your grandmother gave for her didn't seem to be correct."

Of course, Poh-Poh never carried identification. She spent a lifetime giving fake names and addresses. If she didn't protect herself, someone might trick her out of her money. "Where is she?" Benny repeats.

The nurse takes him by the elbow and leads him outside to the hallway. "Why don't you stay here? I need to find someone who might help you with this. Would you like a glass of water?"

Her hips wiggle in an oddly sensual way as she rushes to a desk. Benny watches her whisper to the nurse sitting behind it, who steals a look at him before she picks up a phone.

"Did something happen to her?" he says when the nurse returns. "Did something happen to her?"

He accepts the nurse's outstretched arms, his nose offended by the smell of latex and sweat, and understands her comforting gesture to mean that Poh-Poh's gone. As I mentioned earlier, I am quoting from my own life, except I was several years older, rushing to the hospital after taking a two-hour bus ride from my dorm room on campus, the only one to collect her body because my aunt—the real one—was on a weeklong cruise with her husband. "I'm sorry. It happened quickly this morning, love," the nurse says, confirming it. "The grief counselor will be here—until your parents arrive. She's someone you can talk to."

Benny pulls himself away from the nurse before the grief counselor arrives, weaving past nurses and patients in wheelchairs until he steps into an elevator.

Later, he will have no memory of how he made his way back home. Over the next few days, he feels Poh-Poh everywhere. He wakes up expecting to be chided by her for sleeping in. *Lazy pig*, she'd say, not without tenderness, when he woke up late. He hears shuffling footsteps in the hallway. He opens the door but finds the area outside empty.

He spends five dollars on two cans of Spam and a bottle of soy sauce. Out in Chinatown, old ladies with stooped shoulders and mismatched outerwear look like her from a distance. He washes his hands with her sandalwood soap to produce her smell. He eats both cans of Spam for dinner without frying it, licking the slimy coating of the meat from his fingers, even though they're supposed to last him two days.

He knows Poh-Poh wouldn't approve of him crying. He stuffs up his sobs by imagining her slapping him across his cheek. *No crying*, she would say. *Only children cry.* He needs to be a man. He leaves the house again to sit alone at the park, listening to the Clash, trying not to make eye contact with the big white guy from his building, who's coming home from work. Then he sleepwalks through Monday classes.

He thinks about calling August Pham. His one friend, resourceful and empathetic, would find help. Benny digs through his drawer until he finds the letter August wrote at the beginning of the year.

Yo Benny,

How's life? How's your grandma? Is school too easy for you now that there's only one smart kid? Ha-ha. We are in this town and it's amazing. It's also very different. If I were to tell you how different things are, you'd think I was lying to you. I love it here. Maybe one day I can return to Chinatown and we can hang out again. We can dig up the time capsule we buried in my backyard. You might not recognize me.

Anyhow, I am not much of a writer—not like you. I miss you. Hope that doesn't make you feel weird. We should talk on the phone, okay? My parents say that it costs extra money, but if I call at night on the weekends, it won't be as expensive. So maybe I'll try you. You can call me too.

Later dude,

A

August wrote his phone number under his name. Benny has the phone on his shoulder, the dial tone droning, but he resists dialing. *You might not recognize me*, August wrote, and Benny can detect pride in those words. By contrast, August would never fail to recognize him. Benny is the same loser in ugly clothes, minus his one friend and his parental figure. When the phone makes its off-hook alarm, chirping loudly, he replaces it in the cradle.

On those initial nights, he falls asleep with the TV on, but the solid beep of the broadcast signal at three a.m. wakes him up and makes him shudder at his own loneliness. He dreams about Mommy. He remembers when she died in the hospital. Back when they lived in a basement apartment, and he had his own room, and Mommy promised him a pet hamster soon. (Benny's father assured him that he'd show up at his fourth birthday party, and that he'd come with a pet lizard as a gift. But neither he nor the lizard appeared.) Benny had just turned eight and had gotten used to her being really sick, going to the hospital, then coming back weak at first, getting stronger. She would always regain her vigor, most of it, for a while.

He remembers being at home, playing Transformers with the TV on in the background. Steph spent the day either picking away at her fingernails or flipping listlessly through the magazine she'd brought over, while Poh-Poh stayed with Mommy. Normally his aunt would be on the phone with whichever gwai lo she was dating, but all day she seemed distracted. Twice that morning she hugged him with no warning. When the call came, she leaped for the phone in the kitchen. Benny could hear a sharp gasp, how someone sounds when they touch the heating element on a stove by accident.

Steph rushed him into his coat. It was a winter day, and he remembered how much Mommy liked playing in the snow. He didn't know why he couldn't stomp around in it for a while. The whole time on their way there, he expected to go to the hospital to see his mother still alive. For some reason, Steph thought he already knew.

As it was, he hadn't understood. How could he? And yet he was already watching TV shows like *Family Ties* and *Diff'rent Strokes*, in which families had misunderstandings that would get untangled by the end of the episode, with a discussion and hugs. With his own family, there were plenty of misunderstandings, but no discussion and almost zero hugs. There was also no dad, and everyone spoke Cantonese loudly.

It was only when he saw Poh-Poh standing by the hospital bed, wiping tears from her eyes, that he knew something was wrong. Steph was holding his hand. When she began to enter the room, he pulled away. Mommy's body was a well of shadows, in her cheeks, her clavicle, and the sunken cavities of her closed eyes. Poh-Poh kneeled by the bedside and prayed. Steph played with her sister's hair. Benny stood at the entrance.

"Come, silly pig, come," Poh-Poh said. "See your mother."

Benny shook his head.

"You need to listen to Poh-Poh," she told him. "*I have eaten salt more than you have eaten rice.*"

He always hated it when Poh-Poh used Chinese idioms. It was the hammer on the final nail of any supposed debate, signaling its foregone conclusion. He edged toward his dead mother, steadying a trembling hand on the bed rail. He started sobbing. He felt from Poh-Poh not a sharp smack on his cheek but her hand patting his back. For once, it was not only okay but preferable to cry— not just to cry, even, but to wail. Once he was done crying, he would forever mourn his mother in silence.

To honor Poh-Poh, Benny doesn't weep. He cannot afford to waste his energy, and keeps himself busy. When he runs out of TV and comic books, he starts drawing with a pencil. Despite knowing how much Poh-Poh hated wasting paper, he copies images of Wolverine and Superman. Then he tries to draw images from memories. Of Shirley. Of Mommy. Mrs. Renzullo would show off the illustrations he would produce for assignments so frequently in class, eliciting further taunts, that Benny would do them poorly on purpose. Now he draws until he's so distracted that he doesn't at first hear knocking at the door.

Benny doesn't answer until the apartment manager announces himself on the other side. When Benny opens the door, the manager looks over his shoulder into the room. "Is there something wrong?" he asks. "She's never late with the rent." Benny lies and says Poh-Poh is out volunteering at the nursing home, a job she had last year. "I'll try again tomorrow," the slimy, rodent-faced man says.

Every day, after school, he calls the house of the drummer in Steph's band. The following Tuesday, on his fourth try, the drummer's roommate answers with unexpected cheeriness. "Oh, hey, dude," he says. "You're in luck today. Do you have a pen and paper?" The roommate reels off a list of clubs and cities that takes up most of a page in Benny's notebook. If that list is correct, Steph's band is somewhere in Wisconsin or Minnesota. Their next gig is at a club in Minneapolis in two days. He calls Minneapolis directory assistance and gets the name of a place called Duffy's but reaches an answering machine. His message for Steph is cut off by a beep, so he calls again to leave the rest of it.

He figures Steph will respond immediately. He needs only to last a couple more days until she returns. He buys a Flake bar from Mr. Mah's son, Wai, who doesn't make fun of him today. Maybe it has something to do with Wai's blackened eye. Benny wanders over to the park to celebrate, wishing he'd also bought a Coke. He eats half of the Flake bar instead. Poh-Poh would never have approved, but he should have a treat for being alone. Then he eats the rest of the Flake bar. He's still hungry. He makes a peanut butter sandwich with the last of his peanut butter and stale bread. It doesn't matter if he has no food left. Steph will be back. If he doesn't eat, then it's because he doesn't trust she will be back. And if he has any doubts, then he jinxes himself.

At school during history class, Benny and his classmates move their desks and break into groups to prepare for their ancient-peoples presentations. They have a giant piece of purple poster board and Xeroxed images of Incan people from the *World Book Encyclopedia* in the library. As the de facto team leader, Benny tries to assign the easiest aspects of Incan culture to the least dedicated project members. None of them are very studious, not even Shirley. He sees Bronson flash his canine teeth at him and whisper to Roderick, who wrinkles his nose and snickers. As the project takes shape and they become certain they'll pass, they've become less afraid to laugh at him.

During recess, with his back turned, someone throws a pebble at him and yells, "Take a shower!" He sees Bronson and Roderick snicker and then buries his nose in his shirt and finally acknowledges its sour smell. He has been re-wearing his week's worth of clothes since Poh-Poh was hospitalized.

At lunch hour, he walks aimlessly around the school hallways, unwilling to be caught sitting in the cafeteria without lunch. On his way to the library, he sees half of a barbecue-pork bun left in a garbage can outside the lunchroom. He's too hungry to be repulsed and fishes the bun out. When he's done eating, tears fill his eyes. *Fuck this*, he allows himself to swear in his thoughts. *Fuck this*. In spite of his shame, he's still hungry. Through the cafeteria entrance, he sees Bronson and Roderick eating their lunches with a larger group of friends, including Shirley.

Roderick catches Benny's eye from across the room and sneers at him. He gets up and pushes aside the kid sitting next to Shirley. Once he's seated next to her, he places his arm around her. She elbows him, but this makes him cackle. Finally she shrugs away from him. Still he cackles, as though he's taken something valuable from her.

Benny steams as he circles the school again. When he returns to the lunchroom, Roderick and Bronson have their backs turned to him as he approaches them. He imagines himself fearless and impervious to pain, with mutant healing powers, like Wolverine. Shirley's eyes rise as she catches sight of him. Roderick is slightly closer, and taking a sip from his juice box. Benny runs up to him and punches him in the back of the head. Shirley gasps. The punch is only glancing. But Roderick's surprised, and he coughs the juice out of his mouth.

Some of it gets on his white T-shirt, which makes him mad. He turns around, ready to strike him. Benny should run but he doesn't back away. The teacher assigned to monitor the cafeteria looks over to their table. The bell sounds.

For the rest of the day, Benny is on guard. In Mr. Mason's geometry class, he's alert as Roderick turns around and glares. When the final bell sounds, Benny darts out of the classroom to evade the inevitable payback. He gets away this time, but tomorrow he'll take his licks. Once he arrives back home, he counts the money he has remaining. Fourteen dollars.

He picks up the smallest container of detergent and another Flake bar at the corner store—skipping toothpaste. For sure, he can stretch the money for another couple of days. He'll be able to reach Steph by then. If necessary, he can make it last a week. He watches Shirley's older brother behind the register, talking to the unhoused man turning in bottles for their deposits. Benny has noticed empty bottles and cans in the dumpster before. He decides he'll look for some tomorrow.

"Tuan-four is max-mum," Wai repeats, pushing a selection of empties back at the man. The bruise in his eye is finally fading and his shoulders are no lon- ger rounded. Wai speaks perfect English, but when he's at the register he talks like his dad. "Tuan-four is max-mum."

"Sheesh," the unhoused man says.

Wai, with his crown of moussed hair, has the detached air of a royal as he hands the man his change. When it's Benny's turn, he smirks. "Why haven't you come over to our house recently?" he asks. "Already looked up my sister's shirt?" Benny turns red. Everyone knows about his crush.

When he gets back to the apartment, he soaks all his clothes in the bathtub with warm water and a cupful of detergent. He's glad not to be in Poh-Poh's old apartment, where she didn't even have her own shower and toilet, just one down the hall that she shared with her floor. Right before Poh-Poh moved into the new building, a low-income development, the mayor visited for a ribbon- cutting ceremony. Nowadays, the manager accepts cash payments to look the other way when people sublet illegally from the elderly residents whose kids have moved them into nursing homes.

Dinner is again rice with soy and oil. He works on his part of the Incas project, the bulk of it. He watches TV until he should be asleep. But he's afraid to close his eyes. He brushes his teeth without toothpaste. He listens to his Walkman, to Lou Reed and Iggy Pop, but the batteries die.

No crying. Only children cry.

He sings to himself, curling back his top lip in imitation of Joe Strummer, into the ceiling. In a whisper, and then a full-throated scream. He changes tracks in his head and sings with a poker face, as he imagines Lou Reed would.

No crying. Only children cry.

When he wakes up, he realizes all his clothes are still damp. He has nothing else to wear, so he puts on a shirt and pants and hopes they'll dry before he gets to school. He slips on his backpack.

Benny takes the elevator down and leaves through the back exit to the dumpster. Not tall enough to peer inside, he has to heave himself into it. He breathes through his mouth and digs up four beer bottles and pop cans. There might be more, but he hears rats squeaking and panics and scrambles. He throws his haul out into the alleyway and climbs out himself.

He hears someone screaming at him, the rattling of supermarket shopping-cart wheels, then footsteps. "Those are fucking mine."

Benny cradles the empties in his arms. "Finders keepers."

The man with the shopping cart lunges after him. His grip is hard and tight. Benny pulls back, but it's only in his dreams that he's a comic book superhero like Iggy Samurai, my sword-slinging lizard. With his free hand the man cuffs Benny on the head. "This is my fucking block, kid."

Benny lets the cans fall to the ground as he covers his face. He hears the man growl and braces himself for more of his blows. None come. When Benny dares look up, he sees the man on his backside on the broken alleyway pavement, staring wide-eyed past him. Benny glances back to see the big white guy in some sort of stance, like in a Bruce Lee movie, except he isn't making any cat-in-heat sounds.

The man with the shopping cart scrabbles away and disappears. Before he pushes off, he takes Benny's backpack.

The big white guy engulfs Benny in his shadow and hovers over him like a protector. Can Benny trust this guy?

I don't know yet.

CHAPTER SIX

"**I**s *Iggy Samurai* autobiographical?" I remember being asked at a comic book convention, in my era of Peak Fame after the movie adaptation. This was a more optimistic period of my life. Sure, I replied, Iggy was like me, but he was also like every adventure story hero. A lonely child saved from oblivion by dint of his talent and innate goodness.

What few people bothered to ask was whether my other characters were ripped from reality. In that case, I would have had to offer a mealy-mouthed "yes and no" kind of answer. Like Coyote Sensei, for instance, the benevolent but mysterious mentor figure. He borrowed some mannerisms from C. but was ultimately a character who served a role in the story.

The same answer applies to this less fanciful story with the Samurai—who again adopts certain characteristics from C., like his size and karate training, but none of his more unsavory elements. I'm feeling protective toward this boy I've named Benny, and, in this story, the Samurai is his would-be protector.

Here he is, stooping over to watch the Chinese kid pick himself up. The boy takes a few steps to follow the unhoused man, then stops and doubles back. To the Samurai, he looks even skinnier than he did before, so scrawny that his shirt fits on his body like the sail on a mast. He smells weird. His hair has grown over his ears and his clothes look damp.

The kid's bottom lip trembles. He rubs the side of his head where the other man struck him. "That guy took my backpack. My homework is in it. My textbooks."

"He's gone," the Samurai says after a pause. "If I see your bag again, I'll get it back for you."

At the thought of his missing bag, the boy lets out a yelp but then quickly stuffs back his tears. "I'm fine. I don't think I'm hurt, I think."

The Samurai considers his possible replies. If he were smarter, he would see that the boy is vulnerable, easily taken advantage of. Fortunately, he isn't—not in this version of the story. "You don't look hurt," he ends up saying. "You only smell a little."

"My grandmother has been under the weather the last couple of weeks," the boy says. "She hasn't had time to do the laundry."

"Why are your clothes wet?" the Samurai asks.

"I've got to go to school," the boy says before he staggers off. "I'm Benny."

"Benny." He repeats the name as though it's unusual, even though he knows it's not.

"What's your name?"

"Constantine," he says, mad at himself for not offering his name back right away.

"Thanks for your help," the boy says before wheeling in the other direction.

The Samurai should turn away. The boy doesn't want him in his life. The Samurai will find a way to ruin his own good intentions and get himself in trouble. That's how it always ends up working out. But he watches the boy trudge alone in ill-fitting, wet clothes—of course he sees himself at that age. How many days did the Samurai get himself and Iulia ready for school on his own, filling lunch bags with chunks of cheese and mushy apples? How much did he worry that this fact would be uncovered?

He watches the child disappear around the corner and, in doing so, puts himself behind schedule. But when he arrives at work on time, he has to wait for Mickey. He loads the truck himself and hangs out in the passenger side. For all the time Mickey squanders on side hustles and flirting with female clients, he's always prompt to start.

Nearly an hour late, Mickey rolls up in his Pontiac Fiero. The windshield of the car is cracked in multiple places, maybe from rocks. Its headlights have been smashed, its body dented in other places, maybe from a tire iron. And on the hood of the car, the unmistakable, detailed image of a large, veiny penis has been spray-painted.

"Sorry to make you wait," Mickey says, climbing into the truck.

"What happened to your car?"

Mickey starts the truck's engine. "We're behind schedule. I'll explain later."

The Samurai doesn't recognize the route that Mickey takes. It certainly doesn't fit into their normal circuit. Mickey has turned the radio to a hard-rock station and cranked the volume. His hands pulse on the steering wheel, and the truck jolts to a halt at every intersection. They pull into Chinatown, in front of a convenience store.

"Come with me," Mickey says before he hops out of the truck. Normally he would wait outside the back of the truck to receive the bags of ice. Instead, he rushes into the store.

By the time the Samurai enters, Mickey is already screaming at a teenager, the one the Samurai beat up at the tavern, behind the counter. The teenager wears a sweatshirt and baseball cap, oversize headphones slung across his neck. He flashes his teeth derisively.

"I don't know what you're talking about," the teenager says to Mickey, jutting out his chin. "Why would I touch your stupid car?"

"No one else is such an idiot."

The Samurai notices the teenager catching sight of him, his posture tensing. Then the mean smile resettles on his face. "Maybe there's someone else you cheated," he says to Mickey. "Someone else who did your dirty work."

"Fucking asshole." Mickey charges up to the counter. The teenager winds back his fist.

Someone yells from the rear of the store. Everyone freezes as the teenager's father approaches them carrying a baseball bat. He says something to Mickey in Chinese. When Mickey doesn't move, the teenager's father looks to the Samurai. "Go now," he says in English. "We no order icy today."

The Samurai pulls Mickey away, pushes him back into the truck. Mickey stabs the key in the ignition, then turns to the Samurai. "Not only has the kid destroyed my car, he's screwed up another one of my side hustles," he says.

"Not cigarettes?" the Samurai asks.

Mickey shakes his head. "Harder stuff. He needs to know that's not cool." Looking around first, he says from the corner of his mouth, "If you want to make some money, you could mess him up for me."

"No," the Samurai says. "No."

"Just wanted you to have the first opportunity," Mickey says. He cranks the radio volume as the truck rolls out, and Ozzy Osbourne starts screaming through the speaker. Because of Mickey's bad mood, the day proceeds without his chatter or stops for phone calls. He doesn't even deliver cartons of cigarettes. As a result, their shift feels long, and yet it ends twenty minutes early.

The Samurai needs that extra time to get home. Earlier that week, he arranged for the phone company to install a telephone line in his apartment today. The technician wears blue coveralls, just like Tata did when he worked for the phone company, and has arrived half an hour late, without apology.

The Samurai gathers up his fists and recalls how his father would talk about his coworkers. *Dose lazy fuckers call me Dracula because of accent*, his father would say. *Dey eat deir sandwiches and Cokes while I fix deir mistakes.* By his third beer, Tata would be angry. Someone would have to take his beatings. Mama became too histrionic when he slapped her. The police had dropped by. Tata needed someone who would absorb abuse stoically, someone with the requisite physical stamina and training. Only a samurai could withstand Tata's thrashings.

When the technician leaves, the Samurai plugs in the phone he bought at the discount store and places his ear to the dial tone. From his wallet he removes the scrap of paper with Lorna's phone number on it. *She's probably working now. I'll call her later.* He places the phone back into its cradle. He keeps thinking about their conversation at the bar and how he wants to resume it, and how she watched, tilting toward him when he spoke, as if to catch any stray syllables. Instead, he practices with his bokuto, running through katas until he's sweaty and hungry. He walks to the diner outside Chinatown and orders a hamburger with fries and a milkshake. When he calls over the waitress for the bill, he asks for another burger to go but decides against fries—they don't taste right cold. And another milkshake would melt. He passes the pawnshop and sees the sword through the iron bars.

Chinatown is desolate except aboveground—clubs and gambling parlors on the upper levels of benevolent societies and fraternal associations. He sees rats lope under cantaloupe-amber streetlights. He gets back to the building, knocks on Benny's door. No one answers it, but he can hear the TV playing. He knocks again. "Benny? It's me . . . Constantine," he says, his voice raised. "I brought you something."

Footsteps at the door, a body pressing at the peephole. After a pause, the door opens.

He holds out the brown paper bag for the boy.

The burger is still warm, and its smell seems to melt any resolve the boy has about not accepting it. "Thanks," he says. He begins to close the door but stops. "How do you like living here?" he asks.

"It's okay," the Samurai says. "I stick out a little, don't I? The only white guy among so many, uh, Chinese people."

"But you know kung fu, right? I saw the way you flipped that guy on the street."

He nods. "The stuff I know is Japanese."

"Oh, cool." Benny smiles.

They stand there, each waiting for the other to say something. The Samurai takes a step back. Benny begins to close the door, then stops. "Thanks again for the burger."

That night, the Samurai goes to sleep and tries not to think about the phone technician or Tata. He tries not to think about Mama rotting to death in that psychiatric hospital, the same one he'd end up in. Administrators told Tata that she died of an undetected bacterial infection, but Iulia liked to say she'd been killed by neglect. The hospital had forgotten about her, and so had Tata.

The Samurai's woken up by an unfamiliar sound. A phone ringing. His phone.

He picks it up. It's his daimyo. After so long!

Protect the boy. You must protect the boy.

He holds the phone as he prostrates himself. He tells his daimyo that the boy doesn't need help. He's tried to take care of him. He brought him food. And what did the boy do? He shut the door on him.

Help him. It's the honorable thing to do.

Anytime I try to help anyone, it goes off the rails. How can I help him without hurting him?

You must try.

He says, Yes, my lord.

Why are your body and mind so slack? You must increase your training. How will you teach the boy to fight when you're so soft?

Constantine says, I didn't know I was supposed to train the boy.

I didn't tell you, his daimyo continues, *but he needs the strength for what's to come. You'll be his sensei. But where is your katana?*

I don't have one. I don't have the money yet.

Get it soon. Your orders will come.

In the morning, he takes a long shower. He works to get the grime out of his hands and fingernails, and feels better afterward. He's going to refill his prescriptions. Life's easier without his daimyo, guilty though that makes him feel. He gets the prescriptions filled after work and pops the pills in his mouth on the street. No water. He feels less odd. Better, even. Unlike his real-life inspiration, C., he doesn't choose to insinuate himself in the affairs of a vulnerable child. In this version of the story, he becomes involved in the boy's life because he has no choice.

When the Samurai next uses his new phone, he calls Lorna. She's working tomorrow. Her break is at 11:30. The next day he puts on the same jacket he wore the last time he saw her, choosing a dark shirt that will match the tear. He rushes out the door and gets to the bakery at 11:15. He sees her at the register, using tongs to fit cinnamon buns into a paper bag. She wears a striped lime-green blouse and a matching apron and visor. He sits at a table by the door, and she waves at him between customers. Her shoulders don't hunch when she's working. An old man walks in, and she asks him whether he'll have his usual. When he nods in assent, she wraps up a scone for him.

She brings the Samurai her strudel and an insulated cup of coffee when she's done. "I'm not hungry when I work here," she says. "I get full from smelling it all."

The strudel is in a plastic container. She doesn't make strudels in this bakery. She baked this one at home. He imagines her at her kitchen table, in the basement apartment she shares with Donna, wrapping up the apple slices in the thin dough like a lumpy piece of rolled-up carpet. The dough is flaky, the fruit filling sweet and silky.

She watches him eat.

CHAPTER SEVEN

Benny knows it. That guy, that big white guy, Constantine, is onto him. Constantine knows about Poh-Poh. Even though he seems a little weird, as though he's looking out into the world from behind a frosted window. His eyes narrow in dismay at the sound of the bright, high-pitched voice Benny uses when he lies. It's the only time Benny's voice doesn't drop. And now Constantine comes with an "extra" hamburger, one that smells too good to resist, with a pickle resting atop like a surfboard. Benny realizes he should save it for lunch tomorrow, but he eats half of it right away and then realizes the remaining half is more like a third—and eats that as well.

He still has to redo the Incas assignment that he never delivered. Earlier in the day, his voice squeaked again in the classroom as he lied to Mrs. Renzullo. He had left his bag at home. Poh-Poh was out of the house so she couldn't drop it off for him. He had forgotten his key so he couldn't get it during lunch hour. Mrs. Renzullo let her glasses fall to the tip of her Roman nose and looked over them.

"You haven't been your normal self, Ben," she said. She pinched his wet sleeve. "Is something going on?"

"Nothing."

She scribbled a message on a piece of paper, then folded and stapled it shut. "This is a note for your grandmother. I wouldn't normally tell a student this, but since you'll have to read it to her, I am requesting her presence tomorrow after school."

Take it from me, no Asian boy wants to get in trouble with his teacher. It's almost inconceivable. But here we find Benny, sideswept by circumstance. For the rest of the day, he sat slumped in his chair. He didn't even mind the scowl he got from Shirley for not completing the assignment. Or the displeasure from Roderick Chow when Mrs. Renzullo forced Benny to push his desk next to Roderick's so they could share his world civilizations textbook. "After the assignment is submitted," Roderick growled at him, "you're going to have to pay up."

Now, back at home without the library books he borrowed, he scrambles to finish the assignment from memory, working on a piece of poster board he used for a project on photosynthesis last year. He tries to re-create an earlier pencil drawing of Sacsayhuamán, an Incan archaeological site. He thinks about how August would giggle if he heard it pronounced, as it's supposed to be, as "sexy woman." He even turns off the TV so he can concentrate. *The Incans invented jerky. They invented rope bridges and terrace farming.* He has to guess dates and the names of Incan rulers. It might be better to hand nothing in.

Completing the project distracts him from worrying that he has no plan for Poh-Poh's meeting with Mrs. Renzullo. Perhaps Steph will get the message he left on another answering machine, at a club in Columbus, Ohio. Eventually, he finishes up and reads comic books until he's ready to sleep.

The next morning, he uses Poh-Poh's old Japan Airlines tote bag as a knapsack. As everyone gets to their desks, he carries the assignment over to Mrs. Renzullo. Under the fluorescent classroom lights, the poster project looks even shabbier than it did the night before. Roderick and Bronson can see that from their desks. If they were holding back on retribution, now they'll pay him back double.

At first, he's relieved that Shirley isn't in class to join this chorus of disappointment. But then he notices how classmates look piteously toward her empty desk. He hears her name whispered, then the name of her brother, Wai. At lunch, as he wanders the hallways, dizzy with hunger until he scavenges half of a sandwich, he overhears one female classmate tell the other that Wai was shot. The girl says she knows because her mother plays mahjong with Mrs. Mah. She says that Wai is in the hospital, and that the whole family is with him.

The thought of Shirley in pain, on the heels of his own loss, makes his stomach turn. Or maybe it's the half-eaten sandwich. He runs to the bathroom and throws up in a toilet. Afterward, he rinses out his mouth with water, but his breath still reeks.

As lunch hour draws to a close, he prepares another lie. He approaches Mrs. Renzullo at her desk to tell her that Poh-Poh is not feeling well today and unable to meet after class. She puts down the chopped salad that she's eating from a plastic container.

"Can we reschedule?" she asks. "Maybe for tomorrow."

"I'll ask," he says, his voice steady and flutey. "But I don't think she will be better by then."

"Is this why you've been acting so strangely?" she asks him.

He doesn't look her in the eye. He leaves her question unanswered, which he realizes is its own response when Mrs. Renzullo hugs him. He feels swallowed in her cable-knit sweater-vest. She smells like all white people do to him, like Parmesan cheese. Cheese and perfume. Bile churns up to his throat. He would throw up again if he hadn't already emptied his stomach.

He moves his desk over next to Roderick Chow, who pushes his textbook to the far edge of the desk so Benny can hardly see the chapter on medieval agricultural techniques. "Remember, you're paying up today," Roderick tells him, "after English class."

Benny used to like school. He was laughed at, picked last for teams, but the predictability of his humiliation was comforting. In other moments—in the smell of pencil shavings, for instance, or in his tidy cursive—he found redemptive pleasures. His successes and disappointments came like seasons changing. But now the world of last month has become a lost paradise. He can't even succeed at a class project. Now he wishes he could be an adult, someone who isn't forced to attend classes with sadists in sneakers. Someone with a job who can feed and care for himself. Someone who doesn't have to hide.

Poor kid. Even when he becomes a grown-up, a success of sorts, he won't ever be able to run away from his childhood.

At the end of the day, the students quiver in their seats, engaged in silent reading, until the final bell. As it sounds, Mrs. Renzullo asks Benny to remain at his desk. The rest of the class disperses, except Roderick and Bronson, who wait for him outside the classroom door. "What are you boys hanging around for?" Mrs. Renzullo asks, making a flicking motion until they leave her sight. As the air settles in their wake, a kind of peace fills Benny.

A woman in a teal blazer and a high-collared white blouse appears with a notepad. She wears a jade pendant necklace. Mrs. Renzullo introduces her as Macy. "It seems like it will only be Benny speaking with us today," she tells the woman.

Macy pulls a chair over next to Benny, whose hands feel conspicuous and unoccupied atop his desk. She introduces herself as a social worker and the person who oversees child services in the Chinatown area.

"Does your grandmother speak Cantonese?" she asks Benny.

He nods. "Yes, she does."

"And how is your Chinese?" she asks him in Cantonese. "Do you know how to write in it?"

"My grandmother used to teach Chinese school," he says. "She made me study the Bible in Chinese."

Macy makes a whistling sound. "A very bright child," she says in English to Mrs. Renzullo, who nods in approval.

Macy tells him "off the top" that Benny is not in trouble. It's not uncommon for a child, especially a child in Chinatown, to be living with a grandparent. Sometimes she can help them if the grandparent is ill or has trouble getting access to the right services because of the language barrier. Or if the family has challenges affording groceries.

"We Chinese are very proud people," she explains to Mrs. Renzullo. "We don't want to admit we're struggling."

"I can see that in Benny," his teacher says. "One hundred percent."

It pains me to think of this teacher, someone Benny liked and whose approval he lived for, so clueless about the boy, so ineffectual when he needs her help.

"Sometimes that pressure falls on the kids," Macy says.

Mrs. Renzullo nods. "Maybe that's why Benny looks so burdened the past couple of weeks."

Macy wants details about his family situation. He nods deferentially. "I've got a lot to say. But I need to pee. Maybe I should go to the bathroom first?" he says.

Benny takes a few calm steps down the hall, then picks up his pace toward an exit, pushing through the doors to the outside. He runs home, afraid of what he might see if he were to look back.

At home, he revisits the list of clubs. Tonight, Steph is in New Jersey. He gets the number of Maxwell's from directory assistance. Someone answers on the first ring. Benny rehashes his well-rehearsed request, naming Steph's band and asking to speak to its lead singer. "Yeah, they just finished their sound check," the man on the phone says. "They should be around." He asks Benny to hold.

Benny hears another band in the background. Probably rockabilly, he thinks. He listens to them go through half a song, stop, then go through the song again from the top. He wonders whether he should hang up and call again. Will the phone company cut Poh-Poh's line earlier if he runs up the long-distance charges?

"Hello?" It's Steph's voice.

He whimpers in relief. Then he starts sobbing. He can't speak.

"Benny, is that you?" she asks over the din of the other group's sound check. "What's the matter?"

He explains the whole story through his tears. Poh-Poh in the hospital, living alone, the social worker. Steph asks him to repeat his story over the music.

"Mom is dead," she says finally. "I can't believe it." He hears Steph's voice cracking over the phone at first, and that of a bandmate checking in on her, then her reassurances to him. Benny grows impatient as she absorbs the news.

"Sorry," Steph says finally. "I needed a moment. How long have you been alone?"

He's not sure. "Two or three weeks?"

"*Fuck.*"

"How soon can you be home?"

He hears her sucking through her teeth. "This is a lot. Sorry, Benny, I don't know what to do." She hesitates. "The gig is in an hour. I can figure things out afterward."

Benny starts to cry. She should be returning, right? Then she tells him to calm down. Her voice is sharp, as though she's irritated. It softens, and she tells him she has no money to fly back. The van's transmission had to be replaced.

The guys might want to finish their last week of gigs before they turn back. She'd have to buy her own bus ticket.

"Is there anyone who can take care of you?"

They run through the list. August Pham has moved. Poh-Poh's friend, Mrs. Kwan, died of a stroke last year. And the people at the church would send him to his dad. Last year, when Benny's father tried to contact him through the pastor, Poh-Poh stopped taking Benny to Sunday services. Even her piety took a back seat to her fear of and disgust for Benny's father.

"You can't stay with your dad," Steph says. "He's the least responsible man I know. And I'm a musician."

His heart sinks as Steph tries to connect him with the roommate at the drummer's house. Being looked after by one of her greasy-headed acquaintances is the last thing he wants.

"I have a neighbor. He's nice," he blurts out. "His name is Constantine and we've become friends."

"He's not a creep? Not some pedo?"

"No way," he insists. But what does he know? Constantine's a stranger.

"He doesn't act weird around you?"

"No. Not exactly." *He's just weird, in general.*

"Ask if you can stay with him. Don't go too far from home. I love you, okay? I will get home as fast as I can."

When she hangs up, he listens to the phone click and then spit back a dial tone. He drops the receiver on the cradle. His cheeks flush with indignation. He's finally reached his aunt. And yet nothing has changed, not yet. What did he expect? For her to arrive by magic from across the continent to deliver him from fear, hunger, and loneliness? He thinks about what Poh-Poh said about her. "She should be grown-up by now, but she's no better than you. Worse even."

He runs the water to make rice. He opens up the drawer with the rice bucket. There should be enough to last him through the rest of the week. He hasn't fit the lid on it tightly. Poh-Poh used to dress him down whenever he did that, pulling him by his ear across the apartment to the kitchen so they could wallow in his mistake.

When he removes the lid, he finds a cockroach swimming in the grains of rice. Exactly what Poh-Poh said would happen. He picks it out with a piece of paper towel and flushes it down the toilet. And then he rinses the rice in water and makes another pot. *Sorry, Poh-Poh.*

As the rice cooks, he hears footsteps and voices from outside, down the hall. There's a knock at the door.

"Open up," someone says in Cantonese. He recognizes the voice of the apartment manager.

"Maybe he's not home?" It's a female voice. Macy, the social worker.

"Don't you smell the rice cooking? Of course he's inside. I see him lurking around."

"But you haven't seen his poh?"

"Not for weeks."

"Did something happen to her?"

"Wouldn't know. Do you want me to open the door?"

There's a pause. "No. If we don't hear from him soon, maybe then."

She slides a card under the door, and their footsteps grow distant.

Benny sees his choices, stark and dwindling. He can leave his apartment and wander in the streets, but he can't imagine lasting until Steph's return. Or he can take his chances with Constantine.

He steps outside and knocks on the door.

CHAPTER EIGHT

I remember one of the first times Trina and I went out. The particular get-together I have in mind came after a jittery first date, after our first kiss and some petting, but before we'd slept together. It was a tension that we both enjoyed and didn't want skipped over. Okay, a little more in her case than in mine. We were young and poor enough that dating was uncomplicated insofar as our choices of activity were concerned. We went to an Irish bar that wasn't too obnoxiously Irish, a dark, dank place glazed in the residue of cigarette smoke and spilled Guinness, and shared a couple of pints (which kept me from drinking too quickly). The bartender, who pretended to be surprised when I mentioned a rat scurrying across the room, even allowed us to bring in hot dogs from the street.

Getting to know each other, we obsessed over our pasts, shedding our best anecdotes like baubles we dug out from our pocket linings. And probably in this period of parallel confession, I allowed Trina to tell more about herself than I did in return. I remember that date well because of something she said. She told me she was attracted to me because of my laconic demeanor, the fact that I preferred to listen rather than talk. It was a quality she would later grow disenchanted with, as she suggested to our marriage counselor that it was rooted in secrecy. But at the time she was reacting to a controlling father who'd forced her to dress a certain way for school, prim and feminine, and always passed negative judgment on her choices, especially the men she dated. Ironically, the men she dated, up until she met me, were also controlling and opinionated. They always needed to be right.

"I didn't know better," she told me. "I made my bullies into my protectors."

I remember reaching for her hand. The pulse of desire washed over me, overtaken by a respect for self-knowledge that also explained my own torments. I see myself doing that in my experience with C., and how I work this into Benny's relationship with his blue-eyed would-be yojimbo, who is practicing with his bokuto when he hears the knock at his door. It's the boy.

"My grandmother is dead," he says.

"Okay," the Samurai says. He knows he should be more sympathetic. Would a hug be too forward? Yes, yes, definitely. He offers his hand instead.

The boy doesn't take it. He asks to come inside, and, once admitted, his eyes dart around the Samurai's place. He cowers when the door closes behind him. This makes the Samurai aware of how he might appear to the boy. Shirtless and sweaty, holding a wooden sword. In an apartment with no furniture except his futon. The walls bare except for the poster Herb gave him. He misses his old room with the small white bed, orange desk, pink chair.

"I like doing . . . martial arts," he says. "With a, um, practice sword."

Benny's eyeline bounces from the poster of Toshiro Mifune across the room to the tatami mats that cover most of the floor area, but the Samurai's decor goes unremarked upon. "Do you have anything to eat?" Benny asks instead.

The Samurai doesn't have much to offer the boy except for barley tea and a slice of cold pizza, an odd combination that Benny accepts gratefully, although he picks the cheese off the pizza. Between bites, Benny tells the Samurai about his grandmother dying, about living alone. How he needs to wait for his aunt's return.

The boy leans against the wall by the kitchen counter. "My dad is still around somewhere, but don't get me started." He shakes his head. "I haven't seen him in years. He's not a good guy."

"I had a dad like that."

The boy takes his time chewing the crust. "Did he abandon you and your mom?"

The Samurai doesn't answer. *I wish he had*, he thinks.

Benny mentions a social worker outside his apartment who will likely come back and make him live with his dad, the one who looked like a Hong Kong movie star, before his aunt returns. His dad is my own dad, who I saw only a handful of times after my grandmother's funeral before he died a few years later. Benny doesn't think it would work if he stays down the hall in his grandmother's apartment. The Samurai realizes that the boy wants to stay here—with him. He pushes his headband up into his hair, feels the chill of his drying sweat on his body, observes the boy's practiced nonchalance as the Samurai tries to figure out what to say.

"I mean, you don't need to," the boy says into his silence. "But I won't cause trouble."

"I've got no furniture. I don't have guests over."

"We can bring some from my place. And I won't be your guest."

The Samurai throws up his hands. "I don't know."

"I get it," Benny says. He digs his hands into his pants pockets. "It's all right. Thanks for the pizza."

The Samurai hears his daimyo's voice, guttural and peremptory. *Protect the boy.* "Okay," he says.

Benny stops as he takes the doorknob. "Do you mean I can stay?" he asks.

"Okay," the Samurai repeats.

Benny leans against the door and begins reciting assurances. "I won't cause trouble. I won't leave the house. I don't want to ever go back to school."

The Samurai scans his near-empty apartment. "This place is boring."

They wait until it's well past dark to move the boy's clothes down the hall. They also bring his mattress and his television. The new clutter in his small apartment, the way the boy piles his stuff randomly, makes the Samurai's temples throb. He brushes his teeth and gets dressed for bed in the bathroom.

"Can I turn out the light?" he asks Benny.

The boy looks up from the mattress. He's reading the Samurai's copy of James Clavell's *Shōgun*. "What are you wearing? The skirt?"

"This is my hakama. It actually has two legs. My shirt's called an uwagi and my belt's an obi."

The boy expects more than the terminology for his getup. He wants a rationale, a defense and implicit acknowledgment of the ridiculousness of the outfit. When the Samurai doesn't offer it, he returns to the book. Obviously, this guy is cuckoo, but you can use mental illness as a dodge for transgressive behavior, so he's still better than someone who is evil. At least *I* think so. The Samurai falls asleep with the light on.

He awakes to the sight of Benny, already dressed but otherwise unchanged from the night before. The boy sits cross-legged, further into *Shōgun*.

The Samurai uses the bathroom, shutting the door to change. He does the same thing when he's alone. After he's dressed, he offers the boy some instant oatmeal. They sit, the Samurai on his heels, across from each other on their mattresses, and eat.

"I guess I'm staying here all day," Benny says. "It's okay. I like reading and playing video games."

The Samurai mentions there's some bread and salami in the fridge, then leaves.

Work has a stilted quality, with Mickey conducting business quietly. Midway through the afternoon they get to Chinatown and stop outside the convenience store where Mickey had his argument the other day. "I want you to deliver the ice on your own," Mickey tells him, handing him a clipboard with the billing invoice. "You're a big boy now."

The Samurai carries in two bags from the back of the truck. He expects to see the teenager behind the counter. Instead, it's his father, who scowls at him as he places the bags of ice by the freezer. He presents the invoice for the father to sign and notices his drawn, pale face as he scratches his name in block letters.

"How was that?" Mickey asks him back in the truck. "Did he say anything about his son?"

The Samurai shakes his head.

"That's because it was the kid's fault."

The silence that follows is punctuated by more hard rock on the radio, and vigorous honking from other cars caused by Mickey's aggressive driving. For their own safety, the Samurai, who's learning to be crafty, decides he needs to distract his friend. He mentions his visit to Lorna's bakery, and their plans to meet again soon.

This disclosure does the job, tricking Mickey out of his funk. He ribs the Samurai about his romance even though he's sore that Donna doesn't want to keep seeing him after their night out. "It's her prerogative," he says. "I'm not going to lose any sleep." Later, when Mickey makes crude insinuations about Lorna, the Samurai snaps. Very much unlike C., who was always primed for a dirty joke and used them to prove I was uptight about "natural human behavior." For the Samurai, it's a matter of decorum. He's a gentleman. But Mickey has a big smile on his face. He thinks his coworker is in love. He turns the radio to something softer, and they finish their shift with him serenading the Samurai with "Glory of Love."

After work, the Samurai stops to buy something to eat. He should cook for the kid, but he's only used the stove to boil water and doesn't even know if the oven works. At the diner, he buys hamburgers and milkshakes. For the record, C. loved burgers, meat loaf, and meatballs. I think every meal he shoveled into his sneering face featured ground beef. When the Samurai gets home, the boy's swinging his bokuto with determination but little skill. The TV blares in the background.

"I got in a fight a few days ago," Benny says. He tells him about his altercation with Roderick Chow.

"Are you glad you punched him?" the Samurai asks.

"I wish I could have hit him harder." Benny grunts.

He puts down the wooden sword so they can eat their hamburgers, without a word, as though they're in a race.

"I didn't know white people could be samurai," the boy says between sips of his milkshake.

Sitting in a tate hiza, his left leg under his butt, the right one in lotus position, the Samurai notices the copy of *Shōgun* on the floor. The boy says he finished the last seven hundred pages of that door-stopper in one afternoon. The Samurai didn't take much longer when he read it as a teenager.

"It's based on a true story," the Samurai says. His karate teacher, who gave him the book as a present, told him that. There were real-life European sailors who became samurai in the seventeenth century. "The best stories come from real life. *Shōgun* is one of my favorites." As you might have figured, C. gave me his own copy.

"Is that why you wear your . . . hakama at night?"

"Maybe."

The Samurai rises to turn the TV off. Thinking of the boy helpless around his bullies arouses his pity. He picks up the bokuto that lies between them. "Hold it with two hands. For power. Hands at forty-five degrees, spaced apart."

He sets himself down on his left knee, with his right leg extended forward to demonstrate kirioroshi. He brings down the bokuto with two hands over his head.

When the boy is handed the sword, he chops the air awkwardly. His face reddens.

"Try again," the Samurai tells him. "One quick motion. Imagine slicing your opponent so cleanly that they feel no pain."

They spend half an hour going through other katas, like tsukikage, moon shadows, the one where the warrior rises from one knee and slashes with one hand, and nuki-uchi, the one in which the warrior quickly draws the sword from its saya, its scabbard, and immediately cuts while in seiza, seated from the knees. A quick draw, sudden cut. And just like that, he has followed his daimyo's order to train the boy.

The Samurai is flattered by how closely Benny watches him, how eager he is to learn. The boy puffs up at any word of encouragement. The Samurai hears the cadences of his own karate senseis, and later his kendo and iaido instructors, in his own voice. He and the boy practice later than they should. They're both sweating through their shirts. When he notices the time, he suggests they get some sleep, but both of them are too energized by the physical activity, so once the light is switched off, they lie in their beds with their eyes open. The time passes, with only the sound of someone turning over, the barely audible breathing of another person awake.

"My dad used to take me to see kung fu movies at the Golden Harvest Cinema in Chinatown," the boy confides in the dark. "My mom always thought those films *glorified violence*. Dad would let me have Coke and popcorn. Mom hated that too. Afterward, he would drive me around in his new car. Not to anywhere in particular. He just knew I liked being in cars. And he liked to drive. Mom and Poh-Poh took the bus everywhere."

The Samurai wants to say that the boy's father doesn't sound so bad. But he remembers how much he enjoyed fishing with his own dad—and hated almost everything else. How his own dad became jealous of the Samurai's admiration for his karate instructor and banned the Samurai from his class. *Dat man*, he said, *ease not right*.

A hopeful thought crosses the Samurai's mind. Wouldn't it be nice to admit his actual identity to another person? *I am not Constantine. I am a samurai.* Maybe he'll know the boy long enough to share his truth.

As the Samurai ponders this, the boy starts breathing heavily, then begins to snore.

CHAPTER NINE

Trina and I don't attend church. But we were raised by churchgoers, which means we're vestigially religious. In my case, my Methodist grandmother, who dragged me to Chinese-language services but also worshiped our ancestors as beings who could influence our fortunes, made me hardworking but fatalistic, earning my keep but also waiting for a windfall. Trina's family tied their ardent anti-communism with their Catholicism. Mostly this played out harmlessly, like with the somber painting of Saint Wenceslas she would hang when her parents visited and made randomly cruel remarks about how unhoused people prove capitalism works.

I didn't react as well when Trina suggested that we baptize our daughter. "It wouldn't hurt," she suggested meekly as I wrenched my face in disgust. Ultimately I relented, thinking this would soften her up when I spent a considerable sum on a new car. Give and take, right?

The baptism, witnessed by Trina's family and faculty colleagues of hers roped into serving as godparents, took longer than I wanted in clothes I felt uncomfortable in on a muggy summer day in a room with the Jesus torture porn that disgusted me. This isn't quite hell, I thought. Maybe purgatory.

But the most memorable part of that event was Father Pete, the priest who conducted the ceremony. He was about my age, with moist, darting eyes that belied his leaden recitations. He perked up when he poured water over our daughter's head. "This part's my fave," Father Pete said, holding the jug of water. *Fave.* He made a face, like someone trying to stifle laughter, when baby Adele started crying and Trina and I took turns trying to calm her.

Afterward, we had people from the event to our house, where we served them cold lemonade and pasta salad inside, air-conditioning on full blast. The priest had joined us, stepping out of his white robes into a short-sleeved black shirt and his clerical collar. After putting Adele down for her second nap, I returned to the party. Father Pete was not there. I thought he'd left but caught sight of him through the screen door, smoking. He was wearing sunglasses that slid down his low-bridged nose.

"Cool place," Father Pete said, waving the hand holding his smoke at my newly built dojo and meditation garden. "It's like a movie set."

"May I have one of those?" I asked him, despite the flack I'd catch from Trina for smoking.

Father Pete handed me the pack from his shirt pocket. He had a tattoo of a rose on the underside of his forearm. "I hear you're the comic book guy." I nodded. "I hope you don't mind me saying," he said, lighting one of his menthols for me, "but you don't seem like the type who would go for a baptism."

"Nope, it was Trina's idea," I said, inhaling, then trying not to cough. "But I thought, it wouldn't hurt."

"Gotcha," he said, looking at me over his sunglasses. *Gotcha.*

I remember thinking how hard it was to make friends in one's forties, when the obligations of friendship conflicted with the duties of work and family, and when the agonies of middle age—the personal disappointments, the humiliations of the body—were so similar from one person to the next yet also repulsed us from one another. And yet I wanted to go for a beer with Father Pete. I felt like I could say anything to him, which probably made him a good priest. Maybe talking to him would relieve a burden in the way that speaking to therapists and marriage counselors never did. Just meeting him made those sadnesses, which I had repressed to the point of self-destruction, rise to the surface. But I wouldn't be his friend, because the religion thing was, for me, still a deal-breaker. And those sadnesses were quickly buried again.

The reason why I'm thinking about Father Pete now is because of that conversation in the backyard. I was trying to remember what happened to babies, innocent souls, should they perish before baptism—the thing we were preventing that day with Adele. "What's that place called?"

"Limbo," he said, wagging his menthol in the air. He pronounced it like two words. *Limb. Bow.*

"It's sort of an in-between place."

"You can think of it that way," he said. "But it's better not to think of it now."

Limbo. I was straining to remember that word as I was imagining Benny's plight. And when I did remember the word "limbo," an entire unrelated memory spilled out. I guess the concept still fascinates me, an in-between place that you find yourself in because of poor timing, and maybe that's why I place Benny in Constantine's empty apartment. It's not yet purgatory. He feels safe but temporary.

To pass the time, Benny decides he's training, but for what he doesn't know. He practices the kata he learned the night before until he's toasting from his exertion. He takes off his shirt and keeps practicing, counting silently from one to ten in Japanese, until he needs a glass of water.

If he swings hard enough, he avoids thinking about Poh-Poh or what he's missing out on at school. When he argued with his grandmother over clothes or some food he wouldn't try, she would invite him to imagine her death. *One day I'll be gone and you'll be sorry you acted this way*. Even though he misses her, he doesn't regret asking for Reeboks or refusing to eat stinky tofu or black moss and mushrooms. He wishes he could hold her hand again. He wishes he could feel her presence, even those stinging slaps across his face or that staticky anxiety that gripped her whenever they left the house. He wishes he'd known the last time he saw her would be the last time. Not that he would have behaved differently, but he would have paid attention.

The wooden hockey stick, refashioned as a sword, wobbles above his head before he slices air. Maybe everyone at school will wonder where he is when classes start on Monday. Maybe Roderick Chow and Bronson Su, stymied in their attempt at retribution, will feel the urge to pick on another weakling. And maybe Shirley has returned to class, glad that her brother is healing comfortably at home. Perhaps, once her feeling of relief subsides, she will feel unattended, unwatched.

A child shouldn't be left alone for so long, trapped indoors with a strange man serving as his mentor. He becomes too attached to the stories he rereads, the superheroes he copies over and over, pushed into an abnormally fastidious discipline for a preteen. Even with a benevolent host, Benny is still warped without external contact, dried out and shriveled by house arrest. In my time alone with C., unspeakable things transpired. But it was also like this too. When Constantine returns, he brings back smells of the world outside as he steps into the apartment. Every day, his return is a sudden jolt to Benny's senses.

They have a routine where they practice their katas, then get ready for bed. Constantine is out first. Over his snoring, Benny stares in the darkness, listening to the secret sounds of the apartment building. The anonymous footfalls and key scrapes, the random coughs. Later in the night, Constantine starts muttering to himself. Some words in English, some guttural words in what sounds to Benny like Japanese. Benny is reminded of the sounds of Poh-Poh's nightmares, the plaintive whimpers she would never make when she was awake. She would not talk about it, but Mommy had explained she had been tortured by the Communists, who ransacked her house in Guangzhou for valuables. Thinking she had been holding out her best trinkets, they strung her up by her feet and whipped her.

Whatever affects Constantine in his sleep doesn't bother him in the morning. He's buoyant, getting up to take his pills and brush his teeth before going out to work.

During his days alone, Benny grows bored of TV and comic books, bored of *Shōgun* and *Inside Karate*. Flipping through his things, he rereads his letter from August Pham. Of all the people in his life to miss, he thinks of his old friend the most. He misses the way they laughed together. Or how August would punch him in the arm when he spent too much time staring at Shirley. He misses how unbothered he was by the taunting from Bronson Su and Roderick Chow, both of them in pricey sneakers that always remained ivory white. August would laugh along with their insults. The only way they could irritate him was by poking a finger in his belly as they walked past him. August would tuck his elbows into his ribs and then claw his hands at them like an effeminate Tyrannosaurus rex.

The letter gets quickly stashed away when Constantine returns. He still seems to be in an upbeat mood when he comes home one evening, at five thirty, exactly when he said he would return—Benny appreciates his punctuality—

with groceries and discount-store kitchenware. "Have you ever made a pie crust?" he asks Benny.

Of course, C. never baked, although he loved to eat premade cupcakes shrink-wrapped in plastic. He did once mention to me that his mother had owned a bakery, and it's funny how much I enjoy watching Adele making cookies and pies with Trina.

As I picture it, Constantine measures out the flour and salt without consulting a cookbook. And he then slices pieces of butter and shortening. To Benny's chagrin, Poh-Poh never baked. She stored old takeout containers, which she'd washed for reuse, in her oven. Neither did Mommy, though once she humored Benny and made a chocolate cake from a Betty Crocker box mix. "The bakery in Chinatown is better than this, right?" she asked him after they'd tried it. He agreed with her, knowing to say what she wanted to hear.

"How did you learn to bake?" Benny asks Constantine.

"My mom liked doing it. We baked a lot of cakes and pies. Where's your mom?" Constantine asks, as though it never occurred to him that most kids live with their mothers.

"She's dead."

"My mom's dead too." Constantine pauses for a moment. "Would you like to roll the dough?"

Benny takes his cue and flattens the dough with the newly purchased rolling pin. They slice enough apples for two pies and eat one as dinner with a pint of vanilla ice cream while sitting cross-legged on the floor. The other pie is wrapped in foil. Constantine doesn't say what or who he's saving it for. Benny watches the Samurai lick his bowl of every crumb, holding it to his face. Then the Samurai settles back on his heels with what Benny takes to be a look of contentment.

Afterward, they practice hand-to-hand combat. A baking session's requisite masculine counterpoint. Constantine tells Benny that they will run through the heian shodan, the simplest katas in karate. Benny throws a punch, slices an open hand in the air. He sweeps a socked foot along the tatami floor mat. He throws out his forearms to block punches.

After every kata, he has to remain still as Constantine adjusts his form and guides him. At first Constantine seems afraid to touch him. Very much unlike C., who always took the chance to grab me by my arms and legs and throw me off balance. To make me his bitch. But when he gets frustrated at Benny's inability to follow his verbal instructions, he moves the boy as though he's a friend's prized doll. Benny doesn't like being coaxed into competence. Everything he does well, he started with some natural ability. Everything he does awkwardly—be it playing the recorder or square dancing at school—prompts him to quit at the first available chance.

This is different. He realizes his buried strength can be found in these forms. A one-room apartment no longer seems stuffy or confining. The faces of Poh-Poh and Mommy no longer sneak past his closed eyes. It's like listening to Steph's tapes, but instead of setting something free inside himself while the headphones hug his ears, it's his body in a controlled motion, like a piston in a machine.

An entire week passes stuck in an apartment. He'd be a missing child, his dorky school portrait emblazoned on posters, if anyone noticed. Time wobbles. It feels like years, the days are interchangeable. Benny expected Steph to be back by now. Perhaps she has tried to call him on Poh-Poh's line, but he doubts it. He's embarrassed he had any expectations around his aunt. Why did he think Poh-Poh was wrong about her, and that she wasn't unreliable? After that first week, Benny begins to crave being outside, being able to walk around the block or talk to one of Poh-Poh's former students in a shop. Maybe Shirley, relieved that he's safe, would see him and give him a tearful hug. His longing to leave the apartment becomes a thirst that he can ignore for a while when he practices his katas or listens to the Clash, but it inevitably returns. He could go outside now. But he doesn't have the key to this apartment. He may as well walk into Macy the social worker's office and ask to be whisked away to his father, who always reeked of cologne and once yelled at him for smearing his chocolate-covered fingers on his car's white upholstery.

One day in that second week, Benny hears the apartment manager, his keys jangling, talking to someone else down the hall, near his grandmother's.

"There's not a lot in there," he says in his booming voice. "We have to clear it before the next tenant comes in."

"Did the old lady die there?" the other voice says. "A lot of old people die in their own beds. People shit when they die, gwaa. That will stain a mattress."

"The social worker has been investigating. She told me the old lady died in the hospital," the apartment manager says. "She was a tidy baht-poh, so her furniture is probably in good shape."

"And whatever I find I get to sell?"

"Fifty-fifty. That was our deal."

"That was before you told me you wouldn't pay me to help you empty the place."

"I guess I have no choice now, do I?" the apartment manager says, sucking his teeth. "If we find any jewelry, we can renegotiate."

Poh-Poh always complained about selling her gold to pay Mommy's way through her accounting classes. Now Benny is relieved there's nothing to steal. Through the peephole, he watches as they haul out the couch, the kitchen table, and the bed from Poh-Poh's apartment. Then, in armfuls, her clock radio, the toaster oven she used to make Benny Shake 'n Bake chicken, and the water boiler Steph bought her as a present that Poh-Poh thought was too extravagant but liked too much to return. Even the drawer with Poh-Poh's chopsticks, spoons, and kitchen knife.

"That's it with the valuable items," says the scrawny friend of the apartment manager. He's dressed in jeans and a work shirt and looks familiar to Benny, who hasn't yet placed him as the guy who helped Constantine move in. "Do you need help with her personal items?"

"I can do it myself," the apartment manager says. "Nothing of much value, but I will take a look. It will probably end up in the trash."

In the rush when he left, Benny had taken the items that were most important to him. His pictures of his family (even his father), his honor roll certificates. Only when he sees the apartment manager emptying her place does he realize that things that mattered to Poh-Poh might matter to him. The portraits of ancestors, her Bible and cross, a pair of old reading glasses that belonged to Gong-Gong.

He sits down on his mattress and imagines her face. He wishes he had even a photo of her. Then he realizes what he can do. He takes out a piece of loose-leaf from his binder and begins to draw her portrait from memory until a resemblance emerges. *This is no way for a man to act*, he hears her saying about his drawing. But he disobeys this voice, knowing it's the only way to bring her back.

CHAPTER TEN

With my first love, comic books, heroes and villains were pretty clear-cut. As a young adult, in my desire to acquire cultural power and become a sophisticate in a tailored shirt and tapered slacks and not just a comic book artist with a taste for booze, I started consuming stories with moral ambiguity. No one was totally bad in these tales, no one entirely virtuous. Supposedly, that was like real life. Every would-be hero or villain needed to be complicated, given detail.

The trouble was, that didn't chime with my reality. There were heroes in my life, unstained by ambiguity, in the same way that I came across an absolute monster. Maybe I don't know why the villain acted the way he did, but does it matter? Now as I try to reimagine C., I furnish his alter ego with a backstory and a set of friends to justify his oddness. Maybe that's why the Samurai has become Benny's protector.

And that's why I've introduced Lorna, a woman whose delicacy serves as a mirror to reflect the gentleness submerged in the Samurai's oversize physique and sometimes violent manner. Today, as I picture it, Lorna suggests a picnic. She tells the Samurai to bring something to drink. She will take care of the rest.

On their first outing with Mickey and Donna, she and the Samurai were like pets led on leashes. Being on their own prompts a new hierarchy. If the Samurai's presence were stronger, he figures that Lorna might defer. In a vacuum of assertiveness, she grows more confident. Perhaps she knows, on some level, that he's a ronin—a warrior without orders. Perhaps this is the reason she's drawn to him.

"A gentleman always stands between a lady and the street," she tells him when they leave her workplace. Lorna adds that, "In the olden days, the gentleman would shield the woman from being splattered by puddle water and sewage splashed by carriages. Now it's just polite." He switches positions with her, shifting the two-liter bottle of Coke he brought from one hand to the other.

They walk several blocks until they get to the beach. I picture Lorna being a sort of younger Mia Farrow type, pretty, with soft features and a milky complexion, unconfident in bearing. Maybe I'm imagining her from one of the descriptions that C. would offer up about the women he dated. I don't remember. Lorna's wearing the blue jeans and teal pullover sweater she changed into before leaving work. She has brought a blanket that she removes from a large beach bag, and they lay it in the shade of one of the logs arranged in rows on the sand. She watches the Samurai sit on his heels, her own knees wide apart before she tucks them away.

From the beach bag Lorna takes out her picnic items. Potato salad, fried chicken, grapes—all in plastic boxes—and plastic plates and forks. She says she didn't bring cups. "When you said you were bringing Coke," she says, "I thought you'd bring cans or individual bottles."

"I'm sorry," he says. It's bad enough that the two-liter bottle is lukewarm.

She waves off the apology. "My mother always said, 'You get what you get but you don't get upset.'" Lorna goes on to explain that her father left the two of them months after his investment in a friend's board game made him a millionaire. Her father's lawyers browbeat her mother into accepting much less money than she might have otherwise received. And yet her mother has never complained, despite working two cleaning-lady jobs. She even talks fondly of her former husband.

Lorna cracks open the Coke and they take turns holding the bottle with two hands and sipping from it. They eat their lunch as people walk past them with their dogs. Afterward, she replaces her emptied boxes back into her bag.

"Would you like to kiss me?" she asks later. She says this as though he's crying and she's offering him a hankie.

He says he would. And he does. His sexual instincts are garbled because of Mama, but not to the extent that C.'s were. He has to stoop over to kiss her. She reminds him of his mother, who also wanted him to be a gentleman. Mama was feminine, comforting, and in control when confined to their domestic bubble, and on the right days, but when she wasn't feeling well or was confused by someone speaking English too quickly in a store, it was as though she were the Samurai's own helpless child. He wants to protect Lorna. And even he knows it's wrong to think of Mama when he's kissing her.

The kiss leaves him flustered for the rest of the picnic. He wants more, but then he begins to think, *How would she react if I told her I was a samurai? Horribly.* To keep kissing her, he would have to hold this secret. He would have to lie. Lying is dishonorable.

Lorna smiles at the Samurai, asks him what he's thinking. He says, "Nothing."

He lingers by the picnic area on the edge of the beach where the air is scented from lily and violet blossoms and newly cut grass until he gets on a crowded bus full of people who smell like dust. When he steps off to pick up burgers and fries, he feels the sun baking the pavement. He's aware of the time, how he's keeping the boy waiting. The katas are helping to distract the boy from his wanderlust, to a point. He must be practicing for hours when Constantine's gone because the way he has improved from day to day, the way his body has strengthened, reminds the Samurai of time-lapse videos of a plant emerging from a seed in seconds. They've progressed on to heian nidan. He likes the kid. The Samurai's starting to feel as though he can talk to him. When he gets home, he finds Benny standing by the window, peeking through the curtains to catch the slice of street activity beyond the alley.

"I know I promised I'd stay hidden, but I'm so bored. Can I please go for a walk at night?" Benny asks him. "*Please.* Just once."

The Samurai thinks about what might happen to him if they get caught. There was a time, after being fired from a kitchen job—when he drifted between shelters that kept ejecting him for getting into fights, when he spent weeks sleeping in an underground parking garage—that the one-room apartment he presently occupied might have been all he craved.

Now his apartment is no longer his own. He's already had to blow off his sister, who, despite having recently given birth, wants to paint his home a "happier" color. And Lorna. He's not ready to show her his place. And yet he doesn't want to hide anything from her, to talk around the presence of the boy.

"Give me a couple of days," the Samurai eventually tells him.

Without any solutions, he explains the situation to Mickey the next day at work. His friend pulls over the car. "Aiya, what is wrong with you?" Mickey asks. "I know there's something screwed with your head, but nothing this sick."

"It's not like that," the Samurai says. "I'm a gentleman."

"My buddy stuck out his neck when he rented that apartment to you."

"I know."

Mickey asks more questions about the boy and the whereabouts of his aunt. "The best thing for you to do is to ride it out until she claims her nephew," he decides. "Keep him happy or the next thing you know, you'll be thrown in jail."

He comes up with a plan. The Samurai feels it might be dangerous. But Mickey's right.

That evening, the Samurai comes back to the apartment with a dolly from the ice factory and a large cardboard box. "Climb inside," he tells the kid.

"Where are we going?" the kid asks.

"Trust me," he says with a slanted smile that belongs to someone else.

Benny climbs in and he pushes it down the hall. They take the elevator with a Chinese family and pass the front foyer where the MISSING posters for Benson Yu, featuring his school studio portrait, have been taped up.

He hoofs the dolly down the block to the parking lot behind a tofu factory that is out of sight from pedestrians. He tells the boy it's safe to climb out.

Benny looks at the night sky and the streetlights in the distance with an opened face. His chest heaves as he guzzles the city air. "Okay, thanks," he says. "I can climb back in now and we can go home."

"Just wait," the Samurai tells the kid. "There's more."

A moment later, Mickey's cherry-red Pontiac Fiero, with the penis still spray-painted on it, pulls up. When Mickey climbs out to say hello, Benny steps away from him. His face curls, as though he's being taunted. The boy raises a finger at the Samurai's friend and coworker, pointing at him accusingly.

The Samurai looks back at Benny.

"He took my grandmother's things," the boy says. He looks at Mickey and raises his fists again. "*You took them.*"

The Samurai turns to Mickey for his reaction. His friend, chewing on a toothpick, throws up his hands. "How would I know? I was just trying to help a friend. Just like I have helped you. Don't hate me for being a nice guy!"

The boy starts screaming at Mickey in Chinese. He lunges at him, and strikes him hard in the stomach. Mickey crumples to the ground. The Samurai can't help but be impressed. Even as he holds the boy back, he infers his unseen strength.

"His grandmother had nothing of value," Mickey tells him. And then he turns to the boy. "You caught me off guard."

Slowly picking himself up, he demands that the boy apologize, but the boy refuses. The Samurai shrugs. Finally, Mickey grunts, gets into the car, and starts the engine.

The Samurai tells the boy to climb into the back seat, as Mickey throws the dolly and the folded-up box in the trunk. Mickey drives them out of Chinatown and into the downtown core of the city, past the bars and theaters. He suggests getting burgers, so they find a fast-food drive-through and buy cheeseburgers, fries, and malted chocolate soft serve, and they eat their food in the parking lot.

"Where are we going next?" the boy asks him.

"I don't know," the Samurai says.

"Can we go to a video game arcade?" the boy asks.

The Samurai shakes his head. The thought of the blinking lights, of those noises, makes his stomach quiver.

"How about a movie? I'm not ready to go home."

The Samurai looks at the dashboard clock. They could catch a nine p.m. screening. He turns to Mickey, who shrugs. "Sure."

They find the movie listings in a paper and drive out to a multiplex in a mall. The Samurai wants to watch *Hairspray*, because he likes musicals—and the boy wants to watch *The Unbearable Lightness of Being*, probably because of the half-clothed woman on the poster. They settle on Mickey's pick, *Action Jackson*. The movie is pretty good, but not memorable. The Samurai realizes that he and Lorna are supposed to watch the same movie next week. He'll have to pretend he didn't see it. By the time the film ends, it's nearly eleven.

He knows he's going to be tired at work tomorrow. The boy yawns when the lights come on.

They sit in silence as they return to Chinatown. The Samurai turns back to see whether Benny has fallen asleep, which would complicate their return to the apartment. But he's still awake. His eyes are so alert, they take in everything. Perhaps he already knows the Samurai's true identity. If not, then he understands that "Constantine" is a husk he wears over his true self, something he throws off when they practice. Maybe if the Samurai revealed himself, the boy would say that he knew all along.

The car makes an unexpected stop at the convenience store. Mickey runs outside and pops the trunk of the car. The Samurai sees him place a single rose, the kind of item sold from table to table at taverns, by the shuttered entrance.

When he comes back, Mickey has tears in his eyes. "The kid pulled out a knife," he says. "Why did he have to do that? He should have just taken his beating. He would have survived."

"Shirley's brother?" Benny says. "Mr. Mah's son?"

Mickey nods. "So they—these bad guys I barely know—shot him."

"Because of your argument?" the Samurai asks.

"Not just that," he says. "He made a lot of people angry. It wasn't my idea to take it so far."

"Is he dead?" Benny asks.

Mickey nods, his eyes full of moonlight. He shifts his car out of park, ready to take them home.

But the boy demands they make another stop. His voice deepens and for a moment, to the Samurai, he sounds much older.

CHAPTER ELEVEN

At my desk, in the middle of this moment, my real life intrudes, as it always does. My phone starts pinging with texts from Trina. The university president is throwing a party next month to honor top faculty! she writes. Including me! Dutifully I have to volley back my heart emojis and gauge her feelings before I can return to Benny, urgently seeking Shirley.

It's difficult for me to imagine him this way. How is this preteen, who is too afraid to even talk to a girl, suddenly some romantic lead in a movie? But he's buzzed from everything that's happened this night. He's been outside for the first time in weeks, thrown a hard punch (not the glancing blow he landed on Roderick Chow), and drained a large Coke while watching *Action Jackson*. Benny insists on seeing Shirley with a newfound boldness.

Constantine runs his hand across his brow and looks to Mickey, who shrugs. "What's the address?" he asks. Benny only knows the street but can guide Mickey. That's how Benny ends up at her doorstep. He prepares to face Shirley's parents, readying his demand, maybe plea, to see her. He hears footsteps. Shirley appears. She's surprised to see him at the door, looking drifty-eyed in her pajamas but not displeased.

"Why are you here?" she asks him. "Where have you been?"

When he mentions her brother's name, her face clenches at first, readying for a punch. "I'm sorry," he says. "I just learned."

She remains silent. She glares at him the way you do in conversation when a tacitly forbidden topic is broached. She steps back, but Benny takes her hand—the first time he's touched her since his now-dead mother babysat her for pocket money.

He feels the charge of physical connection. Her eyes shift, thawing into an appreciation for his concern, his pity. When she finally crumbles into high-pitched sobs, she cries the same way Benny always does, with the under-standing that shedding tears in front of another person is a failure of char-acter. Benny cries too, mainly about his own stuff but also about Shirley's brother. For a fraction of a moment, in each other's arms, they grow close out of that shared sense of shame. It doesn't feel unnatural to touch this girl he admires so much, to hold her close. For the first time, until Shirley's mother comes out in her nightgown, scowling at her with puffy, cried-out eyes, he feels unafraid, willing and capable of helping someone else. He feels like a man.

When he returns to the car, Constantine and Mickey look fearfully toward him as they await his next order. He sinks into the back seat, his flushed cheeks cooling in the air of the spring evening even as he tries to hold on to that brief interlude with Shirley.

Back in Constantine's apartment, his night out feels less like a reprieve and more like a taunting reminder of his deprivation. The next few days, then weeks, feel like years, then decades. His thoughts shift from Shirley to his aunt. Why'd he think Steph would save him? He wears his headphones and listens to *London Calling*, throwing his punches and kicks to its slicing minor chords. He stops reading comic books. He stops drawing, even the samurai and katanas he's grown absorbed in re-creating.

His punches prove he has power. A force that comes not from his arms or legs but something that passes through him, whatever makes his limbs move as quickly as his thumb on the A and B buttons at the arcade when he used to play *Double Dragon* with August. Wherever it originates, he feels invincible. He needs this strength when he feels most alone. On those nights Constantine spends with Lorna. Or when he remembers how Steph has abandoned him. He's been with Constantine for over a month now. As nice as Constantine is, Benny knows he's still an unwanted guest. He'll have to leave this apartment eventually, and then he'll need to be ready.

He begins pleading with his host to spar, hand-to-hand, since they don't have two bokuto, much less the shinai used in kendo. Constantine says no. Benny hasn't trained long enough. They don't have protective equipment. There's not enough room in the apartment. None of these justifications convinces Benny to stop. Eventually, Constantine relents, insisting they practice kumite at half speed and with light contact.

When they first practice-fight, Constantine uses his experience and size to gain an advantage. And yet the effort leaves him winded. Benny knows he's not easy to beat, and both of them take pleasure in his progress. He throws off his shirt when he gets sweaty, but Constantine recoils at the sight of his scrawny torso. Formerly embarrassed of his belly, Benny takes pleasure in how starvation and training have made him lean and contoured, if not muscular like his comic book heroes, the Punisher and Cyclops. But Constantine insists that he put on another shirt. Afterward, he talks him through his errors, in a voice Benny finds patronizing. This makes him try harder.

The way he catches Constantine looking at him can feel odd, as though he were Constantine's Shirley, his crush object. Maybe Steph was right to be worried. Maybe there's something wrong with the big white guy. As he wipes his brow, he catches Constantine looking at him once more.

"I need to tell you something," Constantine says in a low, uneven growl. He stares down at the floor. "I haven't been honest with you. I'm ready to tell you."

"What is it?" Benny asks. He braces himself for something uncomfortable to be said.

And I lose it.

"DON'T DO IT!" I start yelling in my office. "DON'T DO IT!" Trina walks in and asks what happened, and I have to slam my laptop shut and lie about a "sports team" I'm cheering for online. And of course, Trina shoots back a skeptical look.

"My name is not Constantine," the Samurai says. "I am a samurai who first lived five centuries ago, one who was reborn into this world. For many years, a time-traveling demon kept me estranged from my daimyo—my lord—who exists outside of time and space. Those were tough years. But my daimyo has returned. He has told me to protect and train you. I didn't trust those instructions until now. There's something special about you."

WHY'D HE HAVE TO DO THAT? I knew it was coming. At some point, after I've stirred the pot of real life with made-up backstory, these semifictional beings always revolt against me, freeing themselves to make their own star-tling, self-defeating choices.

Benny waits for Constantine to finish his confession and then excuses himself to go to the bathroom. He runs water and begins to sob. *How did I end up alone with this maniac? How could I place my trust in him?* Constantine knocks on the door and asks if he's okay. Benny doesn't answer. He knocks again. Benny pushes the tears back into his eyes.

When he steps outs he insists they fight again. He assumes a combat stance and waits until Constantine readies himself. He wishes again there were two bokutos so they could practice sword work. He wishes he were allowed to scream. Fighting hand-to-hand, Benny's not only weaker, he's at a disadvantage because his arms and legs are so much shorter. He can only really connect with his feet.

First, they bow toward each other. Then they wheel around the room, bouncing forward and backward. When Benny's frustrated, Constantine drops his guard to let him get some contact with a roundhouse kick to the kidneys. That's when Benny hits as hard as he can. Constantine winces, but he doesn't make a sound, nor does he tell Benny to stop. He tells him he's done well, which makes Benny want to hit his sensei harder.

They break apart again. After tapping Benny's face with his fists and swat-ting away the boy's kicks, Constantine drops his hands from his face. Although they look good in films, high kicks are pointless in street fights, he has told Benny, because they allow a fighter's body to be vulnerable. This time, Benny's foot reaches just high enough to strike his sensei in the chin.

The kick leaves him stunned, and he steps back toward the wall. Benny starts throwing his fists into Constantine's torso. Normally Constantine blocks him, but Benny can tell he's surprised by the velocity with which his fists fly.

"Time-out," Constantine says in that disembodied sensei voice that comes out of him as though a ventriloquist were standing behind him. "Okay, stop."

But Benny ignores him. He keeps punching until Constantine flinches and strikes back.

At last, I say to myself, quietly this time, *he shows his true self.* In spite of my efforts to dress him up like Don Quixote with a topknot.

Benny hears the crack and feels the blow, but he's almost outside the trauma, like a bystander watching a bar fight. He hears Constantine gasp. Then he feels the blood trickling out of his face. For a moment he thinks he's suffocating. Then he calms down enough to breathe through his mouth.

"I think I might have broken your nose," Constantine says, stooping down to look at it. To Benny, he doesn't sound like the lunatic who admitted, moments ago, to being a samurai. He sounds like Constantine. His voice drops in volume. "We'll need to go to the hospital."

Benny wails until Constantine uses one of his T-shirts to stanch the red ooze. He feels the big white guy at his back hurrying him past the elevator, outside through the rear exit. Benny is being led down the alleyway a couple of blocks until they get to the edge of Chinatown.

"It's easier to find a cab here," Constantine says, reaching into his robe for a twenty-dollar bill.

Benny agrees, but the shock and adrenaline have worn off, leaving a throbbing ache that pushes other feelings to the periphery. A cab pulls up and they climb inside. He watches Constantine stare at his fists throughout the ride as though he is assigning blame to his hands. Benny doesn't fault him. He was hitting Constantine with all his force, angry that his sensei had admitted he was a samurai. He wouldn't stop when Constantine asked. And now they're both exposed.

The taxi drops them off at the emergency room entrance, the same door Poh-Poh must have come through before she was admitted. They arrive at the waiting room. Through colors splotching his vision, Benny sees people coughing, others doubled over in blue armchairs. He sees one person rushed through a set of doors on a wheeled hospital bed. Some watch a TV set playing the eleven o'clock news. At the far end of the room a nurse sits behind glass under a sign that reads RECEPTION.

Constantine stops by the door, his eyes darting. Benny turns back for him, so he lurches toward the door.

"I've got to go, Benny," he says. "I've got to go." He digs up a ten-dollar bill from his pocket and hands it over before he leaves.

When Benny returns to the waiting room, he sees a police officer in a corner. The cop looks at him with narrowed eyes, and then scans past him toward the doors. He says something into the walkie-talkie that he's removed from his belt.

At the reception desk, the nurse twists her brow as Benny removes the T-shirt from his face. "Where are your parents?" she asks him. She presents him a clipboard with a form to be filled out.

When he doesn't answer, she takes back the clipboard and tells him to sit down. Another nurse waves him over to a bed with the back half raised, tells him to lie there, and hands him an ice pack. She asks him how he broke his nose.

"Karate. A friend and I were sparring," he says. "I let down my guard and he got me good."

"He really did," the nurse says as she examines the wound. "And where are your parents?"

"They both work night jobs," Benny says. He's ready this time. "My mom told me over the phone to take a cab here. She's going to pick me up when she's done."

The nurse warns him about a wait. The emergency room is short-staffed, and Benny needs a doctor to reset a misaligned bone.

Benny clamps the ice pack onto his nose, which has stopped bleeding, and brings his feet up. He wonders how long he will be here and worries that Constantine's in trouble. He regrets his reaction. *Of course Constantine thinks he's a samurai. There was no need to overreact. What else would explain his clothes and the tatami mats?* Benny watches the people around him. Some are writhing and groaning. He can smell the scent of alcohol wafting from the body of the patient in the next bed.

The doctor who sees him has a mustache and green eyes that flare with piqued interest at Benny's bloodied nose. He is matter-of-fact, without the kind of cheeriness that adults use with children in public. He sprays an anesthetic on the nose and then gazes at his feet as he waits for it to take effect. After enough time passes, he uses his thumb to shift the bone back into place. The sharp pain has the dissonance of microphone feedback. It ebbs as quickly as it swelled. "Take a Tylenol or two if you're still in pain," he tells Benny before stalking away with his lurching strides.

Benny wonders if he can leave. When he next sees the nurse, he tells her his mother will arrive shortly. "Can I just wait for her outside?" he asks.

The nurse smiles. "Just sit tight," she tells him.

He begins to worry more about Constantine. Is he all right? He thumbs the ten-dollar bill in his pocket and wonders if that's enough to take a cab back—or should he take the bus? Would it even be safe for him to return?

At some point he dozes off, even with the pain of his nose. When the nurse wakes him up, it's one in the morning. She says to follow her. She leads him to a small, windowless room with a table. He recognizes Macy, the social worker, sitting beside a police officer. She asks him to take a seat.

"Good to see you again, Benny," she says. "I know you've been through a lot." She inches toward him and narrows her eyes and switches to Cantonese. "Someone was rough with you, gwaa?"

"I was just playing around with a friend," he responds in English.

She looks across to the police officer. "Are you talking about your neighbor?"

"Is he going to be in any trouble?"

Her eyes skitter. "I wish I knew."

The police officer intercedes and asks Benny how long he's known Constantine and whether he was held there against his will.

"I asked to stay with him, until my aunt came back from tour—he was just helping me," Benny insists. "He shouldn't get in any trouble."

"Well, neither of us will determine that," the police officer says after exchanging glances with Macy.

Benny turns to the social worker, who looks barely older than Steph, and asks her whether she can contact his aunt, a twenty-eight-year-old who steals toilet paper from restaurants and throws parties so she can collect the bottle deposits on the empties. She's supposedly the only person who can raise him.

"I'll reach her," Macy assures him. "Until then, we'll find you somewhere safe to stay. Do you have any other family?"

"No," he lies.

"Where's your father?"

Benny doesn't answer. The social worker already knows the truth, he realizes from her reaction. The best he can do is to keep quiet. And even that strategy, he understands, will only delay what he always knew would happen.

CHAPTER TWELVE

I'm getting ready to teach my last class of the term, trying to overlook the piles of grading ahead of me, but I'm preoccupied by the Samurai, and what an unknown quantity I've jiggered together. From the corner of my eye, as I set up for my class, I catch a glimpse of him, squeezing into a chair in the far corner. On a second look, I see that it's only another student.

Of course, the Samurai is where I left him. He's spent a night awake on a holding cell bench to the sound of a drunk's wet cough. In the morning, he calls Iulia. He blurts out an explanation that puzzles his sister, who tries to speak over her baby's screaming in the background. "Say that again slowly, louder?" He repeats his story and asks her to call in sick at the ice factory on his behalf. He's here at least until he can see a judge. She says she will come to the jail once she finds somebody to watch the baby.

His fist pulses from the punch he threw at the boy—not out of pain, but from shame. He glares at his hand, as though it has betrayed him. He shouldn't have told the boy he was a samurai. It was what he desired most, which was why he should have known better. He couldn't blame the boy for his reaction. The boy fought as though his life had been at stake. The Samurai doesn't know why he hit him so hard. Or maybe he does. It was not the force with which Benny came at him—it was what he saw in the boy's eyes. Hatred and rage. He saw Tata coming at him—the illusion itself the handiwork of the demon—and for once he fought back. Mickey's right. The Samurai's going to be charged with kidnapping. And battery. He'll get hospitalized if he's lucky. Thrown in prison if not.

In the dull morning light, he sleeps as much as possible until he gets moved to another cell. He brushes his teeth and tries to sleep again. He's pulled out and told he has his bail hearing. In a small room, he meets the lawyer assigned to him. They step together into the oak-paneled courtroom. The prosecutor looks at his file and accuses the Samurai of hurting a child intentionally. The Samurai's lawyer notes his history of mental illness as an extenuating circumstance. The judge sets bail and a court date.

The Samurai shakes hands with his lawyer and is returned to jail to await Iulia. He is walked over in a group to a dining hall for lunch, which is a bologna sandwich with a green apple, washed down with fruit punch. He's reminded of the convenience-store sandwiches he fed the boy. He tries to sleep in his bunk bed through the afternoon, but that doesn't work. Another inmate is led in, a man who insists that he was framed for robbery by his ex-wife. They chat for a while, the Samurai dropping his end of the conversation long before it's finished. It's the same way with Mickey, but also with Herb and Tata. People don't care whether he responds. They want to yammer at him. Maybe because he's like a black hole for them, one into which they can void their feelings, knowing their words will go lost in his empty head.

The Samurai finds himself brought out again for dinner, a chicken pot pie, and then returned to his cell. He turns down the offer of a shower and goes to bed.

He stares into darkness from his bottom bunk and drifts off. He hears his daimyo's voice. He prostrates himself in his cell.

How dare you reveal your identity to that boy? his daimyo asks. *You know it's forbidden.*

My lord, it was a mistake. But there's something else I must tell you. I protected the boy as you commanded. There was an accident. The boy and I were separated in the emergency room.

You moron! Do you know who that boy is?

He was my neighbor. His grandmother died. I took him in until his aunt came back.

No, dumbass. He's my heir.

You never told me. How can that be?

A killer was dispatched to my estate as he was born. He needed to be kept safe. We sent him away and concealed his identity. He stayed with the old woman. And then he was placed in your care. Only now you have lost him. And the demon is closing in on him!

My lord, I am deeply sorry. I do not think I can live with this shame. If I had the means—

Never mind that. You must find him. He is in grave danger. Reclaim your katana and take care of him. You must slay the demon and then restore him to the throne.

The next morning, he is bailed out by Iulia. She hugs his slumping form after his release in the reception area. "Sorry it took so long," Iulia says. "Herb has been away at some kind of convention for Communists. And the baby-sitter wasn't available until today."

"It was a misunderstanding," the Samurai explains.

They take a booth at the diner he likes and order coffee. He runs through his story again, the one he botched over the phone the day before. He mentions the child down the hall who needed to be hidden away. He talks about how he trained him in basic kendo and karate, but doesn't talk about the ride in the car with Mickey, or the kid Mickey may have gotten killed. He talks about accidentally hitting Benny. He doesn't admit maintaining the belief he's a samurai.

As he speaks, Iulia starts rummaging through her purse, removing a baby rattle, a pacifier, and a package of Tic Tacs before she finds Mama's old hankie, the one with her monogrammed initials, to dab her tears. She turns away to give her head a brisk shake.

"You've spent all this time with some random Chinese kid—you know samurais are Japanese, right? You endanger your freedom, but you don't check on us," she says. "Not at the hospital, not after. We've spent this morning to-gether and you haven't asked me once about Sarah." She catches the vacant look in his eyes and her jaw clenches with rage. "For fuck's sake, she's your only niece."

"I'm sorry," he says. He tries to find the right language, to remember the cadences of a person engaged with this world and only this world. "There was Benny. And I am seeing someone . . ."

"You're what?" She starts crying again. The waitress tilts her head sympa-thetically toward Iulia when she stops to refill their cups. Her eyes dart on him, prodding him to act. He leans over and grabs his sister's hand. "It's not just you," she adds. "I've been crying a lot lately."

"Being a mom is hard," the Samurai says.

Her eyes bulge with incredulity at his understatement. "You used to take care of me. You took Tata's whippings so he wouldn't touch me, and I will always love you for it. But now I'm the one who takes care of you—and Sarah. Herb isn't as much help as he likes to think."

"I'll do better," he promises.

He goes back to work the next day and excuses his absence with a story about food poisoning, the lie Iulia prepared for him, and it's accepted by the factory manager. While he's in his boss's office, he asks for a raise. His boss promises him another fifty dollars on his next paycheck if he joins the company softball team. Later that week, his court-assigned lawyer calls. The charges have been dismissed. The Samurai's relieved and perplexed.

Once he gets that call, he throws the boy's clothes and mattress into the dumpster. Mickey helps him buy a couch and a kitchen table, cheap, from the garage of another Chinese man. His daimyo returns to him at night, resuming his instructions. He knows these voices aren't considered real by others. Heeding them will only lead to his personal destruction. He resists for a few days. Then he finds himself back in the pawnshop for the first time since he originally discovered the katana.

The shop owner recognizes him. "Find the money for it yet?" he says, one corner of his mouth raised.

"I have it," the Samurai tells him again. "I just need to get it."

He asks to see the blade once more, and the shopkeeper obliges. When it's revealed from the saya, the blade speaks to him in his daimyo's voice. *Remember. Remember. Remember.* He sees the same price tag attached to the sword's tsuka—$2,000.

I never conceived of the Samurai as conniving, just as I didn't see him breaking Benny's nose. Maybe it's that original spark of C., who used to make up stories about all the boys dying to be mentored by him, that has corrupted him and the redemptive undertones of his story. Or it's the circumstances I've placed him in that have led him astray. The following Saturday, the Samurai visits Iulia with flowers for her and a discount-store onesie for Sarah. It's a sunny spring day, and Herb makes burgers and hot dogs on a charcoal grill in his backyard. Everyone sits outside in lawn chairs.

Iulia asks the Samurai if he wants to hold Sarah. He doesn't, but says yes. His sister removes the sleeping infant from her sling and places her in his lap. The child squirms a little in his arms and opens her eyes to see him. He remembers lying in bed next to his sister on nights when she had nightmares. She was six or seven then. She would toss her arms in her sleep, like she was flinging someone off.

"I used to think that Mama was such a bad mother because she was crazy," Iulia says. "Now I wonder whether we didn't make things worse for her. We must have."

Baby Sarah smacks her lips as though she wants to eat, then turns her head toward Constantine's chest. She settles in and falls back asleep.

"I was thinking of buying a used car," the Samurai announces. "It would make it easier for me to get to work and to visit . . . Sarah."

Iulia seems preoccupied watching her daughter with him. Does she trust him? He continues anyway. With his raise, he can afford to pay for gas and insurance. He and a friend, a guy who knows something about cars, have already road-tested a ten-year-old station wagon that's in good condition, with low mileage.

"It's two thousand dollars," he says. "You know I've got the money." The Samurai stares down at the baby on his chest. "But I'll need your help getting it from the bank."

When he looks up again, he sees his poor, tired sister, who only wants her brother to care for his niece as much as he does about the sword he wants to buy. She will do his bidding. When I see the Samurai now, I only see C.'s face.

PART TWO

Elsewhere, the present

PART TWO

CHAPTER THIRTEEN

If I could banish one phrase from the English language, it would be "pick your brain." Those words were inevitably volleyed in my direction after a convention appearance or an undergraduate lecture at the end of the term. Usually from the would-be's I could never coax into realistic self-appraisal, from the "emerging" who did not take "recede" as an answer. And in those moments, my gray matter felt like spit-up chewing gum. But, well, I was a people pleaser. I found it hard to say no. Especially when the request came from someone who looked very much like me twenty years earlier.

By that, I mean an Asian guy in glasses and a cardigan with a messenger bag. The boot-scrapings of most North American social hierarchies. Two decades back, I had that same default expression, looking as though I needed help but not expecting any. This fine young man was holding an early edition of *Iggy Samurai* for me to sign. Probably sourced online, at a markup that I couldn't profit from. At least he wasn't clutching fake merchandise or a movie poster. I was in busy-adjunct-professor mode, cosplaying dignity as I packed away my lecture notes and laptop to schlep back to my shared office, but out of habit I still kept my metallic-silver Sharpie marker in my blazer pocket for signings. It was after the autograph session that he asked for some advice.

His name was Carter. I'd noticed him during the term, present at and punctual to all the classes. He usually sat in an oblique corner of the lecture hall. Once or twice, he'd offered an opinion on Art Spiegelman or Chester Brown. And he was always drawing throughout those talks. I could tell when I strolled the aisles during a quiz. Little margin doodles that would swallow up his notes.

Typically, in this scenario, the request for brain-picking was brought forward with either a compliment or the invocation of a mutual acquaintance.

In this case, Carter talked about how his best friend's older brother had introduced him to *Iggy Samurai* and he'd read the entire series, even the limited edition published only in Japan. He earned bonus points for saying that he thought the character had been watered down in the cynical movie sequels that demolished the value of my intellectual property and future earning power.

"I do some drawing of my own," Carter told me. "I was wondering how you got started. Could I take you out for coffee and—"

Pick your brain. Before I had a moment to respond—and I would have probably offered some advice there, a couple of on-the-spot pointers in lieu of more sustained engagement—he added that he'd forgotten to mention that his mother knew me when we were kids. The sound of her name winded me. I felt the heat of my past ardor, and then the chill of her rejection. Sputtering, I tried to collect myself. I didn't think he'd noticed.

My office hour was canceled because the term had ended. Adele was still with her sitter until dinnertime, and it was Trina's day to pick her up. Normally, that meant I handled dinner. I could bring home pizza that night.

I felt like a beer and suggested the student pub. At this point in history, my decision was suspect. Instructors and students weren't "encouraged" to drink together. Then there was the drinking "problem" I'd once had. But I was tired. And it was always male students who wanted to pick my brain. No one would look askance.

When we got to the pub, the place was full of boys in reversed baseball caps with half-empty pitchers of draft. They were talking across tables to young women in their sweatshirts and flannels—their pre-exam uniform. The music coming out of the speakers made it hard to think, let alone hear, but I didn't mind. The bartender was playing the style of music that made me feel young— with guitars, a rolling wave of fuzz and crunch—the oldies for everyone else. I bought a pitcher of the darker draft, an amber ale, and directed Carter toward a table on the patio.

"You've followed my career. Or maybe only the parts worth following," I told him as I filled his glass. "The first thing you need to know is to find a lawyer to read over your contract. Even if you think it's a lot of money up front."

He laughed at my presumptive piece of advice, his eyes twinkling with arousal. "I don't think I'm that far along in my journey. Not yet. But thanks." His face was red from my flattery. Or maybe it was the Asian flush. "I read about how the royalties for *Iggy Samurai* were diverted. I'll keep that in mind." He took a pull and wiped his lip of foam. "My parents want me to study dentistry, but I'd like to change my major. Did you have to fight anyone to make art?"

"Physically?" I asked him.

The smile sat stubbornly on his face. "That's not what I meant, but sure."

"I fought everyone in every way," I said. "I had to fight to survive."

"So *Iggy Samurai* was autobiographical?" he joked.

Another favorite question of mine. "As much as any work is."

"Why did you stop making comics?"

"What do you mean?"

He shrank back in his chair as though he was afraid I would hit him. He looked as though he'd never taken a punch. He had the face of a boy whose mother kissed away his boo-boos, and now when he was startled, he still expected to be comforted.

"You've got a family, I suppose, and now you're teaching," he started. "I guess you're busy with that . . ."

I told him that I had been working on something else for the last few months, on and off. He asked me what it was about—"You don't have to say." I told him it was a work of prose. He leaned in expectantly, like someone owed an elevator pitch. "I don't remember the writer who said it, who said it's all the same story for him," I continued. "Trying to recapture that first love, that first rupture. No doubt a lot of writers have said the same thing. I'm trying to rework the autobiographical spark of *Iggy Samurai* into a prose narrative. My publisher is excited and has given me a deadline." I dared myself to announce this, to shame myself into completing it. I didn't know what it was other than a busy-making response to C.'s letter.

"That's gonna be great," Carter said unconvincingly. "But it must be hard."

I nodded. Honestly, I was failing. I was trying to distill the truth, instead of skirting it with comic book heroics. My story had gotten away from me, as though it were a house cat I'd let outside, and now I was afraid it was in the bloody jaws of a predator. Maybe that wouldn't have been the case if I could work more regularly. Being married and serving as the kid's primary caregiver took plenty of my hours. I had my priorities. I may have had the social capital in our house, but Trina's tenured professorship put the salad boxes and oat milk in our fridge.

We drained the first pitcher, or mostly I did, but he offered to buy the next one. I asked Carter about his own work, to deflect further questions about *Iggy Samurai*. I tried not to ask the kind of yes-no questions that would prompt him to say something like *It's easier to send you my manuscript if you want to take a look*. And while I avoided queries that felt like invitations for my skull to be further melon-balled, I always told them to contact me if they had any more questions.

Outside the pub, I tossed my keys between my hands. "Your mom. How is she these days?"

Watching the keys with an uneasy smile, he said he would see her at the end of next week when he returned home. I already knew she co-owned a real estate agency, with Carter's father, that sponsored kids' baseball and soccer teams and also a scholarship for at-risk youth named after her dead brother. They took line dancing classes together. She alternated her vacations between China and Hawaii. She liked visiting the same favorite restaurants and beaches. In her photos, I noticed that she had thickened around the waist, but her hair was still glossy and kept long, girlishly long. She liked the pink blossoms of cherry trees and the sheets of gold that hung off laburnums, and I could imagine the wistful sigh she would heave as the seasons changed and she raised her camera phone.

Carter said she was in a good place.

"Well, tell her I said hi."

He stopped and turned back at the sound of my keys dropping to the ground. "Do you want me to call you a cab?" he asked.

I pocketed my keys and pulled out my phone as though to hail a ride, allowing Carter to leave first. He didn't know that I used an app on my phone to unlock my car doors. I only played with my house keys out of habit. Stumbling into my vehicle, I drove without hesitation. There were only two traffic lights and then a cut up the side of the hill with the short blind turn that I could take with my eyes closed. Adele would scream when we went up that way. On our drives home I would always let her choose. "Do you want to take the normal way home—or the scary one?" She invariably chose this path.

Only when I arrived home did I realize I had forgotten to pick up the pizza. But Trina, who either was in a forgiving mood or hadn't remembered it had been my turn to make dinner, was boiling pasta to serve with reheated Bolognese sauce. Adele was in the living room, watching cartoons. When I tried to ask her about her day at school, she waved me off.

"Sorry I'm late," I said, kissing Trina on the cheek. She didn't flinch from me, so I knew she hadn't noticed I'd been drinking. "My brain was picked."

She shook her head. "That's just part of your job."

"Only if I were salaried."

"You have a message," she says. "From a social worker?"

I looked at her and shrugged. "Uh, weird."

"Are you okay tucking in Adele?" she asked me. "I have a second draft of a dissertation to read over tonight. And, of course, my speech for the party at the university president's house."

Trina wouldn't let me forget that party, not even for a day. She was due to get a research award. It was her big deal. I accepted tuck-in chores on my way to the landline. The only calls we got on our legacy connection were from robots, scammers, and bureaucrats. Why didn't we cut off this vestigial limb? Perhaps because we worried we'd miss a call from one of the remaining people who had our number. I listened to the voice-mail message and took down the speaker's information. The register of the woman's voice felt familiar. Since it was dinnertime, I called the number I'd written, expecting to leave my own message back. But the social worker picked up on the fourth ring. She laid out the circumstances that had prompted her initial call. The boy. I let a silence hang over the line that she lurched to fill up. She said she knew his arrival was sudden and I might not be prepared to take someone in.

Hearing this news, I felt relieved, actually. Like a bank robber who'd spent years living under an assumed name, getting pulled over on the highway. Part of me was pleased not to be receiving a speeding ticket.

Without any hesitation, I told the woman on the phone that we could take him immediately. "Oh, great," she replied, with some doubt in her voice.

"How is he doing?" I asked her.

"He's been through so much. But kids are resilient. Even strong, teem," she said, switching to Cantonese.

"Tell him I miss him," I replied in English. I should have told her that I needed to talk to my wife first, but I didn't.

When I returned to the kitchen, dinner was on the table. Watching Adele slurp linguine, I told Trina I had news to share, later. Trina's raised eyebrow matched the curve of the wineglass she tipped back. Afterward, I got Adele into her pull-up and pajamas and charmed her into brushing her teeth and letting me read her a story—then two, three. She wailed for Mommy when the lights went out and continued bleating until she rolled over to her side with a heavy snore.

I stepped out of her darkened bedroom to find Trina slouched in her office armchair with her headphones on, most likely listening to Mahler. The pages of the dissertation were divided into two stacks on her lap. I tried to work in my studio but could never muster much in the evening. I usually answered emails.

Then I started rummaging through old photos that I had digitized a few years back. There was one of me as a child, on a newly purchased bike, the second-to-last present from my mother, that I wanted to print out but never did. I wondered how different the boy looked from that photo.

I decided I was done and was in bed, flipping through a paperback, when Trina turned in. She stepped out of her home jeans and into the bathroom, where I heard the sink faucet run. "So what was the call about?" she asked me while she brushed her teeth.

I told her about how the boy was coming to live with us.

"Who?" she asked.

She had every right to be shocked when I explained that he was not my son, although he might identify that way. That he was something between a distant cousin and a clone. We sat on the edge of the bed holding hands. At first, I was worried she'd think I was losing my mind. But the way she responded—repeating my assertions in her own words, probing my emotional state—suggested she already believed I had crossed that line.

CHAPTER FOURTEEN

In the car with Macy, Benny took in the sight of farmland and cow pasture, and then hills and desert, for the first time in his life. The drive was a knot of silence frayed by bursts of attempted chitchat from the social worker, whose discomfort with gaps in conversation resulted in extraneous personal disclosures. He learned, for instance, that Macy enjoyed thousand-piece jigsaw puzzles of world monuments she wanted to visit. She also had no children of her own, as she was waiting for her gwai lo fiancé, Todd, who worked at an adult-video store, to be ready. "He wants to have kids, laa," she insisted. "We just need to find the right time for him." Benny had loved car rides because it wasn't the bus, because people on TV drove in cars, but he hadn't known he also loved the intimacy—one-sided, in this case—of a long road trip.

Over lunch at a fast-food burger place, Macy shaded in the outline she'd recently given him of his father, how he was a comic book artist and teacher, remarried with a young daughter. He tried to accept this description evenhandedly. It had been a few years since Poh-Poh last mentioned his father, and in that time, maybe he'd stopped working at a nightclub and started a new family. It wouldn't be out of character for his grandmother to describe his father in the most ghoulish fashion. But how did he make comic books?

"We're almost there, Benny," Macy announced, her voice trilling, when they returned to the car. His mind was still clouded with visions of the blue-eyed kids with brush cuts inside the burger place and the way one of them pulled his eyes back and sneered at him. Whether they were Chinese or not, bullies were cast from the same mold.

"Did you notice how funny everyone looked?" Benny asked Macy. "Everyone's clothes and hairstyles are weird. And what about the cars?"

Macy chuckled and looked at him indulgently. "There are lots of gwai lo here in this area. That's why everything seems different," she explained.

"Have you heard from Steph recently?" Benny asked when they were back on the road.

She nodded. "She's on her way back home," she said. "She means well, but I don't think she's ready to care for you." Benny had already been told that Steph's reported income didn't meet the threshold necessary to be Benny's legal guardian. Macy kept her eyes on the highway until she could not keep quiet any longer. "How's your nose feeling?"

Benny squeezed it lightly and gave her a thumbs-up. It had healed quickly in the two days he had spent at a group home, which he already missed. In the home, he'd had his own half of a bunk bed, with house parents, Mr. and Mrs. Douglas, and a wolf pack of other parentless kids. He'd learned everyone's names instantly, and found the experience of being part of a household again heady. And yet he had forgotten all their names the moment he was out the door.

Before they arrived at his father's place, Macy drove through the town center, with its brick buildings and coffee shops built into converted residential homes with mansard roofs, and Benny felt as though he'd seen this place somewhere, probably on television. Noticing the college kids in their college-branded sweatshirts drinking beers on a patio and the childless professional couples window-shopping for "restored vintage Danish modern furniture," he wondered how he would ever *not* be a glitch in this world.

Macy drove up a hill lined with what appeared to be mansions—gated entrances, sloped roofs, and doorways framed by white columns. His expectations momentarily vaulted, so that he felt a thud of disappointment to see his father's modest single-story ranch-style house.

They were waiting for him in the driveway. His father, who held a young child in his arms, and his wife. Again, something about this place seemed askew. The lines of his father's and his family's clothes were rounded in the shoulders, almost lumpy, but otherwise more geometric. Their hair was unstructured with product. Why did everyone dress so strangely? Why did the vehicles look different? Benny stepped out of the car with a knapsack filled only with the clothes that he'd purchased the other day with his house parents.

The woman—his father's new wife, Benny assumed—approached him first. She was as thin-boned as a Chinese woman but had flat white-blond hair cut in an asymmetrical bob and a long, sharp nose. Her fine features and green eyes reminded Benny of a piece of antique crystal he once saw on a field trip to a museum. Her mouth was fixed in a bemused slant. "Call me by my first name. Is that okay?" she said with a voice that was unexpectedly deep and had the hint of a European accent. "We are so glad you are here with us."

Benny kept looking toward Macy, hoping she would sense his uneasiness. Perhaps she would intervene and take him back to the Douglases. But Macy seemed fixated on Benny's father's house and his shiny car in the driveway. "Your son will like it here," she told him. "He's ready for a change."

The girl, maybe five years old, buried her face in her father's chest. "She won't be shy for long," his father said. "You must be tired. We made a room for you."

His father shocked him the most. He didn't look like the father Benny remembered, not even in the badly lit photo he had of him. In that photo, his father did resemble, as Poh-Poh suggested, a movie star. He was as pretty as Leslie Cheung, but with the cocky swagger of Chow Yun-Fat. This man looked like the ugly brother of the beautiful man Benny remembered. He wore a sparse beard and his hair had thinned. Benny had his eyes, his face, his delicate fingers—the ones Poh-Poh, her laughter revealing her fake teeth, described as "ivory chopsticks." He didn't smile as freely as Benny remembered him doing. Maybe his memory was wrong.

This man seemed shy to the point of rudeness, in the way he thanked Macy and, to the dismay of his wife, edged back toward the house without inviting her inside. The social worker seemed reluctant to climb back into her car and asked to use the restroom.

While the house didn't appear as impressive as the mansions at the bottom of the hill, what Benny noticed was how the floor gleamed in the sitting room and how new the couch looked, even without plastic. There was art on the walls, abstract paintings and fine-art photography, instead of a tear-off daily calendar and dusty photos of ancestors he'd never met.

Macy stepped out of the bathroom, her eyes poring over every corner of this house as though she were on the set of a fantasy movie. He expected her to take him by the hand and lead him back to the car. Instead, with a look of satisfaction, she heaved a sigh. "Good luck," she said to Benny. "Pretty soon this will feel normal."

His father took Benny's backpack and led him to a room off the kitchen with a skylight and drafting desk. A folded cot was pushed awkwardly in a corner by a bookshelf. He opened the cot and placed the backpack on it.

"We still need to fix this place up for you," he told Benny. "The trouble is, I own too much junk."

On the wall across from the desk was a framed movie poster of a cartoon figure with a lizard head, samurai armor, and a katana. Benny looked around and saw all the memorabilia. As he inspected the movie poster, he saw his own name on it. *Based on the comic book by Benson Yu.* Poh-Poh had said nothing about this. He hadn't even known he shared a first name with his father, which he correctly believed to be an uncommon practice—bad luck, even—for Chinese. Maybe his dad wasn't the disappointment Poh-Poh made him out to be. Poh-Poh never understood comic books. For her, any success he might achieve would be a failure. "You created your own comic book?"

His father nodded. "Growing up in Chinatown, I always liked to draw."

The boy's eyes flashed. "I'm that way too." When his father said he already knew that, Benny surprised himself with his own unvoiced displeasure. How was it possible for him to know anything about him? The last time he'd seen him, he was four years old.

"As an undergrad," his father continued, "I put out a comic book and it became pretty popular. Then it was turned into movies." There was a drawer in one of the bookcases, and from it he removed an action figure for Benny to inspect.

As Benny looked around the room, he saw other books with his name on them, awards, and framed certificates. There were also family photos of his father with his stepmother and half sister and, strangely enough, a picture of his mother with Benny on a bike from after his father had left. Behind the drafting table, through the window, was a Japanese-style garden with a footbridge over a koi pond, a rock garden, and a small house with sliding bamboo doors. Like Constantine, his father was obsessed with Japanese things. (Despite everything that happened in the war, Benny noted, hating himself a little for thinking like Poh-Poh.) Two deer emerged from the woods the house backed onto, a mother and son.

"Adele calls the little one Bambi," his father told him as he sat down onto the cot. "She calls the bigger one Elsa. I bet you've never seen deer before."

In fact, he found the sight of deer in the yard as unsettling as everything else. "I don't remember you," Benny said. "I don't remember much."

"Of course. There's no way you would," he said. "But I still recognize you. I'm sorry about your poh-poh. I'm sure it was a shock. And I guess I'm sorry too about your mom. Nobody will love you the way she did."

Benny's eyes welled up, and at the thought of how Mommy was mistreated by this man, who acknowledged no responsibility for that mistreatment, his fists balled together. Benny's stepmother knocked on the door to say she still needed another five minutes to prepare dinner. In the meantime, his father could show him around the house. "She's the boss," he said, and rose from the cot. He led Benny to the bathroom and towel closet, the kitchen with its shiny chrome appliances, the living room with the biggest TV he had ever seen.

"Outside in the shed is the dojo," he said as his wife called them to the table. "I'll have to let you see it later."

Benny's stepmother had made elbow macaroni with ground beef and onion in a red sauce. Benny wasn't prepared for the spice. "What's this dish called?" he asked.

"Goulash—I make it every couple of weeks," she said, her smile dimming as she gauged his dismay. "I grew up eating it in Czechoslovakia," she added, almost pitifully. "It's comfort food for me."

Maybe Benny's taste buds had regressed from his time cooking for himself. His eyes throbbed with envy as his half sister forked into her mouth plain elbow macaroni tossed in butter. She smiled back at him before fixing her attention on her father, who chased down his goulash with sips from a glass of red wine. Benny had already drained his glass of water.

In between bites, his stepmother gave him information she thought he might be curious about. She was employed as a college professor at the school where Benny's father taught part-time. "There's not a lot of culture around here," she said. "But it's not a bad place to bring up . . . children." She and his father had been together nearly a decade, and had met at a Halloween party when they both lived in the city. "He was so shy I had to ask him out." Once again, Benny wondered how this description fit with what he already knew about his father—whose girlfriends would call the house. For a year after he left Mommy, these women would call and hang up at the sound of her voice.

Not that his stepmother was ugly. She was warm and engaging, even when she ran him through a checklist of questions at the dinner table. *Do you like school? What are your favorite subjects? What foods do you like? What are your favorite sports?* He fumbled through his responses and realized how sharing his own biography strained him. In a previous life, Poh-Poh tolerated his interests and preferences only if they coincided with her idea of what he needed. To her, wanting anything different from what Benny received—behaving like a child, and not a piece of furniture—was a moral defect. Things were different in this house, as shown by the way his half sister's whining about dessert was indulged. His hands tightened around his fork and knife. To fit in, he'd have to volunteer more information.

"I've started doing karate," Benny decided to offer. "A friend taught me."

She narrowed her eyes at him. "Is that why your nose looks a little funny?"

He blushed. "Yeah."

Her eyes drifted toward his father and she raised an eyebrow. "I can see it's more than a physical resemblance."

His father *mm-hmm*ed into his wineglass. What was this unsmiling, uncharming version of his father thinking? He could barely look at Benny.

Dessert was chocolate ice cream, as requested by his half sister. His stepmother placed a second bowl in front of Benny. Without chiding. Or comments about being fat. His extra serving upset his half sister, who'd eaten a Popsicle earlier in the day. Within a meal, she moved from alarm to indifference, and now to hissing jealousy, at Benny's presence. After some screeching, she accepted her parents' offer of watching a Disney movie, or half of it, before her bedtime. The TV screen, so bright and flat, floored him. He'd never seen such a thing. In its reflected glare, the sight of her around her parents, the ease with which she sat on his father's lap at the table, the way her mother later kissed her feet on the couch, made Benny feel like an extraterrestrial who'd never understand how families behaved.

Before the movie reached its midpoint, Benny claimed to be tired and returned to his room. How good did it feel to air his sweaty feet. Once he'd changed into a new T-shirt, he crawled into bed and opened up an issue of *Iggy Samurai*.

The black-and-white comic was about a fourteen-year-old iguana who was taken from his rain forest home to live with a drug dealer in New York City. When his owner was killed in a turf war, he escaped into Central Park, where he was attacked by a clan of hungry raccoons. At the last moment, he was saved by Coyote Sensei, a samurai master reincarnated in the body of a coyote who solved crimes in the park. The recognition of reading the comic book after spending time with samurai-obsessed Constantine was, in many ways, like meeting a long-lost family member and remarking on similarities in your physical features and personalities. Better, even. In spite of himself, his father was *so cool*. He had a better life than Benny had expected from the version of his father Poh-Poh had presented—a ladies' man who couldn't keep a job.

But when Benny looked at the top of the cover of the first issue and saw the date, *Spring 1999*, his mouth dried out. It must be a joke. And even though the date was over a decade in the future, the comic book was yellowing from age. His eyes weren't working right because he was so tired. They grew heavy and pulled him into a dreamless sleep. When he woke up, he was drenched in sweat, still in the same pants he'd worn through his long road trip here. The sun was beaming through the skylight. How had that blast of daylight not woken him up earlier?

The house was silent. He brushed his teeth with a new toothbrush his father had given him the night before. Where was everybody? How could any-place be as quiet as this house? In the kitchen, he found his stepmother sitting

on a stool at the counter, holding a slab of lit glass in one hand, sipping from a mug of tea in the other.

"You slept well?" she asked warmly. "Your father took your sister to her ballet class."

"What's that?" Benny asked, his interest piqued at the device she held. "Is it like a tricorder in *Star Trek*?"

She laughed, self-deprecating laughter as though he'd made a sardonic comment. "Very funny, it's not that old," she told him. "Your father tells me to upgrade. But it still works fine." She asked him what he wanted to do that day. As he sputtered, she suggested shopping—and he agreed, happy not to decide. The two of them would go to the mall to buy clothes for school, which he would begin the following Monday. "It's better we go without him anyhow," she said about Benny's father as she wheeled around the kitchen looking for her car keys. "He gets very impatient when we shop."

They took her car down the hill onto the highway that opened up to a parched valley. Benny's stepmother was playing music that he liked. Electric guitars strummed, shimmering and shrieky, over the aloof vocalist. Benny turned it up. "What's that?" he asked her.

"The Strokes. Do you like it?"

He nodded, thinking about his aunt's record collection. "It reminds me of the Velvet Underground."

Her eyes brightened. "I think we're going to get along."

Benny's stepmother pulled off the highway into a mall. The scale of the mall multiplied his disorientation. Too many people for Benny to be the victim of a practical joke anymore, so perhaps he was in an extended hallucination. So many people in clothes he didn't understand, fixating on their tricorders. Sometimes their hair was purple and pink, and lots of people had tattoos, even the mothers pushing their kids in strollers.

Their first stop was the boys' section of a department store. Grabbing shirts and hoodies in fistfuls of clothes hangers, his stepmother steered him toward styles that she'd seen on her colleagues' kids. Afterward, she recalled what it had been like to emigrate from Czechoslovakia. "I was more self-conscious about my clothes and hair than my accent," she said over fries and Cokes at the food court. "I was thinking you might want a less conspicuous look." Benny was relieved she'd stopped asking him so many questions. She had a way of giggling, even with her throaty voice, that seemed youthful. Maybe she actually liked him.

He was further relieved that french fries and Cokes hadn't changed.

"I'm sorry to be bombarding you with questions. But your father hasn't told me a lot about you," she says. "He said you were living with your grand-mother before she passed suddenly. And that your mother is already gone." She tilted her head and looked at him softly. "Now you're here in this strange town, with this strange family."

Benny nodded, not wanting to add his confusion about the era they existed in. The details of this one didn't faze her, so he knew he was the person who needed to adjust. He didn't want her to regret taking him in. "I don't know much about my dad either," he told her. "My grandma didn't like to talk about him. I didn't even know he wrote *comic books*. I mean, *holy cow*." He didn't want his voice to squeak in awe, but she smiled in response to it.

"Pretty cool, right? One thing to know about him is he's driven. That means he can be hard on himself. Just watching him with you, I can tell. He sees himself in you." Benny felt his cheeks flush with pride.

"Do you think he likes me?"

Her head bobbed vigorously. "Of course he does. He's thrilled to have you here. He didn't hesitate about you coming to live with us."

He looks at his hands. "He doesn't seem happy I'm here."

"Trust me, that's how he looks. He's standoffish and prickly, I know that too well, but if you show you're passionate about things he's passionate about, the two of you will connect."

They drained their drinks until there was only ice, and she suggested they leave. Because she was easy to talk to, he considered again admitting to his uncertainty about the year they were in. There were too many signs and no explanation. But he didn't want their rapport to be damaged so early. She wouldn't believe him. She'd think he was like Constantine—the so-called samurai.

On the way out, the two of them passed a shoe store. Benny stopped at the window. He saw a pair of shoes that made his chest thrum, the kind Shirley's brother would have worn. They stood, among other sneakers on display, as a reminder of the world he'd left. Looking at them made him lose track, once more, of where he was in time and space. He forgot about Mommy, Poh-Poh, and Constantine, whose faces throbbed in his mind like a toothache. Here they were, his objects of desire, in leather and rubber.

"I like your style—very retro," his stepmother said. "Do you want to try them on?"

Still looking at the swoosh on the shoes, he shook his head. What would be the point?

In the store, she caught the attention of a teenage salesperson, who correctly guessed Benny's shoe size. The shoes he found were a half size bigger, but they fit Benny. Benny looked at himself in the mirror, hands in his pockets, grinning. He'd grow into them.

"We'll take them," his stepmother announced to the salesperson.

"It's too much," Benny called out, following her to the register. "What if you don't like me?"

Her mouth fell open and her eyes widened as though she saw something singular. She apologized. "Sometimes your expression reminds me of your father, when I first met him. A sweetness. I haven't seen that face in a while."

"The shoes are too expensive," he announced. Even accounting for how much more everything cost here, the price seemed too high.

Benny's stepmother seemed touched by his frugality before sliding the shoes across the counter for the clerk to process. "It's a gift," she told Benny as she paid with her slab of glass. "A getting-to-know-you gift. And I already like you."

His face reddened and he tried to blink away the tears. As he left with the box in his hands, his excitement was undercut by fear. In the past two or three months, he'd felt as though he were in one of those video games he had played with August Pham, on the Nintendo Famicom that Mr. Pham had brought home from a trip to Asia, stuck in the same scenario as he battled through a set of challenges. Now he'd finally moved on to the next round. The battleground had changed. Nothing was familiar. There would be new rules. And even though things were calm now, he knew he was going to have to fight harder.

CHAPTER FIFTEEN

The lack of a workspace didn't prove to be an inconvenience, not as I'd feared. Trina accepted this adjustment as my "sacrifice" for having the boy with us. And sure, I missed my studio. But it gave me an excuse not to work and to leave unanswered the anxious emails from my publisher, who was worried I'd not yet delivered the final pages of my "serious" project. Without the distraction of work, I could spend more time with Adele. On the way to and back from ballet class, she wanted to know everything about the boy. *Will he stay with us forever? How old is he? Does he like Pokémon? Is he my brother? Am I his sister? Are you his daddy? Is Mommy his mommy? Am I still your daughter?*

I was too rattled that the boy existed to her and Trina to respond with any certitude.

I created the boy, drew him from my memories, but the rules—were there rules?—that enabled his physical presence were determined outside of me. Was he mine, or was I his? Witnessing him in my current life was an assault on my eyes and ears. He spoke as though he had been born overseas. He had Chinatown manners, slurping everything he drank as though it were wonton noodles. Working a toothpick over his teeth after a meal. Talking over the dinner table as though we were in a three-hundred-seat dim sum hall. He came home from the mall with Trina in the splashy high-tops the cool kids with the moussed hair and parachute pants wore in my day. "These are more than a *hundred dollars,*" he announced, like a tai-tai at a mahjong game talking about a handbag. I could see him on the street, selling fake Rolexes from a felt-backed table. He would brandish the repulsive crassness that I spent years unlearning.

"What he does is cute," Trina insisted when we were in bed. His amazement at his purchase, she noted correctly, reflected his humble circumstances. She could tell how careful the boy was about money, how greedily he pocketed the twenty-dollar bill she gave him for walking around. Her maternal grand-parents credited their survival in World War II to their ability to use a tea bag over two days. Frugality, like her generosity to others, had been bred into her. "If you want to teach him to act the way you want, then you'll need to show him. After all, you're his father."

"I'm not, though. He's my alter ego, my young doppelgänger."

Trina was still convinced that the boy was my son. "The social worker used that term," she insisted. "'Son.' It's okay if you admit being his father. We can share the responsibility." My own explanation—an impossible one, I admit—was too hard to accept as anything other than a symptom of stress and a mid-life crisis.

The next morning, I told Trina I needed a run. She wanted me to go some-where with Adele. She wanted to grade those final essays, and her work moved briskly when she was alone in the house. "Okay, after the run," I said. Some-times you need to save yourself before helping others. That jog was necessary, even though running had messed up my back two days before. On some back-woods trail that cut across the hillside, skipping over deer scat and dodging casual hikers, I tried not to think about the boy, whom I'd protected when he existed in my imagination. Now that I could see him, he looked exactly like myself as a child, and it was *revolting*. His feeble expression and whimpering voice. When I got home, the boy was with Adele in her room, both of them quiet as librarians. He was sitting at her table in her undersize chair, drawing as she watched him in that way a child perceives an older child's abilities as witchcraft. Her eyes drifted away to catch me at the half-open door.

"Daddy, look what Benny's drawing," she announced in a stage whisper.

As I stepped closer, the boy giggled nervously. He showed off a passable re-creation of Iggy Samurai. I still received fan art in the mail, and this was better than half of those attempts.

"Did I do it right?" he asked me.

I shrugged, watching the corners of his mouth fall. His lines were heavy-handed. Seeing him with Adele, and the attachment she had already formed with him, made me realize how easily I could lose her alongside my mostly contented life.

"He can draw what you draw!" Adele squealed.

"I'm going to take a shower," I announced. "When I am finished, the three of us are going to get out of Mom's hair and go for a drive."

Washed and dressed, I found the boy already in his shoes, Adele prepped to leave—no small feat. "Thanks," I told him in the garage, its door churning open. He looked pleased to be of service. "You can ride shotgun."

The boy hopped into the leather passenger seat of the Tesla Model S as I clipped Adele into her booster seat. When I stepped in and the monitor lit up, he gushed, "This is so cool. You drive this car?"

"Hell yeah," I told him, backing out with enough speed to demonstrate how quietly it ran. It had been a splurge, and a sore point with Trina.

"How much does this cost?" he asked. "Twenty thousand?"

I squeezed the steering wheel before I heeded Trina's advice. I stepped on the pedal, still appreciative of its acceleration. "You know, it's not polite, outside of Chinatown, to talk about how much things cost."

"Thirty thousand?"

We ran some errands. I needed to replace a broken showerhead at the big-box hardware store and return a defective dongle at the big-box electronics store. The boy watched me pay with my phone, obviously perplexed by the changes in technology but too afraid to admit it. Afterward, at the coffee shop, I asked him if he drank coffee—I couldn't remember. He shook his head. He didn't like the idea of the steamed milk that Adele always chose either. Approaching the cashier, I settled on a sweetened iced tea for him.

When I returned with the drinks, the kids were both sketching Iggy Samurais.

"Did you draw much at home?" I asked Benny after a gulp of my Americano.

He shook his head. "Poh-Poh thought it was a waste of paper."

My memory was jogged. "She wanted you to practice your calligraphy instead."

He nodded. "One day, I want to make comic books too."

"You will," I answered, and he started sketching more intently as his face reddened. I fell silent, watching this kid with the broken nose drain his iced tea.

"Do you eat Chinese food?" he asked me.

"Not so much," I told him. "The restaurants here aren't very good. And I can't find the right ingredients."

"Oh," he said. He looked stunned. In my head I counted to five, a teacher's trick, as I waited for him to elaborate. "I guess I can get used to goulash."

"There's not much to it. It's dinner," I said. "I can make fried rice. I know how to do that."

He ignored this suggestion. "Why did you invent Iggy Samurai?"

"I liked this musician named Iggy Pop, and for a while I watched a lot of samurai movies. And I did some karate and kendo as a kid. I doodled all the time, even though my grandmother didn't like it either." Should I have bothered to say we had, give or take a few aesthetic refinements and a premature death in the boy's timeline, the same grandmother? "She would even hit me with her broom handle when she found I'd wasted more paper." The boy laughed at this shared memory, the way children do when they interpret a lesser cruelty from a parental figure as affection. "In my dorm room, in the nineties, I kept drawing samurai, but they looked too fierce for my style, so one day I decided to draw a samurai with the face of a lizard."

Enough time had passed that we could go home. In the car, the boy and I periodically engaged with Adele's babble about Pokémon without trying to relaunch our own conversation. When the hill came within sight, Adele started pleading to take the side road. "Please, Daddy," she said. "The scary way!"

I obliged, the sound of the Tesla accelerating like the vengeful ghost of a wronged man overtaking his murderer. To maximize the effect, as we reached the top, I took the turn around the slope as widely as possible. Adele squealed, and the boy balled himself up in the passenger seat as the car nearly grazed the much-dented guardrail.

"Why'd you do that?" the boy said to me afterward. The same preteen who wanted to impress me with his fan art was now murdering me with his dewy eyes.

"We were just having fun."

He clenched his jaw, his mouth pursed reproachfully until we were back home. Sunday was another pizza night, and we ordered a second pie on account of our new arrival. Trina noticed Benny scraping off the cheese from his slices. "Is he lactose intolerant?" she whispered to me when he was in the bathroom.

"He's just picky."

"We should order something else next week."

I waved her off. "It's on him to adjust."

Trina hovered over the boy, taking the time to make him lemonade. Standing over him, then elbow to elbow, as he played with the drawing app on her tablet. Watching the two of them, I finally became curious why this boy might be here, and how long he might stay. Since his arrival came during my creative impasse—his story with the Samurai flaming out after the hulking yojimbo behaved out of turn—I needed to get my manuscript back on track. Once I was done, the boy would vanish from our home, eventually fading from memory.

Until then, I would have to keep him away from my family. After dinner, I led him out to the garden shed that I'd had converted into a training facility. Most of it was taken up with boxes and an ugly leather couch. But the rest was what Trina once described to her colleagues as my "shrine to manly aggression." "Training facility" is what I call it. I had my practice mats laid out, and a limbless rubber mannequin I used to practice my katas. And my collection of swords.

The boy pointed to a movie poster with Toshiro Mifune on it, in one of his many grimacing poses. "He was in *Sanjuro*," the boy said. "My friend Constantine has that poster. He's the guy who showed me karate."

I ignored the clawing in my gut. "We'll watch it sometime soon," I told him. "There's still one video store in town, and they might have it."

He eyed my katana and asked if he could see it. I presented him the blade with its detailing and let him gasp at it for a second. For once, his reaction wasn't inappropriate. I was glad I'd purchased it before I met Trina. She would have flipped out the way she did when I bought the Tesla. It ate up the bulk of the pittance I received for the *Iggy Samurai* movie sequel. But when I'd come upon it in an auction catalog, it felt like another in a series of moments in my life where I was a bystander to my own impulses. In my mind, it already belonged to me. The boy had the same reaction, I could tell. He turned down the chance to hold the sword, as though some dangerous instinct might overtake him should he hold it.

It took me years to return to martial arts, on account of C. For me, karate was about him. And while I was Chinese, I thought kung fu was ridiculous. It felt too choreographed. Too much flying, too many flowing hands. Too much like rhythmic gymnastics. I liked how karate helped my schoolyard brawling. Bruce Lee might have been trained in the sticky-fingered movements of Wing Chun, a style of kung fu, but his fighting style was different. I wasn't surprised to learn that his choreography had been borrowed from samurai movies. And his signature weapon had been nunchucks, which originated in Okinawa.

I took one shinai and handed the boy his own practice sword. He took it with two hands and held it in front of him. It occurred to me that sparring with the boy might help me get through my narrative dead end. You learned so much about people when they became desperate, in that frantic hum between resistance and resignation.

I raised my wooden sword. "Now I'm going to try to kill you."

CHAPTER SIXTEEN

Why bother with school? Benny thought. By now it was May. Nothing important was taught in the impatient final weeks of the school year. He could catch up after being swallowed in the chasm of the summer. But his stepmother insisted that he'd need school to situate himself in the town. "I know it might be awkward," she said as she pulled her car into the school parking lot. Benny's father had taken his daughter to her kindergarten class in his space car. "It's the best way to make friends. You don't want to spend July and August indoors, alone."

He was unfazed by summer's approach, as his struggles with time existed on another plane. By now, he'd seen enough calendars, not to mention electric cars and smartphones, to understand that somehow he was living in a time and era distinct from his own. If the current date was correct, he should be a middle-aged man, his father's age, not a twelve-year-old. He was in the future without having stepped into a time machine. But who could he admit this to? Maybe his father, who never acted as though Benny would understand any news event or technology that had occurred over the past three decades, but he was not the father Benny remembered—he was sure of it. Who else might believe him? Maybe Constantine—the big white guy who'd confessed to being a medieval samurai. If Benny were to tell anyone else, they might think he was also mentally ill. And maybe Benny was. Maybe Constantine had hit him so hard that he suffered brain damage. Believing yourself to be in the future happened to be a side effect. Or maybe he'd been from the 2020s all along, and his memory of the past was imagined. Whatever happened, he would tell no one.

Better to play along with his stepmother's suggestion. The new school sat at the bottom of the hill by the river. Benny's old school was a faded brick building with intersecting gabled roofs, and it felt timeless, the way school should be—as though it had risen from the ground alongside the trees and grass. From the parking lot, his new place of learning appeared to be a cluster of boxlike structures, all with flat roofs except for the library, with its front wall made of glass. It looked to Benny as though an architect had based the school on a set of blocks that had been abandoned by a child.

The school was for intellectually gifted children, and its principal was married to one of his stepmother's colleagues. "When I first learned you were coming, I called her right away—and she pulled some strings for me," his stepmother said as they approached the entrance. "Without even having met you, only going by your father, I figured you needed a more stimulating environment. I was glad to be right."

Other students were streaming in and Benny noted with relief that they wore clothes like his own. When he was younger, he'd daydreamed about life in the twenty-first century, and, even with smartphones and electric cars, he found it underwhelming, the differences more incremental than transformational. He'd expected the future to be neon yellow, but it was beige.

Benny and his stepmother were greeted by the principal, a woman named Ramona in a loose cardigan and jeans, whose freshly applied lipstick and ready-to-please demeanor suggested to Benny that she was interested in impressing his father's wife. Before she left, his stepmother gave Benny another hug—he'd had more physical affection from her in three days than in a lifetime with Poh-Poh. He would never get used to all that touching. He appreciated his stepmother's kindness while, as all hugs did, her embrace made him flinch. Ramona the principal led him to a classroom where students were clustered in groups around tables.

When he entered the room, the teacher nodded at the students. Prompted, they rose from their seats to applaud. On the flat-screen monitor on the wall in front of the room a message was displayed. *Welcome to our class, Benson.*

His cheeks red from attention, Benny found himself led to a chair at a table with classmates who quickly introduced themselves to him. The youthful teacher, in a T-shirt revealing bare arms meshed with tattoos, introduced himself as Gerald. With his hands in the front pockets of his jeans, he explained that that morning each member of the class was presenting their independently guided learning projects, which were intended to highlight both knowledge-gathering and creativity. "Take it all in," he told Benny. "Think about what you want to study for your end-of-year project."

The first student to stand in front of the class showed off a dog he'd built from a robotics set. Another performed a soliloquy from *Henry V*. Another screened a Claymation film he'd made based on Alison Bechdel's *Fun Home*. After each presentation, the class asked questions. Benny's head swam in disbelief. Where he came from, displays of intellectual engagement counted as stains on one's reputation. Here, the opposite rule seemed to be in effect. Demonstrations of intellect were what students offered up as antes in some poker game of precociousness. Maybe this was an example of the progress he'd longed to see.

One student in particular, named Avril, caught Benny's attention as she used the Satanic panic of the 1980s to talk about political censorship. But it wasn't the project drawing his notice. He was convinced he'd met Avril before. Not that he knew how, not in this place or time. And yet her eyes widened when they met his gaze.

The presentations ran through the morning, right until the lunch bell. In the cafeteria, as Benny filed into the line for a shawarma-spiced tofu wrap, a familiar ache, the pains of social isolation, rose within him. Unlike in the morning, when students had been coerced to chat with him, the social herds at the tables felt impenetrable. He was beginning his search for an unwatched corner of the school when he felt a shoulder tap and turned to see Avril.

"Hi," Benny croaked, his voice now betraying him at a predictable interval.

"You don't remember me?" she asked, her own voice teetering between disappointment and a desire to draw out the suspense.

He looked at her. What made her look so familiar, like a celebrity from television or the long-lost relative of a childhood friend? It took another moment.

"August?" he finally asked her. August had become *Avril*. Benny recognized the full mouth and unguarded smile, eyebrows that faded toward the bridge of her nose. Avril's hair, which always fell to her ears, now crested on her shoulders. She was wearing a summer dress over her jeans. She wore black lipstick and eyeliner and silver nail polish. Around her neck, in place of the gold cross August once wore, dangled a silver necklace with two interlocking rings, with the initials "A" in one and "C" in another.

"No one calls me that here." She smiled. "I'm Avril now, but yes."

Benny wanted to hug her, but Benny had never hugged his old friend. The two of them lingered there instead, looking at each other, until a friend at her table, impatient for Avril's return, invited Benny to join them. Benny found a place at the far end of the table from the spot Avril's friend had saved for her. Everyone within Avril's conversational radius hung on her every word, coiling themselves as they awaited her reaction to their attempts to impress her. Benny felt himself acquiring social currency from Avril's interest in him. The boy to his immediate right felt obliged to ask about where he lived, and where he'd come from. Lunch ended. The rest of the day was spent on a group project on democracy and civil rights. When the day concluded, Avril beelined toward him to set up a date for video games at her house. "We have a lot to catch up on," she said.

Afterward, Benny started off for home, optimistic but confused. After all, he didn't know the way back, only that it was uphill. Fortunately, his father was waiting for him in his space car. Benny noticed the way his father propped himself against its gleaming door, arms folded, peacocking. This was not the father, the one with movie-star looks, that he remembered, not at all.

His father climbed into the driver's side. Behind him, his half sister sat in her booster seat with a juice box and a stuffed elephant.

"How was school?" his father asked him. "It's different, isn't it?"

"It was. But it was good."

"Glad she was right," he said about Benny's stepmother. "Funny thing, how I'm an artist but never attended a school for the gifted. Huh. Maybe I became what people like to call, um, a 'creative person' precisely because of all my meathead classmates. I'd worry that being around pampered kids would make me soft. Anyhow, don't tell me you have too much homework to spar tonight."

"Definitely I can spar," Benny said, worried he didn't sound enthusiastic enough.

They approached a familiar fork in the road and Benny's father asked him whether he wanted to take the regular route up the hill or the scary one.

Benny waffled for a moment, worried about how his father would react if he expressed terror at the mention of that blind turn.

"How about the regular turn for a change?" he said, hoping he spoke with enough nonchalance for his father.

"Too late," his father said, and soon they were ascending the hill. When Benny didn't respond with appropriate shrieking, his father raised the ante by slivering shut his wolf eyes ahead of the turn. Thankfully, this kept him from seeing the fear on Benny's face. His half sister squealed in joy.

His father hooted after he made the turn. "Don't tell me you didn't think that was fun. Seriously?"

His efforts to win over his father, to make himself as likable as Trina made him feel, had started with his Iggy Samurai tributes but now felt contingent on his ability to spar. Sword fighting with his father the night before had been the closest Benny felt with him since he had come to live here. In the backyard gym, his father handed Benny some newly purchased protective headwear and body armor that was purposefully loose so he could "grow into it." The new gear allowed him to hit Benny harder, responsibly.

He slipped on the helmet and took hold of the shinai. Constructed from four bamboo slats, it felt lighter than the makeshift bokuto that Constantine had fashioned.

Before sparring, they warmed up with footwork drills, slides and glides, followed by basic solo katas, counting in Japanese. "Louder," his father told him.

"Ichi, ni, san . . ."

With Constantine, Benny could not speak above a whisper. Here he was supposed to shriek after each blow, a kiai, in order to build his core strength and signal his spirit. He realized how counterinstinctual it had been to keep quiet.

"Remember when you asked me about homework?" Benny said during a break. "I was wondering if I could interview you for my first project."

His father slipped his hooded helmet on. "How long will it take?" he said.

They stood two sword-lengths apart, bowing to each other. "Thirty minutes?" Benny said through the metal grille of his own mask.

His father nodded. "Next week works." Their swords lowered toward each other, skittering at their tips.

His father let him attack, occasionally striking him lightly when he found Benny vulnerable. In one exchange, his father pivoted to the side like a dancer to avoid Benny's wooden blade and then struck him in the kidneys. Benny doubled over but got up. By the end of the hour, the two of them were panting and sore.

To spar with him was not the same as it had been with Constantine, who wanted to instruct Benny in their hand-to-hand combat. To build him. His father instructed too, but his words clawed at Benny's confidence. They seemed deliberately chosen to assert dominance. Whenever Benny felt comfortable, his father stopped him. He'd point out his posture was off, as was his grip on his sword. Even worse, Constantine's nose-breaking punch aside, his father struck harder. There were bruises all over his body. Did his father want him to act out, to fight back? Didn't he know Benny well enough to understand that this was his least likely course of action?

That night, he fried rice for dinner in a nonstick frying pan instead of a wok, with honey-glazed ham instead of char siu, and, while moving it around on his plate, Benny made sure to compliment him for this taste of culinary sacrilege. While his stepmother was happy someone else was making dinner, his half sister refused to eat it. Benny offered to clear the table. Benny, who was more self-conscious about his body odor since being made fun of at school, nevertheless hadn't taken a shower since he arrived. Once he was finished loading the dishwasher, a task his father showed him how to do, he found a towel in the closet his father had shown him, walked into the bathroom, and hung up the towel on the hook behind the door. As he turned, his stepmother stepped out of the shower. Seeing him, she wrapped her arms around her breasts, the first breasts he had seen in real life. The breasts he'd seen in magazines were enormous, and he felt partly ashamed to have caught her off guard—he should have known better—because he hadn't given her time to inflate her own pair. She smiled. "Well, I guess there's nothing left to hide," she joked.

Benny apologized quickly and ran back to his room with his gaze fixed on the area rug. He fell on his cot and covered his head with a pillow. He wanted to punish his eyes. He was also reminded of the times, in the months before her death, that Poh-Poh, from her bed, caught him moving his hands at night. He'd thought she was asleep. "Aiya," she said. "You'll mess your sheets."

A few minutes later, Benny heard a knock at the door. The showerhead in the master bathroom was broken, his stepmother explained. And the other bathroom didn't have a lock. "We never needed one before," she told him. "Anyhow, hope I didn't surprise you too much." Benny decided he would shower in the morning.

As he lay on the cot, he pretended to ignore the stirring below his waist, under his covers. In his head, he saw the girl that his friend August Pham had turned into and her new, confident bearing. He wanted to be as at ease in his own body as she was in the one she'd grown into. And then he saw the slender form of the stepmother. Finally, he realized it had been almost a week since he'd last thought about Shirley. Or had it been decades?

CHAPTER SEVENTEEN

With the boy in school, I returned to my studio during the day. His underwear and socks were scattered around the floor like cow patties, my *Iggy Samurai* stuff handled and put back in place (sort of). His grimy fingerprints all over my first editions and collectibles, on the old photos of our saintly, forever-youthful mother. I sat down with an espresso made with the fussy machine that Trina bought and that I always left in disarray. At my desk, I opened my monthly packet of mail and printed-out emails from my publisher (I'd asked that they no longer be forwarded to me electronically). The best decision I'd ever made was to remove my email address from my website, with only a few requests coming to my publicly listed address at the school. Mainly the correspondence was fan art, some tributes from kids, but most from adult males of some indiscernible vintage. I never kept any of it, but I enjoyed it more than the notes.

> Hey Benson, I am just writing to let you know that I grew up reading *Iggy Samurai.* Now my son reads it too. Our favorite characters are the newest members of Iggy Samurai's family. His daughter is so spunky and cute! It's nice to see him grow up and build a family as I am growing up. Please send us an autographed photo made out to "Forrest, Iggy's number-one fan!" If you could add an Iggy "doodle," it would be greatly appreciated. Cheers! The Carlson Family.

In spite of the irritation they can inspire, I can't help reading these notes. I never answer, but I entertain myself for a moment by imagining the response I would write.

Dear "The Carlson Family," Thanks to each and every one of you for your note of appreciation that almost conceals the disproportionate and time-consuming request that accompanies it like a blood-sucking tick on a puppy. As Forrest of your Carlson collective is my "number-one fan," I was dismayed that he seemed unaware of the fact that Iggy's wife and family were character decisions made by a screenwriter at the behest of a toy manufacturer. These choices, in fact, contravene my intentions as to the solitary quality of Iggy's character. May I further suggest that these preferences should disqualify Forrest of the Carlson clan as my "number-one fan" or even a serious reader of my work? In lieu of an autograph or doodle, I have used my own laser printer to produce these words of advice: "Being a casual fan is okay. Own it." I have printed these words on a three-point-five-by-two-inch card. If a senior member of The Carlson Family could get this card laminated so it lasts longer and precludes more correspondence, it would be greatly appreciated. Cheers! Yu

This fan letter was a specimen of one entire category of note I received. And I spent too much time raging about it.

What I should have been toiling on was my manuscript. My intention had been to understand the gauntlet of misfortune and mistreatment that I underwent as a child, but the trouble began when I tried to humanize someone evil. As I delved into the psyche of my abuser, I fabricated a backstory that explained his viciousness—mental illness, cruel parents, et cetera—to the point of erasing, mostly, that original personality. But if I'd left him as he was, a hairy, blue-eyed ghoul in the shadows, it would have been a story without redemption. As I told it, the story got away from me, then stalled on the act of physical violence that inevitably brought that boy to my doorstep. I stared at those pages, searching for a resolution that would leave the boy dispatched from my life, vaporized like a red-shirted ensign on *Star Trek* eating a phaser blast.

Speaking of whom, he appeared at my office door promptly after school, with a notepad and pen in hand. "Are you available for our interview?" he asked me. He backed onto his cot and landed with a squeaky bounce.

"I was in the middle of something . . ." I wrested myself from the desk. "Let's hear what you have."

"First question. Were you always interested in comic books?" he asked me.

I sucked my teeth. "You should learn how to use the internet." His eyes flashed with panic. "Well, after my mother died, I bounced between my poh-poh and father. Mostly my poh-poh." He nodded to acknowledge the biographical overlap. "I didn't have a lot of friends, so I read comic books and copied the drawings."

His breathing was labored as he wrote down my responses. "What were the inspirations for Iggy Samurai?"

"As an undergrad, I was interested in samurai films. And I studied karate as a kid."

"Did you attend a dojo?"

"My father signed me up for classes. I had an instructor who had a big influence on my life. Some of that was good."

"What is your dad like?"

"Was. He's been gone fifteen years. He was, well, a dad."

After I'd gotten beaten up in school, I remembered my dad thinking of karate classes as a substitute for actual parenting. Later on, he'd brag to my grandmother about footing the bill for three years' worth of classes. One day I told him what was happening with C. My dad confronted him and was hospitalized with broken ribs and a black eye. My dad blamed me for his humiliation—he said I was a "sexual deviant"—and I wouldn't see him again for years. After another absence, a relative called me to say his body was found rotting in his apartment. He'd croaked a week earlier of an aneurysm. Only the smell he gave off prompted a neighbor to check in on him.

"Why did you stop writing Iggy Samurai?" the boy asked.

"The movies sucked." While the movies were cheaply made and cynical, and turned my audience off from my work, I stopped writing Iggy Samurai because they highlighted the essential falseness and silliness of my comic book. It was a self-serious and ludicrous whitewashing of personal experience.

I turned back to my desk and announced I was done with the interview. I heard the springs of the cot easing and the boy leaving his own room.

On my laptop, I stared at the pages of my manuscript for a couple of minutes until my eyes glazed over. I had lost track of them. I had no sense of Constantine's whereabouts, and only knew what the boy was doing when we were in the same room. To distract myself, I returned to my fan mail. I found a suitable specimen of another category of correspondence I commonly opened. It came from the type of detail-oriented male I encountered in those lost years when I attended conferences and conventions to make up for the income stolen by an immoral licensing clause in my original publishing contract.

> Dear Mr. Yu, While I am no fan of comic books, your work caught my interest as an independent scholar of Japanese military technology. (Please subscribe to my YouTube channel listed below my signature.) You might be curious to know that, based on the markings on the blade, I have determined that the katana given to Iggy by Coyote Sensei in *Iggy Samurai #4* is from the Azuchi–Momoyama period. However, in *Iggy Samurai #3*, Coyote Sensei clearly states that he comes from the fifteenth century—in other words, the Sengoku period. *Ipso facto*, your detail is historically inaccurate. I hope you can use this information to clarify future editions of your series so that your integrity is not further undermined and the impressionable children who read your work are not misinformed. Sincerely, Ronald Harrison III

This type of letter earned a response, which I did occasionally mail out, after my first glass of scotch-style Japanese whisky.

> Dear Dr. Harrison, I use the honorific because your stunning erudition and modesty no doubt culminated in your choice not to include the doctoral degree you attained from a prestigious institution so elite that its graduates don't even mention it by name—they merely utter the town the campus is located in, in a stage whisper.

Thank you so much for your correction of a comic book I made when I was twenty-two years old and high on weed-butter cookies, intended for other video game–addicted stoners and academically challenged children. In this age of dissembling, the truth matters. Historically accurate military technology matters. Even when it's about an iguana samurai who plays in a punk band. Not *even*, but *especially* when it's that case. If I am so bold, may I also make a suggestion? I submit that you, Dr. Harrison, should speak to someone with a similarly accomplished educational background, a doctor in the field of mental health, who might conscientiously expose you to the breakthroughs toward which the pharmaceutical industry has led us. Sincerely, Yu

The bulk of the forwarded correspondence was gracious fan mail, notes that contained thoughtful appreciations and the "I will understand if you are too busy" dodge affixed to asks that stilled my heart. In my own curdled way, I resented these notes the most, as they required real responses that encroached on my mental space.

I flipped through them until I got to a letter that belonged to a new, exclusive category.

Hi, I am not sure anyone forwards these notes to you so this could be another waste of a stamp. Maybe your assistant reads them. I sent you a letter a few months ago and I was a little sad you didn't write back. But maybe you didn't get that letter. And maybe you don't get this one. But I'm here. I'm pretty old, but in decent shape for an old guy. I can still stare down the little dorks outside the liquor store. Anyhow, in that first letter I wanted to reach out to you. Are you still sore about what happened with your dad? Whatever it was, I was very hurt when you stopped training with me. I know, I know. That was over thirty years ago. But you were my best student. We were very close. I assume you are a man now, or something of a man, and you can look in the mirror and see how much of that I built up in you. From nothing. And yeah, I have read your comic book. I even watched the first movie. I hope you made a lot of money. I hope you are honest enough to cut me in on some of it. Because I know it's for kids and shit, but that sensei character, even if he's a coyote—he definitely looks like me. He definitely sounds like me.

I'm going to make it easy for you. I'll be in your town next month. My cell phone number is at the bottom of the page. You can call me or text me, whatever, and we can arrange to meet. How does that sound? I'm pretty old now and you're a grown-up, so there's no reason to be afraid. If you're reading this, buddy, you owe it to me to get back in touch.

C.

I folded the letter, replaced it in the envelope, returned the envelope to the packet, and then placed the packet into a plastic bin with the other packets. Somewhere in that bin I had the first letter from C., the one that pushed me into my new writing project.

The next morning, I drove the boy to school. He gaped out the window with that same wincing, fatalistic air, like someone in line to be punched.

"Do you have everything you need for your project?" I asked him.

He shrugged. "I've got another week. I'll give the World Wide Web another try."

"For your project, you should use your own illustrations of Iggy Samurai."

He turned to me. "Really?"

"They're just as good as mine. Especially the ones where he holds his katana."

He twisted his face as though he was clinging tight to my praise.

That moment of self-parenting exhausted me and when I got home I lay down until eleven in the morning, when I needed to eat. I poured myself a bowl of cereal. I shaved. I went for a run until endorphins lifted me from despair. I came home to shower in the main bathroom. After I dried off and changed, I got in the car to take care of some errands. Adele had library books that needed to be returned. Trina had dry cleaning that needed to be picked up. When my good-husband labors were completed, it was two o'clock. The remainder of the day yawned at me, a dried-out well into which I tripped and fell. I got behind the wheel of my car and drove around, trying to enjoy the spring scents and the way the sun honeyed the surrounding hills. Before I knew it, I had stopped at the campus bar, caught in that sweet lull between academic terms. There was only one server, and she drifted sluggishly between tables. By the time she came to me, I felt obliged to order enough to last the rest of the afternoon.

I was sitting with so many glasses in front of me that someone might have thought I was trying to coax a tune out of them when I saw that student of mine, Carter, wander in. My former student, my potential protégé, linked to me by a childhood crush, pretended not to see me wave him over. It was only after he failed to find whomever he was meeting, and I cupped my hands and yelled his name, that he made his way to my table.

"I know you're waiting for someone," I said. "Take a seat until they arrive."

His eyes popped at the sight of all my glassware. "Are you sitting with anyone?" he asked me, one hand on the strap of his backpack as he scanned the room. "Meeting your TAs?"

I pushed one of the glasses, one of the few I hadn't downed, toward him. Easing himself down, he picked it up tentatively and looked at it. "I didn't poison it," I said. "I thought you'd be back home by now."

He whipped his phone and began to text. "I'm here for a couple more weeks," he said, still fixated on his phone. "There are some friends I want to hang out with, now that exams are over."

I saw a slyness drift across his face as he skirted the truth. "Are you texting with someone special?" I asked him.

His nose wrinkled reflexively in dismay, not so much because I had caught him but because it was his professor using the words "someone special" to elicit personal gossip. Heaven forfend! "You could say that," he said.

"When's your mom going to meet her?" I asked, arching an eyebrow. "Or him," I added after a beat. "Or them."

"She probably won't," he said, dropping his phone to the table. "It's casual."

I nodded to his phone. "And the person you're texting—she knows that?"

He sipped his beer and shrugged. "She should."

I was emboldened by the coldness in his eyes. We could talk, man to man. "Did you know that I had a huge crush on your mom?" I asked him.

He smiled and shook his head. He was lying.

"For all of middle school, I sat behind her and used to stare at her ponytail. We even studied together. Did you say hi to her for me?"

He pretended not to hear me. If he had responded, maybe I would have told him that in a different version of my life, one where I was bolder or less beaten down, I could have married his mother. And that he could have been my son. My real son. Not some husk of my childhood self who had insinuated himself into my household and would turn my family against me.

Carter took a sip of the whisky I had offered him. "My mom said you were really smart," he said as he caught sight of his friends, all beta males like him, entering the bar. He waved at them. "I'll say hi for you." As he messaged her, I saw her social media profile photo and name appear on his smartphone. Sheryl Mak. "There. Done."

"Your mother really had a shine in her eyes," I recalled, wondering what response Carter's text might elicit. "We both suffered incredible losses—"

He'd stopped interacting with me. He rose from his chair. I watched him loose-talk around his friends, their discourse presumably centered around summer plans and sexy bodies. I returned to my collection of glassware. I paid close attention to the bottoms of those glasses. And my limbs became heavy and gangly. Another older guy, a retired history prof, sat next to me and we complained about the entitlement of students and their up-spoken demands. *Order another round?* the retired prof said to me. *I need to take a piss.* Then he wanted to talk about basketball. My tongue had become a salamander crawling out of my mouth as I spoke.

After the history prof left, I tried to flag down the waitress, who didn't like me tugging on her apron tie. With a bull-necked heavy behind her, she told me to finish what I'd ordered and leave. And as I complied with her instructions, I began to compose, in my head, the response to the note I'd received from this man, the person who had loosely inspired Coyote Sensei, then inspired the Samurai.

> Dear C.—This is a letter to say that I do not want to speak to you, much less see you, again . . .

Getting up to leave, I knocked some glasses onto the floor. Fortunately, this place catered to adult-sized toddlers and the glasses were made of plastic. Still, I wanted to offer an extra tip. But I had no cash. I turned my wallet inside out and stared at the empty pocket for bills for a while until the bruiser marching me outside thought I was stalling. Following the direction of the bouncer's outstretched arm, I found myself on the sidewalk and in the parking lot. Once I located my car, I butted my head on the steering wheel and counted to a hundred, hoping to jostle myself into sobriety.

> We seem to remember things differently. I was a boy raised by his grandmother, estranged from his male parent. I had no father figure, no friends. By circumstance, I ended up in your care. At first you helped me. You paid special attention to me. You told me stories about how you'd been picked on. You gave me presents. You knew I was hungry, so you took me out for hamburgers. You gained my trust. And then you did things to me that, as a parent, I would kill someone over if they were done to my daughter.

I lost count at some point but was roused by the headlights of a taxi approaching the bar for a fare. I powered the car and drove.

> Coyote Sensei is a character I created—a moral and decent teacher I constructed from the negative example you produced. No one would want to read the real story. No matter how many times I've tried. I owe you nothing. That character has nothing to do with you. That character is a good person, a good teacher . . . Fuck you, fuck off.

How I drove, how I got home, was wiped away from my memory, without a smudge. Unlike my greasy head against the cool driver's-side window. I do remember the keys dropping onto the driveway. Jabbing them into a lock. What else happened? I somehow ended up in bed, ready but unable to sleep. It wasn't even seven at night.

CHAPTER EIGHTEEN

Avril's bed, the bed she and Benny were sitting at the edge of, had the same whale-and-dolphin-pattern duvet covers that she'd had in Chinatown. And yet Avril's room was three times the size of the one she had before, in one of those standardized mansions that he'd seen when he first arrived. In the far corner of the room, he found his old Optimus Prime, the one Mommy gave him, on a dresser. When he touched it, his finger collected a thick layer of dust. Avril's posture became slumped and her breathing audible as she played *Dragon Quest* with him. Finally, a video game from his era. When the two of them were alone, she seemed a little more like his old friend. At school, she had a confidence, a way of displacing social vectors with her invitations to her karaoke parties or a pointed look when a white classmate mentioned her "almond-shaped" eyes. Benny didn't know how that person contained his old friend, and it was nice to see she could devolve, a little, to the person he knew.

It was only once *Dragon Quest* had loaded, as his characters wheeled around eight-bit forests and mountains, that he explained everything that had happened, his story halting whenever the game paused to indicate that a slime or a Magidrakee—names they'd never known when playing the original Japanese version of the game on Avril's old Nintendo Famicom—was drawing near. He told Avril about Poh-Poh, impressing her with his account of living alone. When he told her that he'd punched Roderick, her eyes bulged in disbelief before she gave him a high five. He skipped over Constantine, instead saying he had spent some time with a friend, because he knew Avril would rush to judge Constantine as a pedo. He talked about waiting to hear back from his aunt while living with Mr. and Mrs. Douglas and their house full of cast-off boys.

Although Avril had explained how she too had been confused by the time jump, her experiences confirmed Benny's. He was not Constantine. If this place was a hallucination, he was not its only hypnotee. "One day my parents, my sister, and I arrived here, and the world had changed," Avril told him. "We decided not to tell anyone—it wouldn't be believed." In her past life, she had loved science fiction books and movies about time travel. In this case, there was no gadgetry involved. She didn't have an explanation for what had come to pass for them, only that she belonged here. "If I were in Chinatown, in the past, there was no way this would have happened." This prompted Benny to ask how she became Avril.

She said she always understood that she was a girl. "Did you know that about me?" she asked him. She told him that she had taken pains not to confess her feelings of gender dysphoria—a term she had supplied him. Hiding that meant concealing her depression and anxiety, smiling constantly.

"Uh-uh." But maybe Benny did. Her feminine manner had been noticeable to everyone. For kicks, Roderick and Bronson would periodically prod her until she squealed. But he also remembered how sad she could get sometimes when they were alone, crying over a B plus or a fight she had had with her younger sister, and how Benny would calm her down by running his hand along her arm or patting her head. And he remembered how she would self-soothe by drawing patterns, spiraling fractals on the backs of her notebooks, a honeycomb pattern she often drew onto her forearm that would prompt Benny to joke she was an android. She was always pleased by that comparison.

Avril's glass bar, her smartphone, lit up on her bed, and she paused the game to take the call. Her voice shifted again, to a hyperfeminized version of the person Benny had seen at school. When Avril noticed Benny watching her, she took the phone into her walk-in closet and slid the door shut behind her. Through the door he could hear her teasing laughter.

Benny thought about the necklace with the interlocking initials around her neck. "A" and "C." If she was "A," then who was "C"? Was she talking to this person now? In any event, he couldn't play without her—the game was in two-player mode—and as the conversation stretched out, he grew bored. Benny approached the old Optimus Prime and was cleaning the dust from it with the sleeve of his shirt when the closet door slid open.

"Sorry," Avril said. "It was a call from Carter. Actually, he really wants to see me. He's usually busy with classes but now he's got an opening. You and I need to wrap up. Can we hang out tomorrow?"

"Sure," Benny said, relieved he had plans for Saturday away from the house.

Benny followed her downstairs. The house was not only empty but apparently devoid of life. He'd associated visits to his old friend's house with the smells that came from her mother's cooking or the piles of Mr. Pham's loafers gathered around the front door. In the kitchen, he found an opened box of saltines and only Avril's flats under the chandelier in the front vestibule. How could the same parents who'd grounded August for getting a single B minus—for PE, no less!—on a report card teeming with As allow their child to wear makeup and dresses to school? Had the time jump changed them too? But they weren't around to ask.

Benny trudged up the hill until he found the place he called home. His stepmother was making dumplings for dinner—buttery flour-fat bombs, not the kind he grew up eating. Benny's father had not arrived home. His stepmother asked him to watch his half sister, and he drew more Iggy Samurais in crayon with her. His half sister looked more like her father than her mother. She and Benny shared a resemblance that hadn't been apparent when he'd first seen her. Her hair was sienna-colored, almost caramel in the light, and didn't hold a curl. Her eyes were single-folded. Only her long nose and emotional expressiveness came from her mother. At some point that evening, she climbed onto Benny's lap to cut out her drawing.

Benny was still playing with her when the garage door groaned open. His father was home. Benny heard him stagger into his room and slam the door behind him. His stepmother stopped setting the table to check on him. When she came back, she announced that he wasn't feeling well and that the rest of the family would eat without him.

Later, after Benny's half sister was tucked in, as he brushed his teeth, he could hear his stepmother and father arguing. There wasn't any screaming, barely a raised voice. Benny could hear a determination to get a point across in his stepmother's speech, which boiled over into exasperation. In his father's slurred mumbles, Benny heard a few sentences repeated, then muttered with resignation.

Benny was convinced his stepmother wanted him out of the house. She humored him, bought him clothes and shoes, but she expected an end date to his stay. How could he blame her? Because he hated her cooking and had seen her naked. And his father, who didn't seem impressed by his efforts to win him over—what could he say? Would he defend him? Benny was unwanted. If he couldn't make a home out of this place, where would he go next?

In search of distraction, he flipped through old issues of *Iggy Samurai*. The Coyote Sensei character reminded him of Constantine. How he was an almost accidental teacher, someone who reluctantly helped Iggy learn to become a samurai because no one else would help him survive in Central Park.

Brushing his teeth, Benny saw his father taking a pillow and a duvet to the couch in the living room. They did not make eye contact. Benny changed into pajamas and lay on his cot. He listened to his father burp and gurgle from the couch, and then his snoring. But Benny couldn't sleep.

He rose from his cot and pulled his chair up to the side table where his father kept a laptop computer. He had been shy about using computers ever since a classmate compared the glacial pace of his internet research and bemused clucking at his search results to his grandmother going online. Even at home, Benny was reluctant to browse because he would look for the world he left behind—the TV shows he watched, the celebrities—and discover it was gone or disfigured with age. Tonight, though, he would not indulge in nostalgia, which, along with the pornography he was delighted to find, seemed to be the primary purpose of the internet. He would use it to figure out a way to return to the past. *How do I travel BACK in time?* he typed onto the screen. In his day, time travel was a far-fetched dream. But he had taken a highway to this place, which felt, by turns, real and made-up. The screen spat back search results about the theory of relativity and wormholes, and he meticulously clicked through each link. He'd arrived here in a hatchback. All he wanted to know was, could he get a ride home?

CHAPTER NINETEEN

Back in the doghouse again. Not an unusual circumstance, given my absences, boozing, and erratic parenting. For those failings, I was banished to rot on the cot in my office. Forced to yodel my trauma at individual and couples therapy sessions. Made to claw my hands along my face, impotently, as my entire liquor cabinet was drained in the sink. To stave off these foul correctives, I'd usually admit to whatever Trina wanted me to say. That I had daddy issues, problems with ghosts, and that my struggles with addiction and emotional intimacy sprang from some unvoiced wellspring of pain that required professional guidance.

But I didn't grovel last night. The momentum of our marriage, of childcare and career advancement, could not allow for much more than a day of Trina's freeze-out. As well, Adele could feel any tension in her parents and seed her belly with it, prompting her to projectile vomit on a few occasions—one time, after Trina and I'd argued about my spending, throwing up an entire strawberry-and-banana breakfast smoothie onto her clothes and the back seat on the way to daycare. Now there was the boy—the real headache in our household—who got Trina pretending to be much less strict than she would otherwise be about, say, leaving the milk to ferment on the counter or pissing on the toilet seat. Not a word from her for infractions that would get me roundly criticized.

Moreover, I didn't plead for mercy because of the party that night. That would be what counted. This shindig at the university president's house celebrated the end of term, but also touted the researchers who'd scored the big prizes and funding awards. At last, Trina, who'd won an international fellowship in the fall, would be feted and recognized for her scholarship. She wouldn't admit to it being a big deal except that, until the boy arrived, her waking hours had been consumed by the party. Her outfit, my outfit, the colleagues she wanted to schmooze, the rivals she needed me to deflect. Even with the boy's disruptive presence, the date loomed large.

The smell of coffee and bacon woke me from the couch. In the kitchen, Adele stood, aproned, on her stool, stirring batter for waffles. Trina saw me from the corner of her eye and turned and, without any detectable sarcasm, asked me how I'd slept. She took a step toward me. Her breath tasted like toothpaste when we kissed. So far, so good.

"What would you like first?" she asked, pouring the batter into the waffle iron. "Coffee, breakfast, or Tylenol?"

"Waffles," Adele answered for both of us. I nodded.

"Where is he?" I asked.

Trina shrugged. "I know he's already awake. He's out of bed."

I was setting his place on the table when the boy emerged, fully dressed, his backpack slung across one shoulder. He said he was getting ready for a project with his friend Avril. "Is it okay if I spend the night there?" he asked, looking at Trina. "Her parents already said it was okay."

I'd been hoping he would stay at home and watch Adele, so we could cancel the sitter. Before I could share my disappointment, Trina had told him to have fun and call if he needed a ride home tomorrow. Officially, Trina still objected to my explanation for the boy, but his uncanny resemblance to me, and the interest he'd taken in watching old episodes of *Night Court* and *Growing Pains* on YouTube, wobbled her. The boy, flourishing under her attention, bounced out, his stride more sure-footed from our training.

"Isn't it nice he's made friends?" she mused, taking her place at the table. "And with a girl. I know he's interested but wasn't sure he was capable of befriending one."

I grunted, vicariously insulted by her comment. Also, I knew the boy well enough to sense that he'd withheld something from us. While he was getting better at making excuses, even now I could have made him sing. But I didn't want to jinx things with Trina and remove my focus from the party. If tonight went well, she would forget about my recent wrongs.

We spent the morning at the farmers' market. Trina bought some greens and fresh pasta while I towed Adele and faked a shared interest in handmade soaps. Good, clean fun. Even with an Americano, I kept yawning on the way home, and Trina suggested I take a nap. "I want you *perky* tonight," she said, the brightness of her voice barely masking the blunt edge of her directive. Drawing the curtains, I lay down and closed my eyes.

For the first time since the boy arrived, I pictured the Samurai. Maybe it was the most recent letter from C. that led me back to his alter ego. I saw him right now, a tie around his tree-stump neck, being led by the elbow to meet Lorna's mother. The mother lives in an apartment in a house encircled by a metal fence. She watches them from the bay window facing the street as he and Lorna take the faded yellow steps to the porch. Lorna has one arm looped around his. In the other she has a container of home-baked cookies. Since the boy left, the Samurai's relationship with Lorna has progressed. The mother opens the door of the house and hugs her daughter. She shakes the Samurai's hand and welcomes him inside her apartment, which smells like cat piss. The mother is in her fifties, but her hair has prematurely gone white. She is a head shorter than her daughter and has an upturned nose, which gives her an elfin appearance. She makes a show of her daughter's baking, and Lorna compliments her mother on a new sweater-vest she purchased on sale, and there's something dissonant to the Samurai in this niceness. How unused to it he is in his own experiences, and also how it covers some unspoken sadness that seems shared. They spend an afternoon eating Lorna's cookies with egg salad sandwiches and English breakfast tea that Lorna's mother has prepared. Midway through their conversation, Lorna's mother asks Constantine what drew him to Lorna, which makes the Samurai begin to breathe audibly as he thinks. "When I saw her," he says, "it was as though I heard a voice . . ."

"*Remember the boy*," I said to him. "*Leave her*."

The Samurai stands abruptly. Lorna looks up at him.

"Who are you talking to?"

I opened my eyes to see Trina hovering over me. "Hey. What time is it?"

"It's almost five."

"I was having a dream."

"You were pretty animated."

For the past four hours, I'd been sleeping on my side. I sat up, stretching my arms. I wanted to return to sleep, back to my dream. That would be how I ended my impasse with my story, and dissolved the boy. My chance was gone. Would it return, or would I need to find another way out of the boy's grip on my life?

Trina asked me, for the second time that day, whether I'd slept well. Still mourning the end of my dream, I managed to mumble something affirmative. I could smell something, the early dinner she'd made for us. The babysitter arrived, one of Trina's grad students, a young woman from Paraguay, who, to Adele's delight, shared my daughter's love of cat videos. Trina had both of my suits pressed and hanging by the door. Although neither felt appropriate for the weather, I picked the lighter summer suit over its wool counterpart, fingering the flimsy plastic garment bag. If only I could put my brain in a garment bag to attend work parties and run errands, and take it out, unsoiled, for those moments when I needed it most, the book would be done. The Samurai vanquished. The boy dissolved.

We took the Tesla to the party, circling the outer ring of the campus until we spun through a roundabout and were spat out onto a wooded side road. Up ahead, we found a line of sedans and crossovers idling outside the university president's driveway and took our place at the rear. Trina wore a dark-blue dress with a plunging V-neck. I could see her staring at the cue cards in her lap, her mouth moving along to her prepared remarks for the short speech she was expected to deliver.

"Thanks for helping me," she told me, after she caught me looking at her. "A couple of years back."

"Is that on a cue card?" I joked.

"It is, but it just reminded me of that time." She reached over and squeezed my hand.

Two years earlier, I had surrendered the pretense of progression in my work so that Trina could complete her book while triaging her teaching and administrative duties. Trina looked at me wistfully as she recalled that period of my self-sacrifice. In my efforts, I burned pots, turned white shirts gray in the laundry, and, one busy morning, took Adele to preschool without shoes. I was away so long from the liquor store, the cashier thought I'd died. My bumbling was wholehearted, and not what it is now, a by-product of a gaping malaise.

Our car finally inched toward the valet station. The university president's house was built in a Tudor style with stone masonry and oriel windows, the vast lawn uniformly clipped and kelly green, and the hedges sheared into oblong, globular shapes, like lava-lamp emulsions. I had been to this mansion half a dozen times, but I always entered trailing Trina, afraid I'd be collared and shoved out its gated entrance.

Faculty members and their spouses were gathered in a sitting area with leather club chairs and walls lined with sepia-toned photos of the university in the past. The university president held court by a bookcase that displayed a marble bust of one of his distant predecessors. He wore a bow tie and a light-blue Oxford shirt under a plaid sports jacket. Opposite him, in another corner of the room, someone had been hired to play jazz standards at the piano. As soon as we entered, Trina heard her name called. I swiped a couple of glasses of wine from a caterer's serving platter, turning back to find Trina cowed into a corner by the middle school principal, the one who'd fast-tracked the boy into her puppy mill for prodigies. The principal, married to Trina's department chair, held out her iPhone and swiped intently, narrating each image to Trina, who accepted a wineglass gratefully.

"Ramona watches baking shows," Trina informed me with the hollow cadences of a prisoner of war making a televised confession. "She makes the prize-winning cakes from her favorite shows."

"It's easy when you're not baking in front of a TV crew," Ramona said, her index finger on the image of a gingerbread Taj Mahal. She wore a gold-sequined halter, under a sari, and I felt like she had a playlist on her phone primed in case anyone was in the mood for a bhangra dance party.

Remembering to be an obedient husband, I squeezed between the two of them and asked Ramona to start from the beginning, as Trina's attention was pulled by a colleague across the room. Once her slideshow had finished and Trina was safely away from Ramona, chatting with her colleague and the university president, I asked the principal how the boy was doing in her school. Her eyes stilled, her smile doubled.

"His teacher tells me that he's very personable," she started. "For some children, switching schools can be a big adjustment. And once you factor in his change in household and, um, socioeconomic circumstances, you could say he's doing as well as you could expect."

Since I already knew the boy was bombing at his new school, I had only myself to blame for that empty verbiage. But these are the sacrifices you make to maintain an unwanted conversation, which was mercifully squelched when the piano player concluded a version of "Watermelon Man" and the university president called our attention to the opposite end of the room. Trina was already standing behind the bigwig and I could see her searching the room for me.

I'd started sifting through the audience of academics toward her, ready to hold her purse, when I caught sight of a familiar face. I didn't know immediately how we were acquainted, only that, like me, he didn't belong there. He was walking through the crowd, his face red from the scotch he was holding. Without deciding to do it, I turned my back on Trina and her speech and followed the man through the kitchen, where uniformed caterers were reloading their trays of canapés, and outside.

His back was turned to me, fumes of smoke winging his head, when I stepped onto the porch. Hearing my steps and the door shutting behind me, this man turned around. It was him, Father Pete! The priest who had baptized my daughter. The tattooed cleric with whom I felt a strange affinity and urge to unburden myself. The man who made me think of limbo.

"Father Pete!" I called out to him. He tilted his head and once-overed me quizzically. "My name's Benson Yu. You baptized my daughter, Adele."

Offering his hand, he had the same affable face, and around his neck he wore a clerical collar with the top button of his shirt undone.

"And how's Adele's spiritual journey been?" he asked me.

"So-so," I told him. We hadn't been back to church since the baptism. But I wanted to tell him that our spiritual discussion had lingered in my mind.

Father Pete dug into his blazer pockets and retrieved a pack of menthol cigarettes. He held out the pack, offering me one, and I accepted it out of politeness. I cupped a hand around the end of the smoke as he lit it with a lighter.

"So, Benson, are you faculty?" he asked me.

"Not really," I said, trying not to cough. "Married to one."

"My brother's the president guy. Whenever I visit his digs, he throws a party. Never in my honor," he joked. "But he's a pretty good guy, nonetheless. I'm surprised I didn't see you at his last event."

"We must have lost the invite." Smoke scorched my throat. "How long have you been a priest?"

"Seventeen years, almost." He smiled, perhaps fazed by my question.

He didn't seem much older than me, and I had already imagined a rich secular life for him before he received the call from God. I was surprised, perhaps disappointed, by his lengthy tenure. "You just knew?"

"Knew what?"

"That, you know, you wanted to be a priest."

His eyes landed on me softly. Maybe my rapport with him at the baptism had been a projection after all. Or maybe all creeps, be they karate instructors or priests, look at me the same way, more like quarry than a person. "Is there something on your mind?" he finally asked.

"Not really." Exhaling my mentholated smoke, I could hear applause and perhaps what sounded like my wife's trembling voice. It was only when she was nervous that she spoke like an immigrant. By not being there, I was already blowing it, so I might as well go forward with my confession. "Actually, is it okay if I ask you a religious question?"

"All right," he said.

"Is suicide always a sin? I'm asking for a friend, a real person, not just me, someone I'm worried about."

"Short answer, yes."

The answer was what I expected, but I still wanted assurances for the urges that lapped at my brow in my more despondent periods. Like right now, with the optimism of finishing my book subsiding, and my inability to emotionally support Trina once again exposed. "Do people who kill themselves always go to hell? Are they separated from their loved ones forever—assuming their loved ones have achieved salvation?"

Father Pete shook his head. "Not always, dude, not in the case of severe mental illness."

That's what I wanted to hear. I almost fist-pumped. "Because mental illness affects free will?"

"More or less." He paused, maybe considering whether he needed to in-quire about my well-being, given that he was off-duty. "Have you, uh, had those kinds of thoughts?"

I shook my head. "I couldn't take my own life. I'm too squeamish. I'd prob-ably need someone to help me."

"Like a hit man?" Father Pete said, with a laugh. His cigarette was down to the filter. He drained his glass and threw the butt in the tumbler. "I saw a movie with a storyline about that once. The hired killer shoots him with a blank. The moment the person who paid to be murdered thinks he's going to die, he's cured of his depression." The priest's eyes turned inward as he recalled that movie. "Sounds like an effective treatment." Then he looked at the door. "Time to freshen my drink."

I remained outside until my cigarette was finished. But really it was to allow enough time to pass so that Father Pete, whose grip on my imagination as my hip confessor had loosened, would not feel as though I were stalking him. I could hear another burst of applause coming from inside, and then the jazz pianist began to tinkle anew. I could imagine Trina's face, pitched between pleasure and uneasiness, as she accepted huzzahs from her workmates. Ready-ing myself for her unalloyed disgust with me for ghosting her speech, I stepped back into the house.

She wasn't there.

I wandered around, avoiding Ramona, avoiding the priest, until I was cer-tain Trina was not tucked away, waiting to pounce on me. But she wasn't any-where. She had left without me. Who could blame her? I'd leave myself too, if I could.

CHAPTER TWENTY

Unlike Benny, Avril's family had arrived in this town, and time, by bus. Mr. Pham, Avril's father, had never learned to drive. Since immigrating, he had worked at a cannery, gutting fish as he longed to return to his professional career in Vietnam, where he'd been an engineer. Mr. Pham was a slight, serious-looking man who kept a comb in his pocket in case even one hair should fall out of place. On weekends, in ironed dress shirts with their top button open, Avril's father had spent his evenings at classes, improving his English and then getting his credentials all over again. For two years, he would send job applications and résumés to every company in his field. Finally, last summer, he'd received a call for the job that he deserved. Mr. Pham accepted the position right away and the family needed to go before they could even sell their house. His friends and extended family had offered to help him move, which he declined. They only needed to get on the bus. They rented out their house furnished and sold the rest of their belongings because, their father explained, they wouldn't want them in their new life. "He knew we were going somewhere different," Avril suggested on Saturday morning, shortly after Benny's arrival. "He didn't want to tell us, in case we wouldn't go. He knew my mother would argue if she knew we were going so far." Avril and her younger sister, Angel, were each allowed only one small suitcase that she loaded herself into the belly of the Greyhound.

"There's a bus that leaves for Chinatown in an hour," she told Benny, scrolling through her phone as they sat at her marble kitchen table. For breakfast, they were eating saltines with peanut butter, one of their old favorites, chased down with Coke. Neither Mr. Pham nor Avril's mother, who preferred being called Auntie Vicky—an emotional woman who kept scented tissues in a bejeweled fanny pack in case she saw a newborn baby and started crying—were around that morning. Avril had not mentioned them since their arrival. "Do you want me to text you a link?" She looked at Benny's empty hands. To her, they probably seemed naked without a smartphone. "Why don't I buy you a ticket? I can even print it out."

"Come back with me?" Benny pleaded hopefully. "For a visit?"

Avril shook her head. "I've already made plans for later in the day."

"With the person you're seeing? Carter? The one you've been on the phone with?"

The corners of her mouth danced as her eyes sank into her phone. "Maybe," she said. "Okay, I've purchased your tickets. For a round trip."

"I don't think I'm coming back," Benny said. "Get a refund on the trip back."

"What if Chinatown isn't what you think it'll be?" she asked him.

"It wasn't the same place for me after my poh-poh died," Benny answered. "I just want to return."

"I'll buy you both tickets. Just in case."

Before leaving his father's house, Benny had prepared. He'd thrown into his backpack the clothes he'd worn when he arrived, a granola bar, and the first issue of *Iggy Samurai*. He was unable to predict his father's reaction to his plan to return, whether he'd forbid him from going or celebrate his departure, so he chose to keep it secret. He pretended he was spending the night at Avril's, and his cover story went unchallenged as his father, clammy and unkempt after another hangover, scowled at him at the breakfast table.

Benny and Avril said their goodbyes, casually, afraid of the sadness that they'd expose if they'd admitted they might never see one another again. Making his way on foot to the bus station, Benny still relished the freedom he had to go anywhere and how different it was from being stuck in that apartment. He finally felt comfortable here. It was only when he reached downtown, and its more compact city blocks, that he became unsure geographically. Avril had struggled to give him directions to the bus station. "I'm already out of practice. These days, people don't give directions verbally," she said at last. "Not when you can look them up." Eventually, she'd printed out step-by-step walking directions from the internet.

The bus station was on the far edge of town, and he arrived early enough that he was the first person aboard. He took a seat near the back and watched people fill the space. There were grimy backpackers, one of whom had a guitar, some young men in dark suits who might have belonged to a church, and a family that spoke Spanish. Everyone on the bus looked weighted with the excitement of their journey. Most likely they would disembark before him.

At the scheduled departure time, the bus driver started the engine. Benny hugged the backpack on his lap, readying himself to leave. At that moment, he resolved he would tell nobody in Chinatown about his time with his father. People would never believe him anyhow. The front door whooshed shut, and the driver shifted gears. The bus hopped to attention. Benny heard someone knocking on the door, which hissed back open. When Benny saw Avril climb on the bus, his heart tap-danced with joy. Avril searched for Benny until she approached the final rows. A calm settled on her face when she found him. "Of course you'd be in the back, tucked away," she said, taking the empty seat next to him.

"What happened to your other plans?" Benny asked.

She shrugged, eyes fixed on her phone. "Carter was busy. His friends wanted him to go on a hike," she admitted. She covered her mouth as she yawned, her fingernails painted in a clear polish. "Can you imagine me on a hike?"

Benny couldn't, nor could he picture her in a relationship with a hiker. Carter, she confided, went to another school. She wouldn't say which one. They'd become acquainted in a chat room and would hang out when his schedule allowed. His classes were very demanding. She hadn't met his friends. He was cool with her being trans but was worried his friends might not be. He didn't want her to get hurt. They spent most of their time alone, at her house or in his car. Since Carter, the "C" in her necklace, had a car, Benny wanted to know how old he was. Avril wouldn't say.

She was dressed in high-waisted jeans and a loose salmon-pink sweater under a bomber jacket with a lambswool collar. Her look, contemporary but plausible for the era they might be heading toward, was more androgynous than the one she normally adopted. In the restroom across from their back row, Benny changed into the clothes he'd worn when he'd left Chinatown. A knockoff Lacoste polo shirt, acid-washed jeans. A flash of hatred passed across his face as he saw, in the restroom's mirror, the boy others picked on.

"Do you remember anything about your trip here?" Benny asked. "I mean, when did you know you'd crossed over to a different time?"

He was hoping Avril would say that she was overwhelmed by a flood of white light as she leapfrogged the final decades of the twentieth century. "It was when we stepped off the bus," Avril said right away. "We were trying to hail a taxi to the house that my dad had bought sight unseen. Some college kids passed us on the street. They were drunk or high, or maybe both. I hadn't seen anyone look that way before, with tinted hair and body piercings. My mother pulled me closer to her and glared at my dad, as if to say, 'How dare you take us here.' But I kept staring at those college kids, especially the one with the more feminine look. I saw the future—my future." Avril paused, then revealed that she did not want to spend more than the day in Chinatown.

The bus ride felt shorter to Benny than the drive with Macy had. Maybe it was because he knew what to expect. In the morning sun, the terrain that he'd traveled through weeks ago—the mountain pass, the vast checkerboard stretches of farmland and groves of apple trees in clockwork intervals— unfolded no longer as unsettlingly new. He flipped through his copy of *Iggy Samurai* and reread the passage where young Iggy, who looked naked without his hakama, was taken away from his iguana family in a Mexican rain forest by a human smuggler, whose drug-dealing brother then kept him in an empty aquarium until he was murdered. He had reread these pages so many times by now that the story belonged to him. Like Iggy, he would transform himself into someone powerful.

When they reached the outskirts of the city, Benny had the first inkling that they wouldn't get to their destination, at least not chronologically. The people weren't dressed right. The cars on the road didn't look right. Some of them cruised alongside the bus, space cars like his father's. When the bus stopped in Chinatown, Benny was glad Avril had purchased a return ticket for him. In his disappointment, he realized that his hopes were pinned to the idea that the bus might take him farther back in time, not to when he left, not back to the empty apartment next to Constantine's, but earlier, to a safer time when both Mommy and Poh-Poh were still alive. They wouldn't recognize him then, because he hadn't been nearly thirteen when Mommy'd died, but he would plead with them until they were convinced. Maybe he would meet his younger self there—and be the big brother he'd always wanted.

"This is the place," Avril announced.

Benny took the lead in revisiting their old haunts with Avril lagging behind. This version of Chinatown felt diminished, in spite of the pailou, the traditional gateway that now welcomed visitors to this historic area. Some of the shops and restaurants he remembered still stood, operated by unfamiliar Chinese faces. Other buildings had been torn down and replaced by apartment buildings occupied by young, affluent non-Chinese people. The noodle shop that Poh-Poh would take him to on Sundays after church now sold vegan pizza.

Just as Benny was ready to turn back, Avril, her jaw set and her eyes like daggers, surged ahead.

Now he was the one falling behind Avril, who hurried toward the edge of Chinatown, away from storefronts and single-room-occupancy hotels, until they were in the neighboring residential area, the one with wire fences and row houses. The row houses had been renovated with skylights and aluminum siding. Luxury cars lined the street. They cut through the park where he and Avril once played, although the swing set had been replaced, and past their old school.

A few months after they had traveled to their new hometown, Avril explained, her father had announced that he and her mother had decided to return to Chinatown. The world they had arrived in was not what they had expected, and not meant for them. Auntie Vicky had struggled to make friends and missed Asian food. Her hair had started falling out. Angel had been diagnosed with ADHD and placed on a prescription that made her scratch her arms until they bled. Mr. Pham was the last holdout among her family. At first, he'd liked his new job. He was treated courteously and never confused for cleaning staff, and only rarely mistaken for the Korean engineer. His casually dressed CEO was amused by his decision to wear a three-piece suit, even though it was cut in the current style. After those first months, though, Avril's father realized he'd made a mistake. He would never advance. The respect that he had hoped to find three decades in the future would remain withheld. Sitting at the kitchen table in a baggy T-shirt, he'd announced to the family that they would return by bus, even if it meant that he gutted fish for the rest of his days.

Mr. Pham had told Avril that she could also return, but not as their daughter. He had been strangely indifferent to her transition, unlike Auntie Vicky, who repeatedly wept into tissues pulled out of her fanny pack. But they had both agreed that only their son could return with them, and seemed resigned to Avril staying. Avril finally confessed to Benny that she lived alone in that house, subsisting from her parents' savings account.

They passed their old church, which hadn't changed except for wear and tear, toward a mismatched set of shingled homes with porches, originally built in the nineteenth century. Now they were restored and painted exuberant colors, the vegetable gardens replaced with crocuses and rhododendrons. They were back where Avril once lived.

Avril stepped up to the last house, freshly painted mint green, and knocked on a door that now had an inset glass oval. Benny stood at the bottom of the step and saw a middle-aged woman approach the door. At the sight of Avril, her face shadowed.

"Angel," Avril said, announcing her sister's name.

"What are you doing here?" Angel said. The younger sister, the one obsessed with Cabbage Patch Kids and Judy Blume novels, was old enough to be Auntie Vicky. Like her mother, she had a high forehead and a broad face, but she wore glasses with neon pink metal frames. The blush on her cheeks was now powdered. She hugged Avril briefly and then stepped back to acknowledge Benny. "I see the twins have reunited." Benny waved, but Angel seemed uninterested in him. "Do you two want to come inside?"

"We don't want to intrude," Avril said. She spoke softly, her face pallid and bashful. "I stalked you online and saw you were back in the house. Surprised?"

Angel nodded. She turned back into her house and called one of her kids. "Molly, why don't you take Hamish upstairs and watch *PAW Patrol?*" Angel watched her daughter lead her younger brother upstairs. Then she turned to her sister and Benny and insisted they come inside.

The carpets had been pulled up and the hardwood floors sanded and polished. Angel led them to a table in the kitchen where the ugly patterned wallpaper had been removed and exposed brick found in its place. Angel, who worked as an interior designer, had supervised the renovation. Serving them fizzy water from a SodaStream in mason jars with wedges of lime, she explained how her family had returned to this area a few years back, when it became "up and coming," after taking over the home from Auntie Vicky, who had been living in a suburban retirement village since Mr. Pham's death.

"I can't believe it," Angel said through tears. "It's been over thirty years."

"It's only been a few months for me," Avril said, shrugging. She was slightly better than her sister at holding back her emotion.

"And you?" Angel asked Benny. "How did you end up where we were?"

"A social worker took me," Benny explained. "It's a long story."

"After we returned, Mom and Dad told everyone that you passed away in a car accident," she explained to Avril. "It was a tough time. None of us talked about it. We all suffered alone. But we never forgot about you. Mom made regular deposits in the savings account so you had money in the future. And Dad called out your name—Avril—when he was dying."

Avril stared at the hands in her lap. "I couldn't go back with you. I needed to stay."

"I know," Angel said. "I wish I could have kept you company." She got up to make them a plate of goat cheese and water crackers. The sight of the cheese gave Benny a lemon face. Angel laughed.

"Still a picky eater, I see."

Benny apologized.

"I'm sorry I don't have any snack cakes for you two, but my kids aren't allowed added sugar," she told them.

Benny watched Angel and Avril reminisce for the better part of an hour. Eventually, Angel's kids stomped downstairs, asking for food. They giggled, eyeing Avril and Benny as potential playmates. And Angel's husband was due to return from his errand running. Avril decided it was better for her and Benny to leave.

"I won't keep you much longer," Angel told them before disappearing upstairs. "But I've got something for you—both of you." She returned with a small cookie tin. "Here. We built a deck in the backyard and found this when we were digging," she told Avril, giving her another hug. "You know how to find me. Mom would love to see you."

They trudged back into Chinatown, Avril looking, by turns, pensive and pained. "I'm just relieved you and I didn't go back in time," she told Benny. "If we were to see my parents, I'm not sure how they would have reacted. On the bus this morning, I realized I didn't need that kind of drama. I'd rather focus on the relationships that work for me. On my chosen family."

It was a warm night, and the sun was still bright, so Avril suggested they get boba, something that hadn't been popularized outside of Taiwan back in their original time, and wander around until their bus back departed. Watching the shops close for the day, they wondered how many of the middle-aged shopkeepers were former classmates and how many of the seniors, in baseball caps and fleece, were those kids' parents. Many of the faces they saw in this remaining sliver of Chinatown looked familiar and yet neither of them could affix any names to them.

In the boba shop, Avril finally opened the time capsule that she and Benny had buried before they parted ways. From the cookie tin, she held up an old Polaroid and laughed at her previous self. Compared to Avril in the photo, Benny had barely changed—maybe his hair had grown out. Folded up was the front page of a yellowing newspaper from the previous summer. They also dug out action figures and video game disk cards that they'd sworn to play with only in each other's company. Avril held up one of them. "We need to find a way to play *Renegade* again," she said. "We played that game together well."

Benny laughed, remembering the arguments they'd get into over *Renegade*, which was a street-fighting video game precursor to *Double Dragon*. The game play depended on both players moving in the same direction, and Avril and Benny were not only continually moving in opposite directions but each insisting that the other go their way.

"I'm glad we returned to Chinatown," Avril admitted. "I would have kept wondering whether it was that easy to go back in time. Do you think Angel was happy to see me?"

"Yeah," Benny said. "Happy and surprised."

"Maybe I'll message her when we get back." She sucked the last brown-sugar pearl from the ice at the bottom of her cup and sighed. "I think we're here, in this time frame, for a reason. I needed a place I could belong."

"What about me?" Benny asked. "I don't belong here."

She chewed on her straw as she thought. "Maybe it has something to do with your dad and why he's so weird. Even in the old days, you would bring him up. I stayed in this time to get away from my dad. Maybe you're here to connect with yours."

The bus came at dusk, and their feet ached when they boarded. This time, Avril took the window seat, dozing off against the glass. As night fell, there was less to see once they were outside the city. Benny couldn't sleep and slid the phone from Avril's hands and typed in the security code he'd seen her use. He launched the web browser and began searching for people. Steph. Shirley. Macy the social worker. Even Constantine. But he found no results for any of them. No one from his past could help him. He had to fight the urge to fling Avril's phone down the aisle, to stomp on it in a fury. If Avril could find other people from her past, why couldn't he? He was filled with jealousy. She still had family. The heat of that rage eventually faded and left him ashamed as he fit her phone back into her hand and on her chest. Avril, he had just learned, was alone. She was not only the one person he knew from the past but also the one whose situation closely paralleled his own.

When the bus arrived early in the morning, Benny and Avril walked most of the way home, until their paths diverged. They shared, as people did here, a quick hug, and then he watched her enter her big, empty house, where she would wait for her older boyfriend to call. Walking home, Benny knew there would be people waiting for him. He took comfort in that knowledge as much as he enjoyed the sun on his neck and forehead. When he stepped into his kitchen, his stepmother asked if he'd had a good sleepover, her smile insinuating that perhaps Benny had something memorable, like a first kiss, to admit. Benny smiled and said it was okay. She was wearing an old Led Zeppelin T-shirt and pajama pants and was drinking herbal tea. Benny's half sister was at the TV, a treat reserved for weekend mornings. His stepmother said she had some news. He looked around for his father until his stepmother said he had gone running. Then she offered him some cornflakes as a flicker of doubt fell across her face.

"Your sister and I are going to live with friends of mine," she finally told him. "I don't know how long it will be. You can come with us. Actually, I want you to come with us."

"Does it have anything to do with him coming home wasted the other night?" Benny asked her.

"That's only part of it. And it has nothing to do with you or your arrival. The way he's been acting, how erratic he's been, it started earlier. There's a lot about his past that has resurfaced. He needs to sort things through."

Benny told her he wanted to think about it. Crunching his cornflakes, he realized he couldn't go. Avril had been onto something when she suggested that they were here for a reason. Maybe she was right, and he needed to find that explanation through his father. Perhaps his existence in this place, and his escape from it, was contingent on his relationship with his father. Like in *Renegade*, he and his father were in a two-player game, and Benny couldn't move any farther on the screen if his father didn't follow suit. He was here to be tested. Maybe not by some higher power, but by his own father. And his own task was to test his father.

No, he wouldn't go.

CHAPTER TWENTY-ONE

When the boy left for school with the lunch Trina had packed the night before, shortly before she and Adele moved out, my body trembled with that sugar high of solitude. The pores in my skin cheered. An empty house. No, a freshly empty house. It's better than bedsheets out of the dryer. It's better than the smell of coffee in the morning. For the first hour, I lay in bed under my sour duvet, thinking of coffee, listening to birdsong outside. I needed the euphoria to die down. I had to prepare myself for the crash that would come when potential was spoiled by inaction.

I was ready. I showered and shaved, put on a button-up shirt. I pinched the loose skin on my face and puckered my mouth until that gargoyle in the mirror had been tamed. I wanted to be a passable version of that person Trina had met, a person whose superpowers came into effect in solitude. I had toast and pod coffee for breakfast. I tried to speak with Trina, but my call sank like an eight ball into her voice mailbox. To pass the time, I folded up the boy's cot to tidy. Under the bed, there was a Polaroid of Trina from when we first started dating, in a party dress, holding a cigarette. Beside it were some wadded balls of sticky tissue paper. I remembered Trina saying the boy had caught an eyeful of her.

Then I recalled my own first glimpse of her. She and I had met at a Halloween party thrown by a friend of mine at the house he rented. This friend once claimed he could always hook up on that holiday. *For one night a year, you don't have to be yourself,* this friend, who was working on his PhD, insisted. But for Trina's and my first Halloween, I dressed as a pirate, with an eye patch, a plastic sword, and a jug of rum. I engaged in a living room sword fight with someone pretending to be a gladiator. *This is me,* I told myself. *I'm always me.* The gladiator and I both seemed equally engaged in our roles until—*snap*—he was cowering behind the coffee table. One of my blows had demolished his cardboard shield. Then the accusations came. My combatant called me "weird" and "intense," and the expression of my host, who had initially laughed at our mock duel, confirmed this opinion—and his own self-interest. *Nobody will wanna hook up with me if you take this fight too seriously!* Once I agreed to "cool off" on the porch, bright pop music was played to correct the atmosphere I'd tainted inside. That's when Trina, a classmate of my friend's, stepped out for a smoke. "I hate the music," she said, not exactly to me, although I appreciated the sentiment and her throaty voice. Over a football jersey, she wore a black leather jacket that matched her dyed hair and the kohl under her eyes. She had already removed the helmet from the costume (borrowed from her room-mate). "Where I come from, they call soccer football," she said, "and American football 'hand egg.'"

"Where are you from?" I asked.

And she told me, with an accent that was more detectable in those days—Brno, with a pit stop in the UK. She'd grown up a bookworm and had started her graduate studies with a humorlessness that bothered her skeezy supervisor, who suggested she needed to "loosen her hair." The cigarettes were her attempt to be that fun person. But she used them as an excuse to skip meals and abruptly ghost conversations, and they bolstered her coldness. When I told her I wrote comic books, she shook her head in dismay. "But you seem so smart."

Even on that first night, I noticed she had a disconcerting way of talking to people. Looking them in the eye. Then past them, over their shoulder. When she spoke to me, I turned around to see who had entered her line of sight. An attacker? A better option? No one. Just not me.

I was well into my thirties, several years older than Trina, but neither of us had been in a serious relationship. Each of us turned to the other to soften the jagged edge of singlehood. We howled at the callous things we said, which we blamed on our immigrant backgrounds. So many social mores had been lost to us. We were both only children, our parents long dead. And yet our similarities also meant we were each used to seeing our relationship as one that was easy to exit.

The first time we'd split up was on account of Trina's postdoctoral work in a city famous for its snowfall and high rate of death by heroin overdose. Meanwhile, the *Iggy Samurai* franchise drew me to warmer climes—to free lunches and corner-office meetings. My life was set to defy the frown of gravity, and in this slipstream of yeses, things would change. I would no longer crash into days-long funks or drink until someone was picking a fight with me (or so I believed). Trina knew it too, and she would be relieved not to coexist with my simmering silence.

At the lunches and meetings I'd been invited to, I was like a tree shaken for more fruit. I had new ideas but they were all, one way or another, lesser, unprofitable versions of *Iggy Samurai*. Every apple that fell from me was bruised. At each meeting, the people I met would start to tap their desks and look at their watches. I would take my expensed cab back to the hotel and worm into my bed with my minibar hoard, trying to gather the strength not to crawl back to Trina. As it happened, when I gave in, her own resolve had been slipping.

Our second split came as Trina searched for jobs across the continent. She was being wined and dined at faculty clubs and steak houses. The idea of being an academic spouse, ignored at parties I didn't even want to attend by people who were less interesting than stucco, prompted me to look for another out. Meanwhile, the last dribs of money from the waning *Iggy Samurai* franchise had been paid to me, and I was happy teaching at the local community college. Occasionally, when asked for advice, I found someone new to offload my tale of intellectual property theft on. That was enough for me, and I didn't want to leave. Our apartment's rent would be manageable on my own. When Trina returned, I was looking at secondhand couches to replace the one I had been sleeping on. Along with her rolling suitcase, she'd come back with a job offer and a positive pregnancy test.

These developments, we decided, were no coincidence. We were fated to be together. Judging by our reactions to that second pink line, you'd think we planned this. And that our woes had come from this result not happening earlier. Our plans changed. Our dispositions shifted. Trina was transformed. She wasn't just a new mother—she was more confident and generous. And she was fully employed. The person she wanted to be. I became a stay-at-home caregiver, basking in the adulation at a park or a pediatrician's waiting room that comes from clearing the knee-high bar of male competency. And I was more than competent. It was as though I had done this before. I knew what a child who couldn't speak was feeling, and I could address her needs.

And yet I was still me. Miserable me. The baby grew big enough that I didn't think she'd wither away if I looked afield. She crawled and tottered and walked and ran. She drew blotches, then circles, then cats. She left for school, and I had the house to myself again, time on my own. To write. To write about the past. To alter details to get closer to the truth. That was when I had first begun to wait for the boy to return.

And now Trina and I found ourselves at our third break, right here and now, the one that would leave lasting damage. When I got around to checking my email that morning, there was a text message from her. Her schedule had been rearranged. From now on, she would handle pickups and drop-offs for Adele. I could visit whenever I wanted, so long as there was an approved adult present. She asked me only to watch over the boy. He may not be your son. He may be your youthful alter ego. And he may be independent, but he still needs to be protected, she texted, in a way that was too well-punctuated and capitalized to be composed in a thumb-stroke blitz. I wouldn't leave him with you if he couldn't look after himself. But you must check in on him. Spend more time with him, please. It'd be good for both of you.

Morning tripped into afternoon. All this time sitting. I needed to stretch. I thought about going outside, where one deer watched me as she chewed on grass. I thought Bambi had been abandoned by his mother, but Elsa bounded into view a moment later. I remained in that chair. I tried to picture the life I could live on my own, stuck in this town. Unemployable. My one lucrative idea exhausted. Coparenting. It was more unbearable than trying to imagine the conversation I would need to have with Trina to move beyond this "midlife crisis." *How is it different this time?* she might ask. I would make promises. I would be a better husband, better parent. I would find another shrink. I would quit drinking for good.

How is it different this time?

I pictured her staring over my shoulder, staring past me, as she asked this question. It was a habit she kept after all these years. *I'm not looking over your shoulder*, she would tell me. *You're just short.* She couldn't wear heels when we went out. But now I understood she wanted to see who was behind me. I had been waiting for the boy. She had been expecting the puppet master. The monster.

I needed to confront C.

In my fan mail bin, I dug up the packet with the letter from my old mentor. *I'm going to make it easy for you. I'll be in your town next month.* I smoothed it out and placed it on my desk. I picked up my phone.

CHAPTER TWENTY-TWO

That Saturday, Benny's father was unusually attentive. Since his stepmother left, Benny had been stuck on his own, working through the extra groceries that she'd bought before her departure. Today, his father stepped out of his room already shaved and dressed. He started making breakfast sausages and toaster-ready hash browns with orange juice. Benny sat down at the table, angry. All of the food was taken from the refrigerator, food he had been hoping to stretch as long as possible, now that he was fending for himself again.

"How does that taste?" Benny's father asked.

Benny grunted. He was too busy shoveling food in his mouth. He couldn't help it. He was always hungry. His father nodded in approval.

"An old friend is in town," he announced. "I was thinking how you and I could visit him today."

"I've got homework."

There was a ripple of desperation in his eyes. "Come on, it won't be long. There will be more food. And I've known him since I was your age. You can ask him all about me."

Benny stopped eating as he thought of his father as a child. Was Benny as strong as his father was? Or as weak as he was? His father noticed his fork had gone still.

"As a matter of fact, he was my former karate and kendo instructor," he added. "And I told him about you."

"What did you say?" Benny asked.

"He liked that you were already training. I told him about how hard you hit. He wanted to know if that was true."

Benny tried to fork in a hash brown before his father could see him smile. The two of them had to leave in an hour. Benny's father asked him whether he had any nicer clothes than the ones Trina had bought him, but Benny shook his head. His father dug up a dress shirt that fit over Benny's scrawny body like a tablecloth, and a striped tie. Benny picked a pair of dark jeans to go with them.

The meeting was at a coffee shop in a strip mall. Benny staked a table while his father ordered at the counter. When Benny took his seat, he noticed Avril at the far end of the room with an older boy. No, a young man. He wore a button-up shirt and a ball cap from the school where his stepmother taught. He looked as though he shaved. The two of them were sitting at the same side of the table. The man's hands were cupped around his coffee mug, and hers were folded on the table. They seemed to take pleasure in their proximity, in how they risked impropriety. The older boy drained the remainder of his drink and they rose. As she gathered her purse from the back of her chair, Avril's eyes locked with Benny's. She held his gaze for a moment and then followed her boyfriend, who nodded at Benny's father on his way out. Benny's father was carrying a tray.

"Who was he?" Benny asked.

His father sat on the same side of the table and slid a hot chocolate and a doughnut in front of Benny. His face had reddened. "Carter, a student of mine," he said. "A former student."

"I go to school with his friend."

"Why does she look so familiar?" Benny's father asked. Benny didn't answer. For once, it seemed, there was a part of his life that his father couldn't take ownership of.

Benny's father had also bought two paper cups of coffee. Benny watched him put sugar and cream in one of the cups. Then his father set the cup with the sugar and cream across the table. He took a sip from the other and winced when the coffee scalded him. His friend was late. He repeatedly checked his watch.

When the friend finally stepped through the door, Benny's father took one long draw of his coffee, as though he needed it for courage, and stood up from the table to greet him. Benny followed suit.

"Sensei."

Benny's father's friend looked old, grandfather-old. He stood a head taller than Benny's father. He was bulky and soft, with a chest that looked like a garbage bag filled with autumn foliage. Under his red tracksuit he wore a white undershirt. Graying chest hair poked from the top of the collar. Benny noticed his eyes—a pale shade of blue, exactly like Constantine's—when he bowed, Japanese-style, to Benny's father, who withdrew his outstretched hand and bowed back. And then he bowed to Benny.

His formality melted away when everyone sat. He took the chair across from Benny and jabbed a finger at his coffee. "Double cream and sugar." He nodded with pleasure, as though he'd fooled Benny's father into remembering his order.

"It's cold now," his father told his sensei. "I can get you another."

The old man shook his head. "You'd think I would get here on time since this place is so close to where I'm staying." He pointed to a motel across the road. "But I overslept."

"You mentioned in a letter that your sister lives nearby. Why did she move out here?" Benny's father asked.

The old man took a sip of the coffee. It was cold enough for him to swish in his mouth. "When her husband died, she wanted to live closer to my niece, who lives with a fellow from around here. My sister is always on my case about visiting, and I owe her a lot since she helped me out when I lost my job at the ice factory." Benny's eyes widened at this detail. "But her condo is small and we bickered a lot as kids. I thought it'd be nice to have my own space. You know me, I like stretching my legs." He looked out the window at the motel. "Not bad for what you pay. If you've got time, you could check out my room. Use the pool."

Benny's father laughed nervously. His forehead glistened. He sweated easily. Only a few minutes into sparring, he would need to slip on a headband. "We don't have a lot of time."

"I get it. Well, it's nice to see you after all these years. You haven't changed much." He turned his attention to Benny. "And you look exactly like he did thirty years ago. Maybe stronger in the arms." Those eyes fixed on Benny in appraisal. "I understand you started training."

Benny nodded. "My dad said you were his sensei."

The old man placed one arm on the back of the seat next to his and leaned back. "He was a great student. Your dad was pretty serious. Could you tell?"

"He has his own dojo," Benny continued, as he was excited to be spoken to. "And a collection of samurai swords."

The old man looked pleased. He turned to Benny's father, who dragged a napkin across his wet neck. "A dojo? Is that where you keep all my old movie posters?"

"I forget what happened to them," his father said. By now, Benny knew him well enough to know when he was lying.

"It's hot here, isn't it?" The old man removed the wooden stir stick from his coffee and bent it with his hands as he spoke. "Well, I had a lot of students over the years," he said, watching the stir stick break. "They move on and you never hear from them. And you don't think about them either. They studied with you because their mothers thought they had too much energy. Or because their fathers were tired of watching them get pushed around in the schoolyard. They passed some time with me. But other boys were special. They had talent and perseverance. More than that, they looked at you like they needed your guiding hand. Because they didn't have anything, anyone. They needed your spare time. They had trouble with their parents, and you talked to them. And you like to think you left an impression on them."

The old man stilled himself, hands folded on the table. He dug his blue eyes into Benny's father and waited for him to respond. His father sputtered. A moment passed. The old man waited and started talking about an intellectual property lawyer he'd met with. "I could only do the free consult with him," the old man said, "but he believes that you stole my identity, and that I have a good case for restitution. We could do all this legal BS, but wouldn't it be better if you and I could come to an agreement? I'm barely getting by, while I can tell from looking at you now that you lead a nice life."

Benny's father started to cry. His shoulders convulsed as he sobbed. Benny stared at the door, wishing he could leave. "I don't have any money," his father finally told his sensei. "I was cheated out of it."

The old man looked away, trembling with anger. "Should have known. And there's nothing you can do about that?"

Benny's father shook his head. "I tried."

"Well," the old man said. He let out a snort. "At least you manned up to seeing me. I thought you'd never come back. I thought it was because I kicked your dad's ass."

His father shook his head. "What you did to him—it was the right thing to do."

"Exactly. I saved you there. And you just abandoned me. You ran away from that messy scene. And then there were cops."

"I'm sorry."

The old man stood up from his chair and grabbed Benny's father by the front of his shirt. His father flinched and looked away, scowling. But he was otherwise passive. "Those are just words," the old man added. "You owe me. After all these years, you owe me my share of your fortune with interest." He paused and looked at Benny, who felt his skin crawl. "Maybe you could give me something else."

His father's words became scattered and mumbled, the language of a young child accustomed to speaking only within his family. "Before we talk about debts," he finally said, "we need to discuss some other stuff. I don't want to revisit it. But I need to. I need to talk about the stuff that happened to me. That you did to me."

"What exactly do you mean?" But the old man seemed to already know. A cloud shadowed his brow. "Oh, that. *Not that.*" He shook his head in disappointment. "Of all the petty bullshit you want to talk about. You want to talk about that?"

His father nodded.

"It never happened—not that way you made it out to be," the old man said. "The story you told to get me in trouble, to get your pretty-boy father to fight me—that ended poorly for him, didn't it? Besides, we did so many other things. Before you met me, you could never stand up for yourself. You learned so many things from me. Why don't we focus on those instead?"

"Okay," Benny's father said, his head falling into his chest. He held up his hand, unable to take in any more of the old man's disavowals.

Benny's fists pulsed as his father's sobs lessened. There was silence until the old man brought his hand to his forehead in a feigned jolt of remember-ing. "I almost forgot," he said, turning to Benny. "I brought you a present."

The problem was, it was in his motel room. "I lugged it all the way here," the old man said. "I won't take too much more of your time." Benny's father agreed to follow him back across the street. The old man tottered as he walked, and Benny realized the tracksuit was more about comfort than physical activity. The three of them passed the motel front desk and into the parking lot and pool area that the room doors opened onto. "I'm upstairs," the old man said, removing a key from his pants. He forced his bulk up the stairwell.

In his room were twin beds, one unmade. The other had an open suitcase on it. A half-full bottle of Jim Beam sat on his nightstand, next to what were probably decades-old copies of *Penthouse* and *Juggs*. The old man turned on a noisy air conditioner. From the suitcase, he dug out a white gi and held it up to Benny. "It was your father's. He left it with me," he told him. "When he was your age. When he lost interest. Do you want to try it out?"

The sight of the uniform pleased Benny, who looked to his father to see if he could accept it. Standing at the door, his father shrugged.

In the bathroom, Benny changed, leaving the oversize dress shirt and his tie and jeans in a pile. He took a moment to admire himself in the mirror. He never knew he wanted his own gi. It fit him well.

When Benny emerged from the bathroom, it was just the old man, sitting at the foot of the unmade bed, hands on his knees. Benny's father was gone.

"Where is he?" Benny asked.

"He forgot to feed the meter," the old man said. He flashed his teeth. "Look at you. Perfect size, right?" Benny nodded. "Let's see what you can do."

He noticed a table had already been pushed to the wall. In the space that was cleared, he went through the basic kata in order. Gedan barai. Oi zuki. The old man rose. He held up his hand to stop him.

"Well done," the old man said. "You have some raw ability. But you also have some of your father's weaknesses. His stubbornness, his inflexibility, his shaky balance. I bet you already knew that."

Benny didn't answer, but he agreed with the assessment. The old man stood up and asked him to repeat those first kata. When Benny completed gedan barai, the old man asked him to freeze. He placed one hand on Benny's outstretched arm, then another on his hip. Benny felt the power that remained burrowed in the sensei's old body. He smelled the whiskey on this man's breath, commingled with the coffee.

His hand slipped down to Benny's lower back, and his breathing grew heavy. Benny saw his reflection again. He closed his eyes so he didn't have to imagine what would happen if his father didn't return. The old man could still overpower him. And do to him what he'd done to his father.

Benny pushed him away, startling the old man. He retreated a half step, stunned and old. Benny was going to fight this man. He would do everything to hurt him—even if it would hurt Benny more in the end. When he advanced, Benny threw an uppercut at him that was heavier than the punch he'd thrown at Mickey back in Chinatown. Instead of leveling the old man, he bubbled with amusement. When Benny tried to repel him with a side kick, he easily caught his foot and hooked the other one. Flat on his back, Benny felt the old man's hand running along his left side.

As he began to touch him, Benny felt a fog of déjà vu fall on him. He'd experienced this before. In a nightmare. In *Iggy Samurai*. He knew the old man's smile and his smell. And he knew he would endure whatever would happen by stepping out of his body and withdrawing into his mind. By pretending his body was a marionette that could go limp if he let go.

That was when the door was flung open. To Benny's relief, his sweaty, teary-eyed father stood in the frame. "We're running late," Benny's father told him. "Hurry, let's go."

The old man's grip loosened. Benny picked himself up from the floor, slowly at first, but then, heeding his father's words, he ran back to the bathroom to get his clothes.

He exited the room first. He watched as his father bowed once more to his sensei, apologizing for leaving so soon. "We'll have to talk about debts another time," his father told him. The old man shook his head.

When Benny crossed the street, he remembered that his father had parked at the strip mall. There had been no meter to feed.

CHAPTER TWENTY-THREE

I was barely out of Chinatown, years beyond my karate and kendo training, when I started watching samurai movies. At that age, technically an adult, enrolled as a film major, I liked Asian movies as much as I wanted to parade around campus in a bamboo paddy hat. In World Cinema class, the lecturer, a white man, talked about *Seven Samurai*. He paused, as though he were waiting to be swatted. He paused again. When he did, he looked at me. Did he worry I might correct him? Fuck yeah. Before the term "microaggression" gave my irritation a name, I avoided anything that would call attention to my Asian-ness. I stopped eating rice and grew to like the macaroni and cheese served in the cafeteria. I played hacky sack. All my friends had names like Connor and Fritz. But in a darkened room among these budding, alabaster-toned sophisticates, I could be a fan of these movies.

Throughout that screening, I started doodling images of Toshiro Mifune holding a katana over his head. (I couldn't get his expression right, as much as I tried over the weeks that followed. I had always preferred drawing animals. Whenever I drew people, I turned them into monsters.) I was as struck by the swordplay and the robes as any kid who grew up watching the *Star Wars* movies would be. But rewatching the samurai classics now, I found myself moved by the walks those lonely samurai seemed to take in the woods. As I'd grown up in Chinatown, that was my first exposure to what the Japanese call shinrin-yoku, or forest bathing. Not that I hiked often nowadays. There was a lushness in these films that I had forgotten about. Kurosawa helped to conflate the samurai movie with the American western in his portrayals of lawless towns and mysterious outsiders. But the towns in westerns were parched and sand-scaped. And the frontier architecture, the saloons with the batwing doors and spur-bitten floors and the hideout cabins with the black chimney stoves, was a far cry from the bamboo groves and palaces in samurai films. Kurosawa was an exception, and his movies held up the least for me.

I began rewatching these movies the day after we met up with my old sensei. The visit had gone poorly, as I had expected, but I was surprised by how weak C. still made me feel. I had wanted him to admit to his abuse—an apology was unimaginable—and he'd deflected it with a cold glare. He had gotten so old, and yet he could still have his way, at least emotionally, with me. I offered no resistance, not even when he wanted us to go back to his motel room. Drenched in sweat, I'd felt light-headed, the way I did when I drank too much coffee. I knew what he wanted. And in the hotel room, I saw the magazines and the booze. His game plan had remained the same after thirty years. When the boy was changing in the bathroom, C. told me to go. He held out his hand, instead of bowing. "Let's call it even," he told me, staring at the door.

I had turned my back on the kid, leaving him to the fate I had steadfastly avoided when I assigned the Samurai to be his protector. If that didn't make the boy disappear, at least it would kill him in a different way. I was halfway down the steps when I turned back. I would not let C. win one more time, even if it meant that I would ultimately suffer. The boy was trembling when I opened the door. He knew what I'd almost done to him. He sat stone-faced in the car on our way back home.

"Why are you looking at me that way?" I'd said to the boy. "I came back for you, didn't I? Nothing bad happened to you. I wouldn't allow it."

But that was not true.

On my way down the steps of that motel, I had known that leaving the boy there wouldn't lighten my burden. I didn't save him to protect his innocence, or to safeguard him from more searing psychic trauma. In fact, I had something more gruesome in mind for him.

I only needed to get into the right mood. Up until that point in my life, the decisions I had made had been simple ones enacted with scant second-guessing. I survived whatever was necessary, for instance, to get through my childhood. When it came to following Trina across the continent, the choice was simple, even if the adjustment could be painful. And the decision to take in the boy—the suspension of disbelief—was the same. Now another choice was approaching. But I felt paralyzed in the way friends talked about when discussing depression or anxiety. Or addiction. I had never related to that choice, or had that particular set of symptoms that led to it.

For most of a week, I sprawled out on the couch in my kimono, a bottle of Nikka Super Rare Old in front of me, and rewatched all my favorite samurai movies. Sometimes, I would fall asleep during a movie, and day would shake off night. With the nights growing warm, I was sticky from sweating and kept a wet hand towel on the floor to cool myself. The boy would come and go as he wished. He had learned the way to school and walked there on his own without complaint, even though it took forty-five minutes. I ordered pizzas, one without cheese for the boy, on our first night alone. On our second night I forgot about him. He made himself rice with soy sauce and oil. On another night when he ate alone, I found him at the dinner table, hunched over a pile of paper. At first, I thought it was Trina, poring over one of her grad students' dissertations. As it was, the boy had found my manuscript in progress.

He shook his head. "Every detail is here. Every thought. How did you know?"

"I retraced some memories, invented other parts. But I got stuck. How do you think it ends?" I asked the boy. "I'm imagining something violent."

The boy stepped away from the table. He went into the backyard and I could see the doors to my dojo slide open as he practiced with his shinai.

He'd left a bowl of rice for me, with a fried egg and green onions on top. I checked the sink. He had washed the dishes.

I kept watching samurai classics. Even though, for decades, I had cited this genre as an influence, in reality I'd seen the older films only once or twice. Entire scenes and subplots felt new to me. In screening these movies again, I realized how far off my first impressions had been. I had built *Iggy Samurai* around a story of an apprentice and a master, something I thought I'd picked up from these films. Only after these viewings did I see how few samurai actually trained with sensei. Most on-screen samurai appeared fully formed. Either they were beholden and devoted to their daimyo or they were masterless ronin. They fought for them, avenged their deaths, committed seppuku at their behest. I had taken the character of Coyote Sensei from my own karate training, from juvenile samurai-adjacent movies like *Star Wars* and *The Karate Kid*. I was surprised a comic book nerd hadn't emerged from a thicket to "well, actually . . ." me. In my life, I'd always modeled myself after the itinerant ronin, fierce and self-sufficient—literally, the quintessential freelancer—that I'd seen in these films. But there was a part of me, the kid in me, who yearned to be both the sensei and the pupil.

The boy kept training by himself after school. One day, I stood by the sliding screen door and watched the boy in my dojo swing his shinai opposite my practice dummy. I stepped outside. A run of summery weather had come and left, and now the sky was overcast. The garden itself was the work of a land-scaper who was a fan of my comic books. I'd hired him to clear space for my dojo. His enthusiasm about my oeuvre and his offer to perform labor at little cost had resulted in something that looked like a movie backdrop. I stumbled over the footbridge and nearly fell into the koi pond as I approached the dojo and the decision that loomed.

The boy was sweating as he worked a series of blows along the dummy's neck. He stopped only when he saw me unlocking my katana from the glass display case. He was panting as I handed him the blade. It shone like moon-light reflected in water.

"I've been studying your movements," I told him, "and I think you're ready to use this."

"What the hell?" he said. "I need more practice."

I took the blade back from him and strode outside. Behind the dojo there was a separate shed structure where I kept gardening equipment. That was also where I stored my wooden stands and stalks of bamboo.

The boy stood on the deck outside the dojo doors and watched me place one of those stands, a plywood pedestal, in a clearing by the rock garden.

"You've been drinking," the boy said. "Maybe you shouldn't be handling a sword while you're wasted?"

I didn't heed his caution and set the piece of bamboo on the stand. I stead-ied myself on the grass, with most of my weight on my back foot, and held the blade above my head in the hidari jodan stance, with the hilt of the blade against my forehead. I brought down the blade. The bamboo was halved and fell to the ground. *Yes!* Trina had been horrified when I'd suggested doing this at a party. It would have been so cool. I looked at the sword now. The blade was like a high beam through the fog I had lost myself in. I was awake. I could feel the sweat drying on my skin.

"A piece of bamboo offers the same resistance as a human bone," I said to the boy, waving him to come down. He stepped off the platform reluctantly. "The trick is to keep your right and left arms balanced. The cut should be clean, angled. You know samurai were executioners, right? They would behead people who committed seppuku through ritual disembowelment. The samurai finished them off. One slice. It was an act of mercy."

I placed another piece of bamboo on the stand. I handed the boy the sword, which I'd purchased from a collector in Indiana. He held the sword in front of him in the seigan no kamae stance. He closed his eyes and took a deep breath. Raising the sword behind his shoulder. Letting out a yelp.

The top half of the bamboo hopped off its bottom, as though the blade were a piece of jumping rope.

"Pretty good," I said.

The boy smiled, and I squeezed his shoulder. It was the first time I had touched him, outside of combat, since he had moved in. My hand tingled. I set up three other stands and placed them so that they surrounded the boy.

"Were you lucky?" I said to him. "The true test of a samurai in combat is to strike accurately in quick succession."

I took back the sword to demonstrate. A few years before, to brush up on my skills, I'd hired an instructor in iaido, a solo sword-based martial art that involved withdrawing a blade from seiza and striking. He was from Kyoto and washed dishes at a sushi restaurant in town. I paid him in cash, but he felt more comfortable when I brought him cases of beer. Thanks to him, my movements were slick. I closed my eyes and started swinging.

At that moment, I saw the Samurai once more. Like in a training montage in a movie. He's practicing with his katana, the one from the pawnshop, in his little apartment, preparing himself for battle. He senses something bad is happening. I see Lorna in tears as the Samurai ends things with her, taking home an empty cake pan as she leaves his apartment.

When I opened my eyes, three of the four pieces of bamboo were sliced cleanly.

I handed the katana back to him. The boy raised the sword. He hit the first piece of bamboo cleanly again, pivoted, nicked the second, whiffed the third, and then, out of breath, hit the stand.

He cast his eyes at the ground and heaved a sigh. "Your first try," I told him. "Not bad."

I returned to the storage shed for more pieces of bamboo. Thankfully, I had lots. He would soon be ready. Ready enough. Even if he had been rushed, he'd do the job.

CHAPTER TWENTY-FOUR

The next few days alone with his father, as his old man watched samurai movies and drank himself into a sweaty stupor, Benny steered clear of him. At first, he burned with betrayal that his father had left him with his old sensei—who was obviously a pedo. Then he tried to explain away the similarities between the old man and Constantine. But he knew. Whatever reality had brought him three decades into the future was responsible for those qualities that Constantine and his father's sensei shared.

And then he read his father's manuscript in progress, the one about him, about Constantine. No wonder he couldn't go back to Chinatown. In a previous life, he had acted according to the narrative dictates of this man he thought to be his father. But in this world, his alter ego no longer controlled him. After all, here, the man he called his father out of habit could barely control his own bodily functions. The rules of this world, its time and place, were in flux. They moved according to patterns, like the honeycombs that Avril drew on her arms or the apple trees they saw on the highway, except they didn't replicate so much as they echoed and mutated in succession. Perhaps if he anticipated these patterns, he could have some influence on them.

The night he came to this conclusion, another premise took root. He acted on it only later, when the lights went out in the house and he could hear his father's snoring. Benny stepped into the kitchen. He picked up the cordless phone that hung on the wall. He dialed a number he knew from memory—Constantine kept a scrap of paper with it by the phone—but had never called before. He heard a familiar voice.

"Constantine?"

"Speaking," Constantine said, after a pause. "Is this Benny?"

"Yep."

"Hi, Benny."

There was another pause. "Um, my nose is healing. It's fine," Benny said. "Did you go to jail?"

"Only for a day," his friend said.

Benny told him about his new family, the new school. He skipped the time jump—had Constantine crossed the decades as well? He wanted to apologize for his reaction to Constantine's confession about being a samurai, his angry disbelief. Given his current whereabouts, he knew himself to have been closed-minded. But he couldn't muster the words. As their conversation proceeded, he felt his willingness to form sentences fail. It didn't work to interact with Constantine through small talk. It was like speaking on the phone with the family dog.

"I guess I should go to sleep," Benny told him.

"My daimyo says you're in trouble." Constantine had seemingly snapped awake.

"Who?"

"Give me your address."

He paused, uncertain. "I don't think you can find me."

"Mickey will help me. He'll drive me to you."

Where would Constantine take him? "I'm very far away."

"I will leave soon. Mickey and I have Friday off, three days from now. Mickey will drive."

That's when the kitchen lights flicked on.

Hanging up the phone, Benny turned to see his father looking in the refrigerator, staring into it. From across the kitchen he could smell the booze wafting from his father's body. He watched his father dig out his leftover fried rice from the back of a shelf. His father seemed oblivious to his presence.

"Who were you talking to?" he asked, removing a spoon from the drawer. He sat on a stool and cracked open a beer already set on the counter.

"Just a friend from Chinatown," Benny said.

His wolf eyes sharpened. "You have no friends."

Benny flinched. His father was mean because he was drunk. But there was a calculation in his cruel remark, a desire to hide his concern in a welter of insults, that reminded Benny of Poh-Poh. In those moments, he knew they were related. "I know Avril from Chinatown," Benny finally replied.

His father looked at him in disbelief. "You didn't know anyone named Avril." Before Benny could correct him, his father pounced on his evasion.

"Are you calling your old roommate?"

"No," Benny lied. "You have no clue what I've done or thought since I've arrived at your house."

His father tipped back his can of beer. "You better not be calling that guy," he said, wiping his mouth with his wrist. "Whether he means it or not, he's dangerous. Look what he did to your nose. He would have hurt you more if you weren't safe with me."

His father took a bite of his fried rice, then another, and finally pushed it away from himself. It had been sitting in the fridge for weeks. He took a sip of his beer. "I'm going to cook something, maybe for tomorrow. What do you crave eating the most?"

"My poh-poh's jook," Benny told him. "The kind she'd make from leftover rice."

"You'd have to drive all the way back to Chinatown for jook, and it wouldn't even taste the same as hers—you can't get home cooking at a restaurant," his father said. "Your poh-poh was a tough woman. Easier to respect than to love. Not like your mom. You miss them in different ways, don't you?"

Benny couldn't disagree with his father's assessments. The way his father claimed ownership of his thoughts never sat well with him, even now that he knew how, and knew his father was using this knowledge to regain control of their relationship. Benny watched his father drink his beer. His father's face grew as red as the envelopes Poh-Poh used to fold twenty-dollar bills into for the Lunar New Year. Benny took pity on him.

"Why don't you talk to your wife?" Benny asked him. "Is it my fault?"

His father blinked at him. "Yes."

"You're not really my father, are you?"

"In some ways, you're mine," his father, or at least this man he still called by that name, told him. "Anyhow, what's the difference?"

"Can you take me back to Chinatown?" Benny asked. "To my time?"

His father shook his head. "I've closed that door. Or maybe I am that door."

They both went to bed. Lying in his cot, Benny realized he had nowhere to go. He'd already taken the bus to Chinatown and found no one. So far, his only place of refuge had been school. And that was a mixed bag. While Benny wasn't openly ostracized, he had not made any new friends—unless he counted Avril.

After he'd spotted her with Carter, she'd approached him outside their classroom on Monday morning and said, "Don't tell anyone that you saw us."

"How old is he?" Benny asked her. His stylish, poised friend now seemed vulnerable in his eyes. While Avril thought she'd come to this world to find freedom, Benny again perceived this timeline as cruelly repetitive. In Carter's relationship with Avril, a thirteen-year-old living alone, he saw his father and his old sensei. Perhaps he also saw himself with Constantine.

"Older," she said, reflexively touching the necklace with their intertwined first initials. "But we just click. He's going away for the summer, so we just need to spend every spare second together. I've got no one here."

"*You've got me*," he pleaded, taking her hands. "Have you called your sister?"

She kept smiling, but her eyes grew angry, and she pulled herself away. As a group of friends called to her, she turned her back on him. He gave his end-of-year presentation that morning on *Iggy Samurai*, and it was commended as well researched and detailed. His teacher, Gerald, and classmates admired his illustration of a samurai warrior in full battle armor that he had spent an entire night drawing on a poster board. Afterward, the class posed questions that seemed to be about what they'd wanted to see in the project. They wanted to know about the author's portrayal of inequities in the Japanese feudal system or the way the Bushido code contributed to Japanese militarism and colonialism. They asked whether the author's own non-Japanese ancestry made this work culturally appropriative. Benny sputtered through his answers before Gerald cut the question period short and asked for a round of applause.

That afternoon, Benny still ate lunch with Avril's group, but at the far end of the table, between two students who politely concealed their displeasure to be sitting with him. He spent the afternoon at the library reading the graphic novels of Frank Miller, inspired by an edition of Miller's work *Ronin* he'd used for his project. When he returned to retrieve his books from the classroom, Gerald asked if he could set up an appointment with his father.

"He's not feeling well," Benny told him, parroting the lie he'd told to Mrs. Renzullo, a lifetime before, about Poh-Poh. "Maybe you could write a note for me to take home."

"A conversation might be better," Gerald said, asking him to sit.

He pulled a chair over to Benny and explained that the school normally had a rigorous interview-based admissions process. They had skipped those steps at the discretion of the school's principal, the one who was a friend of Benny's stepmother's. It had been irregular.

"Not everyone is suited to independent learning," Gerald explained, hands, as always, in the front pockets of his jeans. "Others prefer a more hierarchical, structured educational environment—with less advanced internet literacy. I mean, how do you think our classroom suits you?"

Benny expressed how much he enjoyed the freedom to choose his own course of study with an intensity derived from his desire not to change schools. In his heart, he wanted a teacher he could address as "Mister" or "Missus," school days portioned off by subject, and worksheets and quizzes. He felt like a failure for not taking to this school's format. Finally, he agreed with Gerald to check in when the term ended and "reassess for the fall."

He doubled his normally lazy pace up the hill to the house and found his father wearing the gray light of his television like an undershirt on his bare chest. Benny made dinner for himself and then headed to his father's backyard dojo. He needed to hit someone. The training dummy would do, and he threw his calloused fists and feet at it. He noticed his father watching him from the house, and then the screen door opening. It annoyed Benny to see his father enter, but he knew that if his father, who had put on a kimono, wanted to spar, he would be too drunk to put up much of a defense. Benny could strike him in the face fairly easily, break his nose, knock out his teeth.

Benny's father alarmed him by unlocking the glass case that held his katana. The moment he'd unsheathed it, a few weeks back, had been the moment Benny fell in love with it. Now he handed it over to Benny. It felt lighter than the wooden blade Benny had been practicing with, and when his father set up the pieces of bamboo in the yard, he tightened his grip around its tsuka, worried the sword would fly out of his hand.

Benny imagined his father's head when he sliced that piece of bamboo perfectly. And both the act and his implicit intention seemed to please his father. There was a high five and a fist bump. For the first time in Benny's memory, his father seemed to be proud of him. He asked Benny if he was hungry and suggested going out for dinner.

Benny's father showered and shaved and slipped out of his kimono into a button-up shirt and chinos. Benny accepted his invitation, in spite of his obvious buzz, only so they could drive. He missed being in the car, if not every part of the drive. He was sad it was only a few minutes on the highway to a chain restaurant. The two of them got country-fried steaks with gravy and mashed potatoes. His father encouraged him to get the larger steak, and when it arrived it was the size of James Clavell's *Shōgun*. Benny worked through it but gave up with the meal halfway finished.

"I finally found something you couldn't finish," his father said. "You even finished Trina's goulash."

"It was too big," Benny said. "At least it wasn't rice. Poh-Poh always said that I needed to clean my rice bowl to have a wife with a clear complexion," Benny told him. "If I left any rice uneaten, she'd be pockmarked like the bowl."

"Everyone's poh-poh says that."

"Is that why you married someone with such smooth skin?" Benny asked. His father rolled his eyes. He knew about Benny's crush.

The glass of wine at the table had been recently refilled. He pushed it toward Benny and asked if he wanted a sip. Benny held the glass, and the first taste of it was sour and astringent. Benny gagged. When his father laughed, Benny took a longer pull. That's when Benny sense the warmth rush through him. The tension he'd felt since arriving in his father's house eased momentarily. When his father called over for the bill, the glass was empty.

Leaving the restaurant, Benny's father asked if Benny wanted to go for a drive, and he agreed. Benny felt confident that dinner had blotted out the booze still coursing through his father's body. Mostly, Benny, who felt buzzed from his own glass of wine, didn't care. He loved being in a car. His father took the on-ramp from the restaurant onto the highway. When he got to a stretch of straight road, he floored the accelerator pedal. Benny was embarrassed to let out a squeal. Only a couple of hours earlier, Benny had wanted to split this man's head in two with a samurai sword.

Benny's father took the car off an exit Benny was not familiar with. His father drove past strip malls and gas stations until he got to the parking lot of an empty supermarket with a FOR LEASE sign in the front window.

"Get out of the car," he told Benny, after unbuckling his seat belt. He opened the door. By the time Benny was out, his father had tossed the keys at him. Benny climbed into the driver's seat.

"Since you've already handled a lethal weapon," Benny's father said to him, with a gassy hiccup, "we may as well see how you drive."

The leather steering wheel was warm and sweaty. Benny needed to move the seat up, but not as far as he had feared. His father wasn't that tall. Then he shifted the automatic transmission on the screen from park to drive. Instructed to tap the accelerator, Benny touched it harder than he thought he had, and the car lurched forward. His stomach flipped as the car darted. He forgot to lift his foot from the accelerator so it would stop. His father screamed at him to lift his foot.

Benny drove from one end of the lot to the other, then practiced his turning. Eventually, he went faster. As he grew more confident, his father taught him to do a doughnut.

How much time passed from when Benny entered that empty parking lot to when his father sat behind the wheel again? It felt like minutes, but the dashboard clock told him it had been over an hour. The clouds had darkened, and as the two of them returned home on the highway, rain fell heavy and straight.

"When can I drive again?" Benny asked. "That was amazing."

"Tomorrow night," Benny's father promised.

Benny could no longer see this man as his father, not really. And yet he could not accept him as an alter ego, even though they resembled each other in appearance and temperament to such a degree that it antagonized them both. In that moment, however, they were linked by the wine buzzing through their bloodstream and the exhilaration they felt to be racing down the road. The car sped up the side of the hill with a sharp turn, accelerating quicker than normal. Benny made sure he didn't yelp this time the way he always did when his father veered hard. Not even when a pickup truck came wide in the opposite direction.

CHAPTER TWENTY-FIVE

The Tesla's Autopilot chirped a warning half a second before I noticed the truck barreling toward us. "Dad!" I heard the boy say, even though he knew better. The pickup was red with a Chevy logo on its grille. Behind the wheel was a young man, blond-haired, with a beard and sunglasses on despite the night. He had the casual attitude of a local, taking the turn with one hand on the steering and the other hand out the window. Going a little fast because, sharp as that bend felt, no one had ever been hurt on that road. There had been no accidents on the hill.

The truck was coming wide. I swerved into the opposite lane and the oncoming vehicle's passenger side connected with the rear passenger side of our car. My foot dug into the brake. Inflating airbags filled our front seats. Our car fishtailed into the hillside. The force of the collision pushed my body against my door and I felt the seat belt hold tight and cut into my ribs. My neck snapped to the left.

The stereo was still playing sports radio. We hadn't been listening to it, but I had lowered the volume instead of turning it off altogether. As a result, broadcasters chirping about free-agent signings provided the soundtrack to this carnage. The windshield wipers swished almost in time with the splatter of the rain outside. The air smelled like wet dust and burnt rubber. I turned to see the boy. His face was to one side of the airbag, as though it were a giant breast. He was grimacing stoically. I asked if he was okay. He nodded. Was he hurt?

"No," he said. "I don't think so."

I reached over and unbuckled his seat belt. I could open my door far enough that I could squeeze myself out between the car and the rocky hillside. As I climbed over the hood of the car, my left knee and shoulder felt as though they had been tenderized with a ball-peen hammer. Perhaps the adrenaline was already wearing off. I opened the door for the boy, who staggered out, looking dazed but otherwise unscathed.

Another car inched down the hill toward our wreck. The driver stepped out and called the police. We followed him as he crossed the road until we saw the flattened guardrail. The red truck had rolled down the hill toward the creek. Its wheels still spun in the air.

I called for a tow truck as a police car and ambulance arrived at the scene shortly thereafter. The police officer wanted to know why I was on the phone. Then he wrote down my account of the accident. Afterward, he asked a few follow-up questions. One of them was whether I had been drinking. I shook my head. "No, sir." So what if I had? I sure didn't feel drunk then. He asked me to take a voluntary Breathalyzer test. Having gone through some similar situations, I knew I had the right to decline. He said I'd pass if I hadn't been drinking. I belched my final "No." He might have pressed me, even threatened me with an arrest, but he was distracted by a call from the station. Then a paramedic suggested we come with him to the hospital for an examination, but I waved him off. We were getting soaked in the rain. The boy stood next to me without complaint, steadily collecting rain. Like me, he'd had practice in tuning out during difficult moments. After the tow truck arrived, I used my phone to order a ride-hailing service back home.

The shower in the master bedroom still hadn't been fixed. I let the boy wash and change first, and then I checked in with him.

"Any bruising?" I asked him. "Any headaches or dizziness?"

The boy was pulling his pajama shirt onto his body. "I'm good. I think I should go to sleep."

"I probably shouldn't have been drinking tonight. I'm sorry to have scared you."

"That wasn't scary, maybe a little loud." He flashed his teeth, his eyes betraying him. "I think I'm ready for bed."

"Yes, I have a big day for us."

"You do? Like what?"

"It's a surprise."

"I should get some rest, then."

"Yes, you need to be well rested." I clicked off the ceiling light for him and turned to the shower.

As the hot water finally hit me, I felt the impact of the crash on my body. I was tired but could not fathom sleeping.

Afterward, I had no attention span for a movie, nor could I read, so I played Texas Hold'em on my phone. But even that was too much. What stayed in my mind was the sight of the red truck that had plunged down the hillside, its wheels spinning in the air. And how it could have been us, if not that night, then many other nights before. And how I wished it had been us in the wreckage. Perhaps we'd have survived. Maybe not.

I tried to sleep on my right side, the one that didn't hurt. Normally I slept facing out from the bed, but now I was staring toward Trina's empty half. She had texted me a couple of times before the accident that she knew nothing about. *How are you?* texts. Not seeing a point to replying, I'd left them unanswered. Rereading those messages, I was heartened to see that Trina had created an escape hatch for me. In her questions, in her reflections on recent events, she allowed me the space that I only needed to fill in for my life to be restored. I began drafting my reply as the picture of a typical weekend morning formed in my mind. Trina singing along to Jonathan Richman as she prepared smoothies. The smell of Adele's hair when she climbed into my lap at the breakfast table. The tension lifted from my battered shoulders as I thought about stepping back from my plans.

I couldn't fit the boy in my tableau, but we could coexist. We could orbit each other's lives, occasionally pushing against each other but mostly keeping apart. In a handful of years, he would be an adult, old enough to continue his life without me.

Having reversed course, I was too giddy to sleep. Things would be different, starting now. I didn't want to ruin it by drinking that night. I lay in bed feeling the aches from the car crash. After a couple of hours passed, I thought a little wouldn't hurt. Leaving my bedroom, I could see the kitchen light. And then I heard the boy's voice. He was on our landline.

"I feel okay," he said.

"It's just the two of us in the house," he said.

"You need to hurry," he said. "Friday might be too late."

"I wanted someone to talk to," he said.

"His sword is pretty amazing. I've got to admit that," he said. "What kind of designs are engraved on yours?"

"Driving is so cool. Will you teach me to drive on the highway?" he said.

"Okay, this is our address," he said. "Hurry. I think it might happen tomorrow."

"Thanks for listening," he said.

"I know something bad is going to happen," he said. "Please come as soon as possible."

Overhearing this conversation, I felt the cognitive whiplash of the boy's betrayal while knowing that he was merely enabling the scheme I had already set in motion as the Samurai's daimyo. The adrenaline from earlier in the evening reboiled. My last-second efforts to bring Trina and Adele back to the house now felt like a distraction. I had to refocus on my plan for inner peace. I had little time to fulfill it. The last day had been squandered on our joyride—a final, positive memory I wanted to leave with the boy. Served me right for being so sentimental. I retreated to my room and lay on my unbruised side. On my phone's Notes app, I composed some thoughts to write out tomorrow in longhand. I placed a pillow underneath my sore ribs, and that allowed me to sleep.

The next morning, I got up early, before the boy was awake, to make breakfast. I found a recipe online for jook, one with pork, peanuts, and green onions, that I assembled in the pressure cooker. It wasn't the same as his poh-poh's, not enough bones—and no century egg—but when he woke up, he smiled at the bowl I put in front of him. We both needed this meal together. He finished it quickly, then asked for another serving.

We spent the morning practicing with the katana. I wanted him to strike down with more force and accuracy. Afterward, we ate lunch together. I let him watch television while I prepared my manuscript, accompanied by a letter of apology to Trina, and composed my jisei, or farewell poem, on stationery.

A truck spins its wheels
At the bottom of the wet hillside

I struggle to hear a voice, or a silence, over the beating of windshield wipers.

I made copies of the poem on my printer and put them in envelopes addressed to C. and Carter's mom, Sheryl, whose address I found online.

I soaked in the tub and then changed into my kimono. I dug out the sake bottle and serving set from the liquor cabinet. I found the boy watching *Lone Wolf and Cub* and told him to follow me into the dojo.

"What are we doing?" he asked me.

"You'll find out," I told him.

"What if I say no?" he asked me.

"It's nothing bad," I lied. "I promise you."

As we hesitated outside my training facility, Elsa and Bambi edged from the woods into the yard. They stopped their foraging to look at us. The baby deer minced toward the boy, almost hopping playfully. "You need to go," the boy said, as though he were pleading with him to save himself. Finally, the mama deer made a croaking noise and Bambi skittered back up the hill.

I slid the door open. The boy followed me inside. He stood by the wall as I set up the low table in the middle of the room. I unlocked the tanto from the case and placed it on the table next to the sake set and the jisei. I poured out two glasses and told the boy to drink his down, all at once. "This is what men do," I said. His face wrinkled as the rice wine warmed his body. And yet I knew how quickly he was developing a taste for it, how a stiff drink rearranges time into an expanse of possibility. Lowering to the floor, I took a drink myself.

"Grab the sword," I instructed him.

The boy snapped to attention. I made sure he held the katana correctly, his hands at forty-five-degree angles and spaced on the tsuka. The blade was a spear of moonlight. I nodded appreciatively at him and opened my kimono. Here we go. Once I began to disembowel myself, his blow should be the one that did me in. He already knew this from his school project. I'd made sure he read up on it. It should leave my head hanging from my body by a flap of skin, although that combination of precision and strength might be too much to ask from a twelve-year-old.

"Go on," I told the boy, "pick my brain."

I gripped the tanto with both hands and pointed the blade toward my belly. Focusing on the deep thrust I would need to make, the horizontal slash that would follow, I heard the thud of the katana on the floor. As I had feared. As I had dreaded with disgust. And as I had envisioned when I saw this day come together.

The boy was shaking his head. "He's almost here," he said. "Just wait for him."

"Who are you talking about?" I asked coyly.

"You know who," he spat back. "He's coming. Why do you need me here?"

"He won't come without you," I said. His face remained defiant. "You need to do this. It's the only way you'll be able to return home."

Did that entice him enough? His eyes glinted hopefully. But when I picked up the katana to hand to the boy, he still edged away. Finally, I rose. With both hands on the tsuka, I raised the blade so it ran parallel to my forehead. As he backed away, he fell, and I inched toward him.

"It's either you or me," I told him.

"Dad!"

He was trolling me. "Shut up!"

This change of plans had been the plan all along.

Although I should have known better, I heard the gate door open and half thought it was Trina. Adele might be nearby. In case it was them, I lurched toward the boy. I would need to end this quickly. But of course it wasn't Trina and Adele. When I heard the male voice that called for the boy, all hope of another fate dropped away. I saw the boy's sensei carrying his own katana.

The Samurai looked the way I'd imagined him to look, and yet it still took my breath away. Here was young C., with the same blue eyes and bulk, but with a guilelessness in the way he carried himself. He was wearing a kamishimo, the whole warrior getup. Even though he had no armor, the front of his scalp was shaved to accept a helmet. The hair on the back of his head, however, was not long enough to be tied in a knot.

The Samurai, the idealized version of my abuser, the boy's protector, stood on the footbridge. He held his sword in front of him at waist level, in seigan no kamae, and I followed his stance so that we were tsukikage, "moon shadows," mirroring one another. As he stepped over the footbridge, he moved to the ichi no kamae stance, raising his sword out in front. I lowered my sword below my waist to gedan no kamae. I always loved the tension that preceded the sound of screams and blades clashing, and I had watched enough samurai movies recently that I scored the soundtrack in my head with solitary martial drumming. If only I could storyboard this.

He stepped toward me as he swung down, slashing from left to right, and I met him outside with my own blade. When he grunted, I could smell his sour breath. He was quiet, probably from all the training in his one-room apartment. At that moment, I saw the storyline for a new *Iggy Samurai* in my eyes. Is that what happens in the moments before your own death, not a flashing back of your own life, but the sudden unspooling of creative possibility?

Our swords were crossed in the air, and his blue eyes bulged with exertion. C. wore contact lenses to show them off, and as a rule, I never trusted anyone with blue eyes, avoiding potential creative partners and roommates for that irrational reason. As we pushed into each other, our swords drew closer until they met at their collars. The drumming kept playing in my head. We struggled to get a blade to each other's neck, but there was no space. With guttural screams, we pushed back and returned to a waki-gamae, our swords behind us at waist level.

The Samurai was briefly distracted as he looked around, trying to locate the boy in the gym. I searched for an opening and decided to strike his torso with a straight cut. My reach was shorter than his, and he shuffled back easily to avoid me. I was disappointed but not afraid. My goal wasn't to win the duel, but only to extend our choreography. To prove myself using a live blade for the first time. And to savor my last moments. He lowered his sword back to seigan no kamae and I reversed.

When the boy slid the screen door and rushed out, his sensei told him to run behind him and hide in the house. Those blue eyes tracked him watchfully. I remembered how C. seemed ancient to me when I was twelve, with timeless knowledge and an authority that even exceeded my grandmother's, but he was not even thirty years old when we first met.

"Always the protector," I said to him. "*Right.*"

"Demon, I'm here for the boy," the Samurai said, as though he didn't know me. He didn't have C.'s silver tongue, his ability to dissemble his horrific acts, to shame me into keeping his secrets. He spoke as though he were reading subtitles aloud—a failure of my own imagination. "If you put down your katana now, I won't kill you."

"*Demon?* What makes you think that?" I screamed derisively. "I'm your *daimyo*. Don't you recognize my voice? Drop your katana. I command you."

I saw his eyes pop. The voice that he heard in his head matched mine. His blade lowered in doubt. I was worried he'd lay down his katana. Then what would I do? I'd outthought myself.

When I raised my katana, his blade rose in parallel. His original directives from me took precedence. All this time, I thought I'd created him to guard the boy from C. But really, I'd invented the Samurai for this moment, to protect the boy from me. We circled the patch of lawn until I grew impatient and slashed at him from above my head. After all this buildup, I suddenly wanted it to be over. He took two long steps back, and then a short one, so that he blocked me with the blade he held horizontally. I was fully extended, vulnerable. He withdrew his sword and jabbed at me. I tried to step aside but the sword pierced my soft torso.

The sight of my own blood on my kimono sent me into a sort of very still shock. *Holy shit, it's happening.* I fell to my knees. I saw the boy's face from behind my dojo's screen door and tried to mouth a goodbye. Then I turned to the Samurai and looked up, for the final time, at his blue eyes. They were strangely round and devoid of malice. Eyes pregnant with pity. I was at his mercy, once again.

POSTSCRIPT

For the rest of June, after the police arrive, Benny returns to live with the Douglases, whom he stayed with for two days before being sent to his father. Dressed in a business suit with shoulder pads, Macy drives Benny there in the middle of the night. Throughout their drive, he waits again for her to say something about the change in time, but her small talk revolves around her upcoming marriage to Todd, who's been promoted to manager of his adult-video store.

The Douglases have an entire house with a porch swing and couches and family photos. In their bathrobes, they greet him kindly without remembering that Benny's stayed there before. They give Benny another toothbrush and a towel, and show him to a new bunk.

He tries not to think much about his father, Yu, or the would-be samurai, Constantine. It's easier to block out the backyard scene in his head than the question of whether it happened yesterday or is something that will occur in his future. He picks over the puzzle to the point of exhaustion. When he wakes up, he feels lighter.

In the morning, Benny meets the new set of boys living in the house. They're told to introduce themselves at the two picnic tables in the dining room, where cornflakes and toasted Wonder Bread are served. The boys range in age from eleven to fourteen. They're all sorts of skin tones and ethnicities. Some haven't hit puberty, while others look like full-grown men with ugly mustaches. But they all seem to have the same kind of face. U-shaped but hungry. Eyes that don't reflect but slice through you.

It's at breakfast that he recognizes the laminated signs everywhere. KNIVES MUST NOT LEAVE THE KITCHEN/DINING AREA, they read. TRASH BAG LINERS MUST BE REPLACED AFTER TRASH IS TAKEN OUT. On a wall-mounted chalkboard, he sees his name already added to a chore chart.

Mrs. Douglas has skin the color of the baked turkey meat that she'll later serve at lunch, and she wears a sweatshirt with *He Loved Me First* written in cursive. In the basement is a makeshift classroom with desks and a shelf of textbooks, where class starts after breakfast. She explains, again, that since none of the kids stay very long, they're expected to study on their own until lunchtime.

During the class period, as the other boys draw the logos of death metal bands onto their arms, he finds the math and social studies textbooks and tries to catch up on what he's missed. Mrs. Douglas sits at a desk in the front, reading a copy of *People* magazine. The cover, featuring actor Robin Givens and her husband, boxer Mike Tyson, is the first sign that he's returned to his original timeline.

At lunch, baby carrots and glasses of milk are served alongside turkey sandwiches. In the afternoon, it's "outside time." They're allowed to either play in the park down the street or help Mr. Douglas run errands. The other boys pick basketballs and baseball gloves from a bin in the garage to bring to the park. Benny volunteers to go with Mr. Douglas. They take his van onto the highway and over a bridge, and then they're in an area with strip malls. Mr. Douglas listens to a talk radio show until the topic changes to AIDS education for high school students. "Not appropriate," he announces, turning off his radio.

They arrive at an aircraft hangar, except that people are pushing gigantic shopping carts. Mr. Douglas smiles for the first time. "Have you never been to a Costco?"

Mr. Douglas takes out his own large shopping cart and starts filling it with bulk-size items from a list. Cereal, hot dogs and hamburgers, pasta, spaghetti sauce, frozen peas, and carrots. Once again, they get new packages of underwear and plain T-shirts, and a pair of jeans for Benny. Mr. Douglas catches Benny eyeing a box of Reese's Peanut Butter Cups and laughs. "Tempting, but we stick to the list or I answer to a higher power—Mrs. Douglas."

On the ride home, Benny turns to look at the food in the back of the van. He will enjoy his latest stint here. He likes being regularly fed and his freedom to get books and wander off in the afternoon. The other boys look mean and unfriendly, but they haven't said or done anything unkind, and there's a severity in the way Mr. Douglas hikes up his belt and Mrs. Douglas whacks a cleaver to dice an onion that suggests it won't happen. He takes comfort in how temporary this situation looks, in the way boys are shuffled through this house. Even if things get bad, he won't be here for long.

When July rolls around, the boys no longer need to attend class in the basement. Mr. Douglas takes Benny and two of the other boys to a soccer camp, which Benny enjoys despite his dearth of ability. At the end of the month, Macy picks him up to reunite him with Steph. It's taken his aunt until then to find steady work and an apartment, Macy explains. "She's really stepped up," Macy says. "I'm impressed." Benny already knows everything she's told him because he talked to Steph on the phone a couple of weeks earlier. "You look taller," Macy suggests. "Have you put on some weight?" Mr. and Mrs. Douglas hug him goodbye with more feeling than he expected. They must do the same with all the other boys.

Slowly, as they enter the city limits, he begins to recognize businesses and landmarks. And then everything becomes as familiar as home. The awnings of greengrocers and their boxes of bok choy and dou miao. The amber hue of the barbecued pigs in the butcher shops. The old men with wispy beards smoking cigarettes at the windows of their single-room-occupancy hotels. The signs for the benevolent associations above buildings with recessed balconies. The smell of ginger and sesame oil. The yowls and gongs of Cantonese opera.

"Can you tell me how we went forward in time?" Benny finally blurts out in the car. Up to this point, he was worried that he'd upset Macy and that she'd keep him with the Douglases forever.

Macy wrinkles her forehead. "What are you talking about?" she asks in Cantonese, breaking into nervous laughter. "You've got a bright future, laa."

Benny mentions the calendar year when he stayed with his father. He mentions smartphones and electric cars. "You can't tell me you didn't see that," he says. "Please tell me the truth."

Macy seems to ignore his plea. But then at a stoplight, she turns to him. "When Chinatown first started, it was a ghetto for railway workers. Lonely bachelor men, heavy in debt and far from home. They had it bad, but not as bad as the women, gwaa. There were only a few women and most of them were mistreated. They came from poor families who sold them off to be slaves or prostitutes." The traffic light changes and Macy continues her story while driving. "Imagine how different that time was from now, laa. If you had the chance to change time frames, what would you do? Maybe if you were a young woman from that time you'd be thrilled to find yourself, for some reason, able to leave that world and enter another world that was more enlightened. If you did, don't you think you'd put yourself in a position to help other people?"

Benny understands Macy's implication. "Maybe that person could be a social worker, laa, like you?" he asks.

Macy smiles. "Indeed, a very good suggestion," she says. "And if that's the case, you might ask how or why things came to be. But you would not let it bother you. No one would believe you anyway."

Benny nods. This will be the only explanation for his recent experiences that he will ever receive.

Steph waits for them on the street. His aunt has found a place just outside Chinatown, Macy explains, because Steph wants him to be somewhere familiar. Benny thinks he'll be chill when he sees her. They've talked on the phone regularly, but they both lose it at the sight of each other. "You've grown so much," Steph insists, and it's true—he's almost as tall as she is. "I'm so sorry I wasn't there for you." She looks the same at first glance. It's only in the days after, as they settle into their life together, that he sees the weariness in her eyes.

He arrives on a Saturday night. The basement apartment that Steph signed a lease on a week earlier is two blocks from Poh-Poh's apartment. He has his own room, but the air mattress there leaks when he tries it, so they both crash on her bed. Steph sleeps in, leaving Benny to eat half a container of yogurt for his breakfast. "You know what we need to do? We should have fun and catch up," she says when she rises after ten in the morning. Steph's idea of fun is to pick flowers from a neighbor's garden and take the bus to the cemetery to bow three times each for Mommy and Gong-Gong. Benny goes along with it, since they missed Tomb Sweeping Day a few months earlier. Steph says that Poh-Poh's cremated remains still need to be picked up. Years earlier, Poh-Poh gave up her own half of the plot so Mommy would have a place to be buried. Now she will have to stay in an urn in Steph's closet until Steph can afford another spot.

They take the bus downtown to spend the rest of the day window-shopping. They sample the new R.E.M. album in a listening booth at the re-cord store. They go to a jeweler's so Steph can try a pair of earrings. "You'd look great with an earring," Steph insists. "Or maybe a nose ring." Benny can only giggle in response.

As the afternoon winds down, Steph leads them back to Chinatown. She takes them to a wonton noodle shop—at a location that might one day sell vegan pizza. She counts the money in her wallet, down to the change in her pocket, and orders in her broken Cantonese a plate of curry beef brisket in green peppers with rice, a bowl of barbecue duck hor fun in soup, a plate of gai lan, and an order of Chinese doughnut. She gets Benny a Coke.

"Somewhere in the Midwest on tour I started craving Mom's cooking—the bowls of soup and plates of stir-fry that I would never finish," she tells him, taking a sip of tea from a plastic cup. "This isn't the same, but it's close enough."

Neither of them speaks until every morsel is consumed. They eat slowly and fastidiously, cleaning each duck bone of meat and gristle, slurping every drop of soup. Benny subsisted for over a month on rice and soy sauce, then hamburgers and sandwiches, and then took care of himself again with that man who wasn't really his dad—the ghost of a future he's determined to change. Then Mrs. Douglas's menu of casseroles and potpies. Only on the other side of it all—after the kind of meal that Poh-Poh would take him to when Mommy was still alive, once they'd gone to church—can he fully taste his deprivation.

When dinner is completed, they return to the basement apartment. His bedroom is empty. He's starting from scratch again. His aunt has taken a job at a medical office across town, near the hospital.

"I always wondered how your mother worked at an office," Steph says. "It's not as bad as I thought it would be, once you get into the rhythm."

He apologizes for being a burden. Without him, she could still be a mu-sician, living on the road. She waves off his apology as though it were a bad smell. She's getting too old to be in a band anyhow. "And you're the only fam-ily I have left," she tells him. "Besides, you'll be an adult in another five years." She makes a gulping sound. "I can wait that long before I have sex again."

Until her next paycheck, they are perilously short on money. He is happy to make do with donated clothes and rice with vegetables for dinner. When he turns thirteen in August and doesn't receive a gift, only a Hostess chocolate cupcake to share between them, he understands. He wishes he could find a job, but he's too young. Classes will start soon anyhow. He's been reenrolled in his old school.

Steph insists on walking during the weekends. They circle the park where the old folks do their qigong and window-shop for a new rice cooker in China-town. Along the way, people recognize them, often ladies whose tottering steps and hand-knit clothing remind him of Poh-Poh. Steph tries to answer their questions in Cantonese, but lets Benny take over once she falters. When they buy groceries, Benny insists on carrying them home, and the handles of the plastic bags cut into his palms. In those moments, he'll think about the cart he used to pull for Poh-Poh. One Sunday they see Shirley on the street. She's holding hands with Roderick Chow, who scowls at him. Shirley pretends not to see him. When he gets home, he finishes the entire box of Oreos that he'd been carefully rationing.

He has nightmares regularly, horror-movie scenarios that he will never share with others. On those bad nights, he winds up in his aunt's bed, even though he's too old for it. When Steph asks him about his dreams, he insists he can't remember them. He declines her attempts to set up a meeting with a therapist.

"What a resilient child, woh!" Macy exclaims in Cantonese during a follow-up visit. Steph smiles nervously.

Benny spends his remaining summer days at the library, reading books about history and philosophy. He's anxious about school—partly the social interaction, but mainly the academic stuff. He's missed a lot of it. So he flips through titles on algebra and English grammar until he grows bored. When he gets home, alone, he is greeted by a pile of mail in the foyer that has come through the slot in the door. Most of it consists of bills and junk mail. Today, for the first time, there's a letter addressed to him.

Hi Benny,

It's me. My old friend Mickey tipped me off to your new address. Mickey knows everything that happens in Chinatown. He's a good friend, and I don't have a lot of those these days.

I'm writing from the psychiatric hospital. I'm not in the same room I used to be but I'm not far. I already know everyone here. I have everything I need. My hakama, a tatami mat for meditation. I guess I'm not allowed to use a wooden sword anymore but I don't miss that. The doctors here have me on a nice set of medications, and I feel better now. Things are a lot clearer. Thanks for vouching for me. I know if your story went another way, things wouldn't be so easy.

I'm writing to see how you are doing. I am glad you are back in Chinatown. You fit in really well there. I get nice visits from my sister, Iulia, and niece, Sarah. She's cute and growing up quick. Iulia and I have nice chats about things that happened in our childhood, especially with our parents, that help to ease some of the bad feelings that overwhelm me.

It gets me thinking about your own relationship with the demon. He was a shape-shifter who pretended to be many things— your father, my daimyo, you—and he needed to be slain. I'm sorry about what happened, and what you had to see. I hope you talk about it with someone. The thing I want to say is that when you don't admit your pain, if you don't call it what it is, it turns into something else. Sometimes that thing it turns into can be good. It can be art or karate. Everyone loves it. Other times it'll be something no one likes. It can be a monster. Something no one can control. Does that make sense? I don't know.

You've been through a lot with me. Some of that was pretty awful. But I also had good times with you. Thanks for that. You don't have to write me back. But if you do I will give you a response. I'm pretty sure the return address is a permanent one.

Okay, pal. Nice talking to you. Hang in there.

Constantine

Benny grabs some scrap paper and a pen and tries to think of something to say. He's not mad at Constantine, not at all. He also feels a little guilty. He likes him too. He doesn't wish him harm. He has so much to tell him but not enough courage or patience to commit it to paper. Maybe he'll write when things settle down.

By this time, Steph has come home. She's bought a block of tofu to serve alongside the mustard greens that she stir-fries with shallots, oyster sauce, and chili oil. Poh-Poh never cooked with spice, so it takes time to get used to it.

They talk about their days. Steph has made a work friend she went for hot dogs with outside their office. She also got hit with her share of the bill for the last repair job on their tour van. Her hill of debt has grown steeper.

Benny has nothing to report, so their meal is finished in silence.

After dinner, he wishes they could just watch TV. But Steph doesn't have a TV. And even if she did, she thinks TV is stupid. So they dance to Blondie and James Brown on her tape deck. It's hot even in this basement suite, and Steph suggests Benny take a shower to cool down before he goes to bed on his patched-up air mattress.

But he's not tired yet. He insists on playing cards first. As Steph shuffles the cards for a game of Big Two, she finds a doodle that he made on the scrap paper he'd intended to use to write his letter to Constantine. She holds it up so she can see it better in the fluorescent ceiling light. She points to his rendition of the comic book lizard. "You drew this yourself? Did you create this character? Holy shit, you could go to art school with this, Benny."

"No way," he says, surprising himself with the sound of his dropped voice. He thinks about how Poh-Poh wanted him to be a lawyer. She always saw him speaking in front of a crowd. What he draws, what he writes, he knows for certain, will only be for himself, like his copy of *Iggy Samurai #1*, which he still keeps, hidden away.

ACKNOWLEDGMENTS

First off, I'll be forever thankful that Loan Le decided to read this book. Loan, your enthusiasm and editorial acuity have been a blessing to me.

Thanks to my agents, Sam Haywood and Carolyn Forde, for picking up this book and seeing its potential. Thanks also to their colleagues at Transatlantic Agency, and Naben Ruthnum for the referral.

Thanks, Liz Byer and Laura Cherkas at Atria/Simon & Schuster.

I moved between two jobs while writing this book. I'm grateful to the School of Creative Writing and Department of Creative Studies at the University of British Columbia, and my colleagues at both institutions, for providing me with rewarding, stimulating employment.

I received funding from the BC Arts Council and the Canada Council for the Arts and am indebted to both groups.

I'd also like to thank more folks. Chloe Chan did the wonderful Iggy Samurai illustration. Calvin Dang provided some assistance on Japanese sword terminology. Any remaining errors are undoubtedly mine.

I received some valuable freelance editorial feedback from Peter Norman, Vivian Lee, and Brian Lynch. Justin Ridgeway and Lindsay Wong also gave their time to read drafts and ask probing, necessary questions.

Shannon Farr didn't read this book, but working with her on another project as she tirelessly fine-tuned a draft showed me how I could apply that same relentlessness to everything I wrote.

Thanks to my amazing wife, Holly, for making me whole. Finally, thank you to my family, including Holly, Joe, and Franny, Mom, Dan, and Judy, for being my world.

ABOUT THE AUTHOR

K evin Chong is the author of seven books of fiction and nonfiction, most recently the novel *The Plague*. His creative nonfiction and journalism have appeared in the *Guardian*, the *Times Literary Supplement*, the *Rumpus*, and the *South China Morning Post*. He lives in Vancouver with his family and is currently an associate professor at the University of British Columbia, Okanagan.